Romantic Times praises Norah Hess,
Winner of the Reviewer's Choice
Award for Frontier Romance!

LACEY
"Norah Hess has done it again! You'll savor every word,
yet rush to turn the pages."

WINTER LOVE
"Powerful and historically accurate as always, Norah
Hess depicts the American West with all its harsh
realities, yet with compassion and sensitivity."

FANCY
"The talented Ms. Hess is sure to catch your *Fancy*
with this release!"

STORM
"A charming story filled with warm, real, and
likeable characters."

SAGE
"Earthy, sincere, realistic, and heartwarming....
Norah Hess continues to craft wonderful
stories of the frontier!"

BROKEN VOWS

When the reverend asked him, "Do you take this woman to love and to honor, forsaking all others?" Big John had to give Kane a hard poke in the back to bring him back to the present.

The preacher was looking at him expectantly and he imagined this was when he was supposed to say, "I do." He almost choked on the two words as he uttered them.

A minute later Jade said in a low voice, "I do."

When Hart saw that no wedding band was forthcoming, he said, "I now pronounce you man and wife." He smiled at Kane and said, "You may kiss the bride."

Kane made a growling sound in his throat and, taking Jade by the elbow, said, "Let's get the hell out of here."

"Take your hands off her, Roemer," Big John ordered, the chill in his voice slicing the air.

"She's not going with you."

"What do you mean, she's not going with me?" Kane demanded. "She's my wife, isn't she?"

Jade

NORAH HESS

LEISURE BOOKS      NEW YORK CITY

I dedicate Jade *to Betty Moredock,*
my good friend in Texas.

A LEISURE BOOK®

March 2000

Published by
Dorchester Publishing Co., Inc.
276 Fifth Avenue
New York, NY 10001

ISBN 0-8439-4310-6

The name "Leisure Books" and the stylized "L" with design are trademarks of Dorchester Publishing Co., Inc.

Printed in the United States of America.

Jade

Chapter One

Wyoming, 1875

The first scarlet streak of dawn illuminated the uncurtained window as Jade Farrow awakened. The air in her bedroom had grown quite chilly and she drew the covers closer around her shoulders.

In the next bedroom her uncle, Big John, snored away. Her full lips lifted in amusement. She'd stay clear of him today, for when he rolled out of bed he was going to have a grand headache. He and two of his trapper friends had been drinking for the better part of the night.

Silent mirth glittered in her dark green eyes. This morning—or whenever he crawled out of bed—Uncle John would ask her the same question as usual. Had he and his friends made too much noise, had they kept her awake?

From the first she had known instinctively that her big, rough uncle would be embarrassed if she told him the truth. So her answer was always the same. "I didn't hear a thing, Uncle John. I fell asleep as soon as my head hit the pillow."

The hangdog look on his face would disappear then and he would be his usual rough, laughing self.

John Farrow was a big, robust man, strong as an ox. In his early fifties, he had a thick head of black hair peppered with gray. He also wore a heavy beard, which he was very proud of and kept neatly trimmed.

In the beginning, when four-year-old Jade had been practically dumped on his doorstep, Big John Farrow had been gruff and awkward with her. But she had soon learned that was because he was frightened of her. Having never been around children before, he was at a loss how to behave around the little girl who had suddenly been thrust upon him.

But he had taken up the job of rearing his niece the best way he knew how. He had hurriedly added another room to his sturdy two-room cabin and knocked together a bed made of small poles. He then sewed a fustian sack and filled the rough mattress with fresh-smelling hay. It had been near sundown when he saddled his stallion, put her in front of him, and rode down the mountain to Laramie. There he had purchased bed linens, which included a feather comforter for when freezing weather descended on the mountain.

That evening, after he had made a supper of fried steak and potatoes baked in the fireplace, he sat down in his rocker and lit his pipe. When Jade climbed up on his lap and nestled her head against his broad chest, he was clearly at a loss what to do. He finally did what came naturally to him. He put an arm around her and set the rocker in motion. She still remembered the lullaby he sang to her, one that he'd said his mother used to croon to him. Just before she had fallen asleep, he raised a hand and awkwardly smoothed his callused palm over her long, soft hair.

Jade could only vaguely remember sleeping in a bed that had flowers painted on the headboard, a soft mattress and a dainty bedspread. Her mother and father were dim memories also. She could recall that there was always a lot of laughter in the house, and she remembered her mother singing as she went about her work. And she remembered her father as being kind and gentle, not at all like his rough-speaking brother. She thought that they might look alike, but it was hard to tell, what with Uncle John's long hair and beard.

But Jade knew that her uncle loved her dearly despite his rough ways. Sometimes when walking past her he would let his hand rest briefly on her head.

Jade's old rooster, Pansy, which she had named when he was a little piece of yellow fluff and she had thought him a hen, crowed from his roost in the lean-to that sheltered their riding horses. She smiled and stretched. The old dickens was announcing that it was daylight and that he wanted to eat.

With a sigh Jade threw back the covers and sat up. She might as well go feed her spoiled, raggedy-feathered pet. He wouldn't quiet down until she did. He would keep it up until the horses started stamping around, agitated by his racket.

She reached for her dress, which she had carelessly tossed over the bed's end rail, and pulled it over her head. She frowned when she stood up and, tugging the faded gray garment down over her hips, heard seams ripping apart. It was time to start nagging Uncle John for some new clothes. She was almost afraid to breathe in her old ones, they were so threadbare. And she needed a winter jacket also. She had outgrown her old one four years ago. Besides, the elbows were worn out. The winter air crept into the holes and chilled her arms and shoulders.

And a new pair of boots, too, she thought. Last winter she had lined her old ones with folded paper to cover up the holes in the soles. But she wouldn't be able to do that this winter. The bottom of the right boot had cracked straight across. It was time they joined the trash pile outside.

Jade curled her bare toes off the wooden floor

as she left her room and walked into the room where the living and cooking was done. It was late September and pretty soon she would drag out the carpet pieces she had stored away for the summer. Twelve years ago Uncle John had paid an Indian woman to weave them for him. They had been woven to size, one for each room. But before she could spread them out and tack them down, Uncle John had to lay a thick layer of straw on the floor to prevent cold air from drifting up through the wide cracks between the floorboards. The straw did such a good job of insulating against the cold air, she could walk barefoot on the floor if she wanted to.

Shivering, Jade hurriedly built a fire in the rusty range that sat in a corner of the kitchen area. When she had started a pot of coffee brewing she stepped outside to visit the privy, which had also been built after she came to live with Uncle John.

She paused a moment on the small stoop, breathing in the freshness of the morning. Uncle John had built his cabin high up on the mountain beyond the usual haunts of men. On a clear day one could see for miles around, even a very dim view of Laramie. There was a low-lying fog in the valley today, but she could still see the silver sheen of the Platte River half-hidden behind a fringe of cottonwood lining its banks. When her old hound scrambled his way out of the hole he had dug for himself under the small porch, she laid a callused palm on his head and said, "That ol' river is a beautiful sight in the mornings, isn't it?"

When the dog answered with a wag of his tail she stepped off the porch, and barefoot she walked toward the outhouse, the rocky ground not bothering her in the least. She had been running around shoeless since the first of May. Her feet would bother her the first week they were once again confined in a pair of stiff boots, though, she reminded herself.

After Jade had answered nature's call she walked to the lean-to and unbarred the heavy door of hewed planks hung on rawhide hinges. Cougars roamed the mountains, and the long, deep scratches on the door, some old and some recently made, had been put there by the big, hungry cats trying to get to the horses inside.

When she stepped inside the building she was greeted by an uproarious noise of crowing and whinnying. Shaking her head at the earsplitting noise, she walked over to a barrel that held cracked corn. She lifted its lid and, picking up a battered tin cup inside, she scooped it full of the chicken feed. She was scattering it on the dirt floor when the leghorn swept down from his perch on one of the rafters.

"Get your stomach full and hush up, you old pain," Jade said, affection in her tone as her pet of many years pecked and scratched away at his breakfast.

A soft whinny from the back stall brought a smile to Jade's lips. It was her little chestnut-

colored mare, Cinnamon. Uncle John had captured her from a wild herd when she was only a
filly. She had been a gentle little animal and quite
intelligent and it hadn't been at all hard to tame
her and break her to the saddle.

And she was fast. She could outrun any horse
that had been put up against her. "Except for you,
my handsome fellow," Jade said, moving to the
next stall. "You run like the wind."

But the sleek, all-white stallion hadn't been at
all easy to train. He had fought Uncle John at
every turn. She remembered the day her uncle's
friends had warned him he should put the devil
down. "He's just like his sire, that big brute that
finally became a killer. Remember how that
rancher had to shoot him?" one of the men had
said. "He'll stomp you to death one of these days,
see if he don't."

Uncle John had reluctantly agreed that his
friends were right. "I don't want to take a chance
on Jade gettin' hurt, or maybe killed by the brute."

When he started to walk to the cabin to get his
rifle, she had stepped in front of him. Her eyes
bright with defiance, she cried out, "You will not
kill him, Uncle. He can be tamed. I can do it. He
likes me."

"What he would like is to trample you in the
dust," John retorted. Stepping around her, he continued on toward the cabin.

Jade ran after him and got in front of him again.
This time she resorted to tears. She had learned

at an early age that tears would get her most anything from her gruff uncle.

"Please, Uncle John"—she grabbed his arm—"give me a chance to tame him," she implored. "I'll be very careful. Just give me a month."

For a moment Jade thought her plea had fallen on deaf ears, that this time her wet cheeks and pleading eyes weren't going to work. Then, as usual, Big John gave in.

"I know I'm making a big mistake, listenin' to you," he said. "But the first time he charges you, or lays back his ears, that whelp of Satan is dead."

"Oh, thank you, Uncle John," Jade cried, embarrassing him by throwing her arms around his waist and planting a loud kiss on his leathery cheek.

"Go on with you now," the big man muttered, pulling Jade's arms away and sliding a sideways look at his cronies to see if they were snickering at him for giving in to his niece's pleading.

When the trappers' rough features remained the same as usual he said, "If by some miracle you're able to tame the beast, I don't want you takin' him out of the corral until I'm satisfied he can be trusted."

"It's a deal." Jade nodded happily, her green eyes shining. "Satan will be gentle as a kitten when I've finished taming him."

She had at that moment unconsciously given the white stallion his name. Ever afterward he was called Satan.

It hadn't been as easy as she had thought, taming the big stallion, but it had not been impossible either. It had just taken time and much kindness. He was very much like his sire: proud, untrusting of humans, and as defiant as a female cougar protecting her cubs.

It had taken two days before he would let Jade touch him, and that was only because a sugar lump lay in her palm. Those pieces of sweetness had gone a long way toward gaining his acceptance. Being very intelligent, he soon learned that there would be no treat until he allowed her to stroke him gently between the eyes.

He grew used to her gentle touch and seemed to look forward to it after a while. Encouraged by her success, Jade dared to stroke his proud, arched neck one morning. She wanted to shout her elation when he stood quietly, even sticking his head over the stall door to nudge her shoulder.

Three days later she ventured into his stall. Her movements slow, her voice gentle, she talked soothingly to him as she ran her hand down his neck, along his back and over his rump. When this was done and he didn't so much as move a muscle or nervously ripple his skin, she wondered if she dared take the curry comb to him. He was quite shaggy from his life spent in the wild.

I'll try it, she decided, and, leaving the stall she walked over to where all the paraphernalia pertaining to the horses was kept. She picked up a curry comb and, keeping it hidden behind her back, she entered the stall again. Holding her breath she brought the comb slowly down on the white rear end. She breathed a sigh of relief when the big stallion's muscles relaxed and he leaned into her.

At the beginning of the third week Jade eased a folded blanket over Satan's back. He looked over his shoulder at the unfamiliar weight, but at her gentle assurance that everything was all right he turned back to the oats she had poured into a pail for him. He paid no more attention to the unaccustomed weight on his back.

She kept the blanket on him for three days, and on the fourth day carefully slid her saddle onto his broad back. This upset Satan and he began to move around in the cramped space of the stall, trying to shake the heavy bulk off his back. It took Jade at least ten minutes to calm him down.

Although still nervous and upset, he stood quietly and took the sugar lump from her palm. The next two days were spent getting him used to the bridle, and to the bit in his mouth.

On the seventh day of the third week Jade tightened the cinches under Satan's belly and then slowly climbed into the saddle. He turned his head and looked at her as if to say, "What are you doing, sitting up there?" She leaned forward and patted his neck and he paid no more attention to her being on his back.

The next morning Jade led Satan outside. Looping the reins over the top corral pole she called to her uncle to come see the progress she had made with the wild stallion.

Big John came bursting through the cabin door, swearing so loudly a flock of birds erupted from the pine tree at the corner of the corral. "What did I tell you about bringin' that animal outside before I looked him over?" he yelled. "You're standin' too close to him! Move away from the devil!"

At the sound of Big John's angry voice Satan rolled his eyes and tried to rear up on his hind legs. Jade grabbed his reins and, talking quietly to him, held him steady. Her own anger rising, she said sharply, "Will you please lower your voice? You're scaring him."

"You're loco, you know that?" Big John retorted. His tone was much lower, however. "Now stand away from him."

"Uncle John, he's not going to hurt me. I'm going to mount him now and ride him around the corral."

"You'll do no such thing." Big John took a step forward to stop Jade. He was too late. She had slipped a bare foot into the left stirrup and swung into the saddle. At a slight pressure of the reins Satan moved out.

Beetle browed, John could only watch helplessly as his niece rode the big stallion, which wasn't yet sure how to respond to the silent order of the reins. But the stallion was very intelligent, and it wasn't long before he had figured out what each tug of the reins meant.

When Jade motioned to her uncle to open the corral gate, he shook his head vehemently.

"Uncle John," Jade warned, "I'll make him jump over the gate if I have to."

Slowly, John swung open the barrier.

Jade steered her pet through the wide opening and walked him down the mountain until she came to the open range. She loosened her grip on the reins a bit then and touched her heels lightly to his white belly. Satan responded by lunging forward and settling into a ground-eating gallop. Her hair streaming behind her like a small banner, Jade let him race along, to stretch the muscles that hadn't been exercised for close to two months.

But knowing that her uncle waited nervously, Jade shortly pulled Satan to a walk and pointed his nose up the mountain. When she pulled rein in front of her waiting uncle she was sure that his face would split apart if his smile grew any wider.

"I've got to hand it to you, girl," he said. "You've done all you claimed. We'll get a good piece of money for him when I take my wild herd down to Laramie. Get down and let me try him out."

Jade started to say that since she had tamed the stallion, he belonged to her. She held her tongue. If and when the time came to sell the horse, she would give her uncle a good argument.

"I don't know, Uncle John," she began doubtfully. "He's not used to you. Why don't you wait until he gets to know you?"

"Hell, he knows me well enough. I handled him

for three weeks before you took over. Come on down," he ordered impatiently.

"I hope you're right," Jade said as she slipped out of the saddle. "He has a tender mouth, so don't saw on the reins."

"Are you tryin' to tell me how to handle a horse, girl?" John grumbled as he climbed onto the big stallion.

At first it looked as though Satan was going to allow the new rider to sit astride him. But if Big John had noticed the flicking of the pointed ears, he would have been warned of what was to come. When he picked up the reins and ordered Satan to move out, the big white went into action. He arched his back and crow-hopped with John gripping the saddle horn. In seconds John was flying over Satan's head.

Jade ran to her uncle. Kneeling beside him she asked anxiously, "Are you all right, Uncle John?"

"Yes, damn it," the big man growled, pushing himself up. "Just winded a bit." He looked over at Satan, who now looked as docile as a newborn calf. "That devil is not to be trusted," he raged. "I'm gettin' rid of him as soon as possible."

Jade still didn't argue with him. It would be a losing battle when her uncle was so angry and upset. She wasn't too concerned about someone buying her pet. Uncle John had had him penned up all summer and no one had come to look at the horses he kept in the corral. Snow would start falling on the mountain any week now and her pet would be safe until next spring, Jade thought with a secret smile.

"We'll go for a ride this afternoon," she said now to the stallion, as though he were human. "Right now I've got to get back to the cabin and make Uncle John some breakfast."

She barred the lean-to door behind her, and then hurried up the rocky path, humming to herself.

Chapter Two

Loneliness enveloped Kane Roemer as he sat alone on the wide porch watching the red ball of the sun disappear over the western mountains. Maria, his housekeeper of many years, had left to visit her sister right after supper. And Jeb, the old man he had known all his life, had gone off to the Longhorn Saloon in Laramie. Right about now he'd be belly-up to the bar, aggravating someone with one of his tall tales.

But the tall, lean man knew that, deep down, it was the absence of his laughing, teasing sister Storm that caused his low spirits. She had married his best friend, Wade Magallen, and was busy with her husband and new baby, little Ben. Kane didn't see nearly enough of her anymore.

"Don't you think it's time you got married and started your own family?" a voice inside him said. "You are thirty-five years old. You should have been wed a long time ago."

Kane ignored the voice. He was not interested in getting married. He liked his life just the way it was. He wasn't about to become like his friend, Wade, who never went to town to drink and whoop it up anymore. Wade claimed that he was content to stay home with his little family.

Every once in a while the rancher rubbed his forehead. His head still ached from the whiskey he had consumed last night at Jake Magallen's saloon, the Longhorn. The latter part of the evening was pretty vague to him. He dimly remembered leaving the saloon at one point and going to the Pleasure House. He guessed that he had passed out there, for he couldn't remember anything after that. He couldn't even remember if one of the whores had pleasured him. He didn't think so, because when he woke up this morning he was alone and fully dressed, even to his boots.

He grinned wryly. He hoped he hadn't given one of the girls any money before falling asleep. He didn't like to pay good money for nothing.

The sun disappeared and the gray of twilight was near at hand when Kane heard the clang of a horseshoe striking against stone. Good, he thought, he'd have some company for a while. He peered through the semidarkness, then gave a grunt. A gaunt-looking old mule was approaching the house with an obese man overflowing the saddle on its back.

Yancy Jones, Kane thought with a frown. He disliked the man heartily. The homesteader was a lazy man who considered farming women's work and had taken little care choosing his grant of land. It was not the rich soil of the range but wooded and rocky land in the foothills of the mountain. His skinny wife and two sons, aged thirteen and fourteen, tilled what soil they could, but eked out a living by the backbreaking work of chopping down trees and selling the wood to ranchers. There were five other children, one an infant, crowded into a derelict three-room cabin a trapper had built fifteen years ago. It had an earthen floor and only one small window, and the roof leaked.

"Howdy, Kane," Jones said as he pulled the mule in at the foot of the steps.

"Jones," Kane acknowledged, but he didn't invite the man to join him.

That he might not be welcome didn't bother Jones. He was used to being shunned. "I saw somethin' the other day that might interest you," he said, swinging his heavy weight to the ground and puffing up the two steps to the porch, where he sat down beside Kane.

Kane slid over, putting a couple of feet between him and the odor of stale sweat and unwashed body. "I was out huntin' rabbits on my land day before yesterday," Yancy continued, "when suddenly down from the mountain came the biggest, whitest stallion a man ever seen. There was a slip of a girl on its back, handlin' that big brute easy as you please.

"It was some picture, I tell you. I just sat my mule watchin' them. Well, when they hit the flat range the girl loosened her grip on the reins and that animal flattened himself out. I only saw a white blur, he took off so fast. That girl was laughin' and whoopin' like a wild Injun.

"I told Jake Magallen about it and he reckoned I was lyin'. Said it right to my face."

"Well, were you?" Kane gave him a narrow look. It was well known that Yancy Jones could lie with the best of them.

"Hell no! I swear to you, Roemer, I saw that white horse and the girl plain as day. Wonder where they come from? Does anybody live up there in the mountains with the varmints and all? Do you reckon that stallion is the get of that white killer stallion folks say you shot?"

Kane made no answer to the question fired at him. He was only half listening to the fat man as he rambled on. He was asking himself if it was likely the white stallion had sired a son in his exact image.

Excitement began to pump in his veins. It might be possible that another such horse lived somewhere in the mountains. Although Yancy wasn't aware of it, there were several mountain men up there. Most were trappers and didn't come down to Laramie more than twice a year to buy supplies and to bring in their winter's catch. Had one of them somehow captured the white stallion?

By hell, he was going to find out, Kane decided. He still regretted having to put a bullet between the eyes of that handsome white, and it would be some consolation if there was another like him he could purchase. He could well afford to spend a few days away from the ranch. The fall cattle drive had been made and the cowhands could easily keep an eye on the ranch and the few hundred head he had kept back.

When the fat man saw that he wasn't going to be offered a glass of whiskey, he said good night and climbed back on his sorry-looking mule.

Kane hardly noticed his leaving. His mind was on only one thing—how soon he could take off to go up the mountain the next morning.

There was a mist in the air when Jade stepped outside the following day. It wouldn't last, she knew. When the sun grew brighter the fog would disappear.

There was no wind today and Jade decided it was an ideal time to visit some of her old haunts on the mountain, secret places that only she knew of. There weren't too many days left when she would be able to travel about freely. Once winter set in and the ground wore a white blanket often two or three feet deep, no one but the hardy trappers moved about.

I'm surprised it hasn't snowed yet, she thought, on her way to the lean-to to prepare the white stallion for the ride. This time last year a foot of snow had covered the ground.

When she stepped into the animal shelter, Big John looked up from pitching hay to the three horses that were kept inside at night. They were valuable pieces of horseflesh and he never left them outside at night. They would be at the mercy of cougars, wolves and bears. He worried some about the wild horses he had captured and kept penned up in the corral. He depended on the hound to raise a ruckus if any varmint came around.

"Are you doin' some ridin' today?" Big John asked, setting aside the pitchfork.

"Yes. Satan needs some exercise. There won't be too many days left in which I can ride him."

"Yeah, there's definitely a bite to the air these days. We can expect snow any day now."

As Jade slipped the bridle over Satan's head and then tugged his saddle off the wall, John said, "You'd better ride to the east today. I saw that buck Long Feather skulking around last night just before I went to bed. I guess he didn't pay any attention to that talk I gave him. I guess I'm gonna have to talk to his chief, Soaring Bird."

"Don't worry about Long Feather, Uncle John. He would never harm me."

"I know that, but he might grab you and take

you to his village and have the medicine man marry you to him."

"Uncle John," Jade chided, "I'd never allow that to happen."

"You probably wouldn't even know it was happenin'. They'd be talkin' Injun and you wouldn't know what was goin' on. Long Feather could say that you was willin' to be his woman, and that would be the end of it.

"I'd have to go after you then, and the whole tribe would be mad. They've been friendly to the mountain folks all these years. I don't want to start a fight with them."

"I don't think any of that is going to happen," Jade said as she cinched Satan's belly strap, "but I'll ride to the east." She grinned and added, "And I'll keep an eye out for my lovelorn Indian."

"You think it's funny, missy, but it could all come about," John said as Jade led Satan outside and swung onto his back.

As she rode out, Jade's thoughts were on the young brave she had grown up with, along with his sisters and brothers and cousins. She had learned many things from the Arapaho youths. They had taught her how to shoot a bow and arrow and hit her mark most of the time. She had learned from them how to spear a fish, even how to catch one with her hands. She knew how to start a fire without a match, how to swim and which berries not to eat.

Those had been such happy times, Jade remembered. But everything had changed once she started to mature. She began to notice then how Long Feather, two years older than she, would stare at her breasts when they went swimming. It made her very nervous and she stopped going to the mountain pools with her friends on hot summer days. When they begged to know why, she answered that the cold spring water cramped her legs.

All but Long Feather believed her. His mocking eyes would look into hers, then drop to her breasts. When he started trying to get her off by herself, it made her uneasy. She didn't know why, but something told her it wouldn't be wise to go off alone with him.

Gradually she had stopped running and playing with her childhood friends because of the brave. The young maidens in the village were happy about that. Long Feather was growing into a handsome man and many yearning looks were sent his way.

Uncle John had noticed her withdrawal from her Indian friends and had approved of it. "When you get married," he said, "I don't want it to be to some young buck who might not treat you right. The Indian man is boss in his tepee, and you're not cut out to take orders. Also, some of them are cruel to their wives."

Jade could have pointed out that many white men were also cruel, that she knew of two mountain men who beat their wives regularly. But why waste her breath? she thought; she didn't plan on ever getting married. She liked it just fine living with Uncle John on the mountain. Besides, she had a vague idea of what went on in the marriage bed and she wanted no part of that. The sounds that came from her uncle's bedroom when he and his friends took whores in there disgusted her. She had seen stallions mount mares and she imagined that was what went on in her uncle's bedroom.

The thought of it revolted her.

As he rode down the main street of Laramie, a crooked grin lifted the corners of Kane's lips. The town was like a whore in the mornings, exhausted by a night of drinking and tending to the lusts of men. The gaudy, false-front saloons and gambling dens, the littered street, the drunken men passed out in front of the Longhorn, all made one think that the town was sleeping off a debauch.

But soon Laramie would come alive with humanity, people going about the business that had brought them to town, Kane thought, as he rode past the mercantile, the hotel, the restaurant and finally the livery. He was on his way to the mountain this morning, and as soon as he hit the open range, he gave Renegade his head.

After about forty-five minutes they arrived in the foothills. Now, where to start climbing? he wondered. He had hunted bighorn sheep halfway up the mountain a few times, but he had never seen a trail. But if he was to find the mountain settlement, he must find the way its inhabitants came down.

It took about fifteen minutes, but finally he saw a trail, pounded into the ground by the many feet and hooves that had traveled that way over the years. He turned Renegade onto the path and started climbing.

The higher they traveled, the rougher the trail became, strewn with rocks and low-growing bushes. He grunted impatiently when suddenly four paths led off from what he imagined was the main track.

"Now what?" he muttered, reining Renegade in. Which of the paths should he take? He dismounted and worked his way through some brush to a large, tall boulder the size of a small cabin. He climbed to its top and there he had a good view of the surrounding area. He slowly studied the terrain to the east, looking for a dwelling.

The only living thing he saw was an eagle soaring high in the blue sky. He was about to turn around and look west when he heard a sudden noise just as a rock thudded against his shoulder. Startled and caught off balance, he slipped, tried to catch himself, failed and tumbled awkwardly down the boulder, scrambling and cursing.

Sprawled on his back with the wind knocked out of him, Kane lay quietly for a moment, his eyes closed. When there came the sound of feet crunching on stone his eyes flew open and he stared up at the face of a girl, the likes of which he had never seen before.

Kane stared and stared at the light-colored, long, snarled hair that hid most of the girl's dirty face. He could see only a pair of dark green eyes looking down at him, and they were shimmering with silent mirth.

"You think it's funny, do you?" he asked, glaring up at Jade. "Do you make it a habit to throw rocks at people?"

"You're not hurt," Jade said contemptuously, "and I didn't throw any rock. It came off the cliff as Satan went down the trail. What are you doing up here on my mountain?"

"Your mountain!" Kane sat up. "I didn't know that anyone could own a mountain."

"That goes to show that you don't know as much as you think you do." Jade's lips curled scornfully.

"I know that you don't own this mountain. It belongs to anyone who wants to climb it," Kane snapped testily.

"That's where you're wrong again. Big John Farrow owns this strip of the mountain."

"They sure do raise some big liars up here," Kane drawled derisively, walking away from her.

"I am not a liar!" Jade cried after him, her green eyes snapping.

"No, you're a rag-tailed wildcat," Kane grated out as he whirled around. "Get your ugly puss off to your cave."

For the first time in her life Jade felt humiliation. No one had ever remarked on her looks or called her names. Was she ugly? she wondered. She had no way of knowing. Her only mirror was a mountain pool, and when she gazed down into it all she saw was her long hair falling in her face.

For a moment she wished she could crawl into a cave as the hateful stranger had said she should. She wanted to hide, to lick her wounds like her old hound Jelly might do.

But the pride that Big John had instilled in her made Jade push back her tears, clear her throat and give a peculiar whistle. As Kane wondered what that was all about, he stepped away from her. She had probably alerted a male relative, and it was well known that mountain men thought nothing of killing a stranger.

He caught his breath when a magnificent pure white stallion walked from behind a boulder and advanced toward them, his ears erect, his eyes wide and alert, snorting suspiciously.

Excitement fired Kane's blood. There was no doubt in his mind but that this young stallion was the son of the wild horse he had been forced to put down.

When Jade swung onto the stallion, her dress rode up midthigh, and Kane was further astonished by the fine lines of her legs. They were more beautiful than any he had ever seen. When she kicked a dirty, bare foot into the stallion and urged him farther up the mountain, Kane hurried to mount Renegade and took off after her. He had no intention of losing sight of the big white that had brought him climbing the mountain. He wanted to meet the owner of the horse, to buy him, no matter what price was put on him.

Jade knew the stranger was following her and her nerves were stretched to the breaking point by the time the old cabin came in sight. She relaxed a bit when she saw her uncle sitting on a stump, a pile of traps at his feet. He tossed one that he had been greasing to the ground, looked at Kane, and then turned questioning eyes to her. She shrugged her shoulders and rode on to the corral.

John Farrow stood up, a wary look on his face. It was rare for a lowlander to climb so far up the mountain. His voice was gruff as he said, "Howdy, stranger."

"Howdy." Kane returned the big man's greeting but stayed in the saddle. He'd dismount only if he was invited to. Mountain people were a strange breed. That unfriendly girl might have brothers training rifles on him, watching his every move.

"I can tell by your garb you're a ranch hand," the bearded man said, hooking his thumbs in his suspenders. "What brings you up here where eagles and bighorns live, not to mention a few cougars and bears?"

He's as tough as an old buffalo, Kane thought. He knew he'd better weigh every one of his words if he was to strike a deal concerning the stallion.

"The bighorn sheep brought me up here," Kane

said, thinking quickly. "I'd like to shoot a big one and have his head mounted over my fireplace."

"Well, we've got plenty of them up here. They're all in hiding this time of the day though. They come out in the early mornin' and late afternoon to graze. After that they just disappear."

"I didn't know that," Kane lied, gazing around. "There's no place in the world more beautiful than these mountains," he said, changing the subject.

Such a pleased smile stirred the graying beard, Kane almost believed that maybe the girl was right. Maybe the big man did own a piece of the mountain.

"Why don't you get down and set a spell, rest your horse," the big man invited. "Try some of my corn likker. You ain't gonna find any sheep until much later on."

"Don't mind if I do." Kane swung to the ground just as the girl came stomping up to the cabin. Ignoring her, he said, "A glass of whiskey would sit right well with me."

"The name's John Farrow," the mountain man said, offering a callused palm to Kane. "Folks around here call me Big John."

"Kane Roemer." Kane shook the big hand and laughingly said, "I can't imagine why they would call you that."

Farrow laughed too. "My maw didn't raise any runts. We'll sit on the porch, if you don't mind. I try to stay out in the sunshine as much as possible. The weather is gonna change one of these days and we won't see much sun all winter. We trappers sure miss its warmth." He turned his head toward the cabin door and called loudly, "Jade, bring out the whiskey jug and a couple glasses."

"What do you mainly trap for, Farrow?" Kane asked.

"I take anything that goes after my bait, but I prefer catchin' mink, silver fox and beaver. They fetch the most money."

"I expect there's pretty good money in trapping." Kane made his words sound more like a statement than a question. He knew that mountain people didn't like being questioned, especially by a stranger.

Evidently John took Kane's words as he had hoped he would, for he nodded in agreement and said, "A man can make a good enough livin' trappin' if he ain't lazy. It all depends on how many miles you're willin' to walk a day.

"But I make more money catching wild horses in the summer. I tame them and sell them."

Kane couldn't believe his good luck. He had resigned himself to wasting most of the afternoon before he could bring up the topic of wild horses. It was all he could do to keep his elation from showing on his face. The scruffy young girl came out of the cabin carrying two empty jelly glasses and a brown jug. From the scowling look she gave him, he knew that if any problem should arise in his purchasing the stallion, it would come from her. In his anger he had lashed out at her with some pretty harsh words.

Now he wished he hadn't spoken so bluntly to her. No matter what age, a female didn't like to hear that she was ugly. She would get her revenge on him by trying to block the sale of the stallion.

"Do you want to take a look at my horses?" John asked. "You might see one that strikes your fancy." At those words the girl stiffened and gave him a look through her tangled hair that reminded him of a cornered cougar.

He tried to dismiss the girl from his mind as Farrow splashed whiskey into the glasses and said, "Drink up. Then we'll go see what I've got penned up in the corral."

The raw whiskey burned its way down Kane's throat, making his eyes water. Good Lord, he thought, this is pure alcohol. He watched in amazement as the other man drank his as if it were springwater.

Big John placed his empty glass down beside him and stood up. "You ready to go look at the horses?" he asked.

Kane nodded, forced himself to finish his drink, then followed the bearded man, who stepped out on a path that led to the back of the cabin.

As they made their way along a rocky ridge, Kane looked over his shoulder at the sound of a rolling rock. He wasn't surprised to see the girl trailing behind them. Big John seemed to realize at the same time that she was following them.

"She's my niece," he explained gruffly. "Jade, we don't need your company. This is men's business. Go on back to the cabin."

She gave him a sullen look but turned around and walked away. However, as he and John approached the penned-up horses, Kane noticed from the corner of his eye that the girl was again slipping along behind them. She's a stubborn miss, he thought, and then forgot all about her when he saw a dozen or so horses milling around in a corral constructed of sturdy poles.

There were draft horses, blue roans, claybanks, buckskins and sturdy little mustangs. And of course the white stallion. His heart beat faster at the sight of him. But not by a flick of an eyelash did he let his interest in the white show. He pretended more interest in a claybank. "All the horses aren't wild," he said to John, who was leaning on the corral beside him. "Especially those draft horses. How do you come to have them?"

"I'm no horse thief, if that's what you're thinkin'," the big man said testily. "Most of the tame ones was running with the wild ones I captured. But the tame mares you see was stole from different ranchers by that white stallion over there."

"I didn't mean to imply that you stole the horses, Farrow. I was just curious." When the trapper nodded that he accepted the apology, Kane said, "It must take a lot of hard work rounding up the wild ones."

"Not really. When I have a mare in heat I take her for a ride. It doesn't take a stallion long to smell her. When he and his harem start following her I turn the mare around toward the corral. Then, pretty as you please, they all walk into the pen." John's whiskers stirred with a smile. "Boy, does that stallion scream when I take the mare away before he can mount her."

"You've got some good horseflesh in there." Kane still didn't show any interest in the white stallion. "That claybank looks built for speed," he said. "I could probably turn him into a good quarter horse."

"I guess he could run pretty fast"—John shrugged—"but if it's speed you're after, the white stallion is the fastest I've ever seen."

When Kane pretended not to be interested, Farrow said, "I can let you have him cheap. He fights with the other stallions all the time. I keep him penned up in the barn most of the time and he sure hates that."

Kane didn't let his face show what he was thinking. For some reason the mountain man wanted to get rid of the handsome white, and it wasn't because the horse fought with the other stallions. There were only two in the pen and they were still too young to give the older, larger stallion any competition.

Kane wondered what was really wrong with the stallion. Could it be that his hooves were too small to carry his great weight? Was his mouth too wide for a bit, or could it be that he was blind in one eye? He prayed that none of this was true as he said, half interest in his voice, "I'll take a look at him."

When he started to climb into the corral Big John cautioned, "He's a little skittish of strangers. He might shy away from you at first."

Kane approached the stallion, his heart pounding in anticipation of owning this magnificent animal. He spoke quietly to the nervous stallion, holding out his hand for the animal to sniff.

The horse shook his head a little, but allowed Kane to stroke his neck. "We're going to be good friends, fellow," he whispered as he checked out all the things that might be wrong with the animal. When he found the handsome white perfect in every way, he said, "Now we'll put a saddle on you and see if you're an easy ride."

When Kane walked back to where he had left John, he found the mountain man and the girl in a heated argument. He thought the girl looked wilder than ever, practically jumping up and down as she yelled, "You promised that Satan would be mine, that he wouldn't be sold!"

"I never told you that, girl," Farrow thundered back. "You said it, but I didn't agree."

"You didn't disagree either." Jade glared at her uncle with clenched fists. "All this time you let me think that Satan was mine, knowing all the time that you would sell him the first chance you got."

"I told you why I want to get rid of him. He's—"

John broke off when he saw Kane standing only a few feet away listening to their argument.

"Well, Roemer"—he turned his back on the irate girl—"you didn't find anything wrong with him, did you?"

"He looks all right," Kane said hesitantly, feeling in his bones that the stallion had a fault, after all, since Big John Farrow was anxious to get rid of the animal. "I'd like to put a saddle on him and see how he responds to the rein."

John nodded, but as Kane watched him lift a saddle off the top rail of the corral he saw reluctance in his movements. Kane took the saddle away from him, saying that he would prepare the stallion for a test ride. He had no trouble getting the animal to accept the bridle and bit, nor any problem in settling the saddle on his broad back. There was a small hitch when it came to cinching the belly strap. Each time he attempted it the horse puffed out his belly. It was a trick many horses played. When the cinch strap was fastened around a ballooned-out belly, the animal could release the air after being mounted. Then the belly strap would loosen, the saddle would slip, and the rider would find himself on the ground.

But Kane was used to such tricks from other mounts, so he gave the stallion an unexpected jab in the belly and the air rushed out in a great rush. Before Satan could puff himself up again, Kane hurriedly pulled the strap tight and buckled it.

That little byplay made the mountain man

laugh. The dirty-faced girl, however, only scowled at him.

That was until Kane climbed into the saddle. He had barely settled himself when the stallion sprang into action. Before he could grab up the reins, the horse was bucking, and in moments Kane found himself on the ground. The girl let out peals of laughter as he lay there, his face buried in the dirt.

He stood up, wiped his eyes clean and swung back into the saddle again, only to be thrown again. Three more times he mounted the wild stallion, and three more times he found himself on the ground.

As Kane's face plowed the dirt the last time, his suspicions about the horse became a certainty. The blasted brute wouldn't let anyone but the girl ride him.

But with patience, that could be changed, he told himself as he pushed himself off the ground. Kane still wanted him and was willing to wait however much time it took for the stallion to come around.

Kane limped across the churned-up dirt of the corral to confront a worried-looking Big John and the highly amused dirty-faced girl. Pinning John with a dark look he said, "You forgot to mention that the devil will only let your niece ride him. I don't want a horse just to look at like I would a painting on a wall."

"Jade has turned him into a pet," John explained, "treating him the same way she does the old hound and that raggedy rooster of hers. But once the stallion is away from her coddlin' ways, he'll forget her. You can learn him your ways then."

"That's right!" Jade was suddenly in front of Kane, her eyes spitting green fire. "You can take a whip to him, break his spirit."

"Now, Jade," John began, but Kane was talking over him.

"Listen to me, you little imp from hell," he grated out. "I've never struck a horse in my life and I'll never lay a rough hand on this one. He'll either grow to accept and like me, or he won't. But whatever happens, he'll never have his spirit broken."

Kane turned away from the angry girl to look at the mountain man. "He's a stubborn son of a gun, but I'll take a chance on him if the price is right. What are you asking for him?"

Practically rubbing his hands together in thankfulness that he was going to get rid of the white before he crippled or killed somebody, John said, "Come on down to the cabin and we'll parley about it."

Kane heard the almost inaudible cry that escaped the girl before she spun around and sped off up the mountain. He felt a momentary twinge of guilt. It was plain she loved the stallion, but as soon as word got out about the white, half a dozen men would climb up here, anxious to buy the handsome animal. And some among them *would* use a whip to break him.

Feeling that he was right in his assumption that the girl's pet could fall into the wrong hands, Kane felt less blameworthy for her tears. It was better that she suffer a little than to have the proud stallion suffer the bite of a whip and the rake of spurs the rest of his life. He climbed out of the corral and followed Big John as he led the way.

Hot tears running down her cheeks, Jade ran but a short distance before darting behind a clump of brush and sinking down. She was too overcome with grief to go any farther. Huddled there on the ground, she dwelt for some time on the hatred she felt for her uncle and the stranger.

But as her tears dried she gradually understood her uncle's wish to be rid of Satan. Although he was gentle as a lamb with her, he might be a danger to someone else. However, to let him go to the man who had set her teeth on edge the moment he spoke to her was almost more than she could bear.

As Jade was coming to terms with losing her pet, Big John and Kane agreed on a price for the stallion. "What ranch do you work for, Roemer?" Farrow asked as Kane handed over the amount agreed upon.

"I work for myself, John," Kane said. "I have a spread on the other side of Laramie."

John stared at Kane, remembering. It was a dim thread at first, changing swiftly into clear recollection. "By God," he exclaimed, "you're that rancher who had to put that killer stallion down, ain't you?"

"Yes." Kane nodded. "It was the hardest thing I ever had to do in my life. But he was a mean devil and almost did my sister in."

"I remember that," John said. "Nobody faulted you for doin' it."

"I hope I never have to do the same to his son."

"I don't think you will. His offspring is gentle by nature. He just don't like anyone but my niece ridin' him. She's spoiled him somethin' awful."

A thought came to Kane. "Has she taught him how to respond to a lead rope?"

John shook his head. "I don't think she has. There ain't been any cause for her to do that. She always rides him."

Now that the big man had Kane's money in his hand, he opened up more about the stallion. "He's a stubborn cuss and I ain't got any idea how he'll act when you try to lead him down the mountain. He's unusually strong and he might break away from you."

Kane gave the uncle an irritated look and asked stiffly, "Do you have an idea how I might get him down to my ranch?"

John stared thoughtfully at the ground a minute, and then answered, "The onlyest way I can think of is to have Jade ride him down for you."

"Ha!" Kane snorted. "I can just see her doing

that. I'm not her favorite person right now, in case you haven't noticed."

"She'll do it. She'd rather ride him down than see him frightened by a rope. He don't like ropes a'tall. He's been lassoed too many times. He knows they take away his freedom."

"It's getting late." Kane stood up and pushed his rickety chair under the table. "Will you call your niece in, see if she'll do the favor of helping me get the white down off the mountain? It's still sunny up here, but in another hour or so the sun will get ready to set down below. I'd like to reach the ranch before dark."

They walked out on the porch and John cupped his hands around his mouth to call for Jade. Then he suddenly let his arms drop and looked at Kane. "I just thought of somethin'. Jade's not gonna have a mount to ride home. Her little filly is in heat and them two stallions will fight over her all the way to your ranch. Either one, or both, could get hurt real bad.

"Besides, I never let Jade ride alone after dark. There's too many animals prowlin' 'round, includin' two-legged ones."

Kane didn't dare speak his thoughts for fear of offending the big man looking earnestly at him. How could he say that in his opinion the girl was safe from attracting any man, and she was so dirty he doubted that a wolf would follow her either?

"I'll see that she has a mount to ride home, and she can spend the night at the ranch."

When John eyed him suspiciously, Kane said impatiently, "My housekeeper lives with me. Your niece won't have to beat me off her."

"A feller can't be too careful of his womenfolk," John said. "The men around here are always after Jade."

It was all Kane could do not to throw back his head and roar with laughter. He couldn't imagine even a blind man coming to court the scraggly looking girl. He jumped when John gave a loud shout for his niece.

Several minutes passed and Kane was swearing to himself at the waste of time when the sullen-faced girl finally walked into view. He could see she had been crying from the dirt streaks around her eyes and cheeks. He felt a twinge of guilt and pity for Big John's half-wild niece. As far as he could see she didn't have much of anything but her pets, and he was taking away her favorite one.

All soft feelings for her faded when she gave gave him a heated scowl, full of hatred and scorn. No woman had ever looked at him that way.

Next, she turned her green gaze on her uncle and ungraciously asked, "What do you want?"

"The first thing I want from you is that you watch that sharp tongue of yours. You know I don't stand for any sass. The reason I called you is that you're gonna have to ride Satan to Roemer's ranch. That is, if you ain't learned him to be led, to follow another horse."

In the charged silence that descended, niece

and uncle faced each other. The girl's eyes blazed with indignation and the bearded man glared back at her, his eyes saying that she had better do as he had ordered.

"I haven't trained him to a lead yet," Jade said, breaking the silence, "but you're asking too much, Uncle. It's bad enough he is taking Satan away from me, and now you expect me to help him."

"Well then, if that's how you feel about it, there's nothin' to be done but put a rope around his neck and let Roemer drag him down the mountain."

"No!" The cry was one of helpless fury. "That would frighten him and undo all the work I've done to tame him."

"Well then, are you willin' to ride him down?"

Kane saw that he was about to receive another contemptuous look and turned his back on Jade. One such look was enough for one day. He was beginning to think that she was a witch who could put a spell on him with those snapping green eyes. He slowly sighed his relief when the girl finally conceded the battle.

The husky quality of her voice showed she was near tears when she said, "As usual, you have won, Uncle. I'll ride him down."

"Now Jade, girl, I don't want you feelin' that way about it. Deep down you know I had to sell him or let him go. We owe it to our neighbors to get rid of him. What if one of their younguns tried to pet him and he stomped them to death? I haven't told you, but some of the fathers have complained

49

about Satan. Sutter Jenkins has threatened to shoot him. You know that mean devil is capable of puttin' a bullet between Satan's eyes."

Jade's face paled beneath the dirt at this news. She knew that half the mountain people were afraid of her pet, but she hadn't known they wanted Uncle John to get rid of him. Her shoulders sagging in defeat, she said, "I'll go saddle him."

As John was pointing out to his niece all the bad things that could happen to her pet if they kept him, Kane was beginning to regret that he had bought the stallion. The animal sounded as though he might become a killer, like the stallion that had sired him.

He gave the mountain man a narrowed, cold look and expressed his uneasy feelings.

"Don't pay any attention to what I said to the girl." John gave a dismissive wave of his hand. "I just told her that so she'd ride Satan down the mountain."

"That was a hell of a thing to do to her," Kane said angrily.

"I know it," John said regretfully. "But I knew that was the onlyest way I could get her to accommodate you."

"I feel bad, taking her pet away from her," Kane said.

"I do, too, but some of the things I said to her was true. A couple neighbors have been pressing me to sell the white or return him to the wild. I couldn't bring myself to turn him loose, he's such a grand-looking piece of horseflesh. I'm right pleased that he's gonna be with you. He'll be well taken care of."

"Let's hope she comes to that conclusion after a while."

"She'll grieve a while, but then she'll realize it was all for the good, sellin' him to you," Big John said as Jade rode toward them, looking very small astride the white stallion.

When she reined in, Kane ran his gaze over her slender body, frowning slightly at her thin dress, the dirty feet and grubby knees. "You'd better put on a coat and shoes," he said. "The air is getting colder by the minute."

Jade gave him one of the looks that he was beginning to think she saved especially for him. Then she swung out of the saddle and went into the cabin. She was gone but a moment before she returned, drawing on a threadbare jacket. The garment was sizes too small for her, the sleeves coming well above her wrists, and half the buttons were missing. When he saw that her feet were still bare, an angry glint shone in his eyes. "Hadn't you better put on some shoes?"

When Jade made no response, her uncle cleared his throat and said gruffly, "We ain't had time to go down to Laramie and buy her some new duds. We'll do that the first thing when she gets back."

Kane started to say angrily that the girl would be nearly frozen by the time they reached his

51

ranch, but remembered in time how proud the mountain people were. He climbed into the saddle and said shortly, "Come on, then; light's fading fast."

Jade would have ridden past John without a word had he not grabbed the bridle, bringing the stallion to a halt. "Jade, girl," he warned, "don't go gettin' any wild ideas in your head. I'll look for you back sometime tomorrow."

Jade nodded, then waited for Kane to move out ahead of her. He started to nudge Renegade into motion, then held him back. "You lead," he said. "I can keep an eye on you if you're in front of me."

Jade's response was a cold look. Then she touched Satan lightly with her heels, signaling him to move out.

John stood on the porch looking after Jade and Kane until they were out of sight. "They make a fine-lookin' pair, don't they, Jelly?" he said to the hound he had tied up so it couldn't follow its mistress. "That rancher is the kind of man I want Jade to marry one day. Wouldn't it be nice if they hit it off and ended up together?" The hound's tail thumped the porch planks in agreement.

Chapter Three

Jade took a path other than the one Kane had used on his way up. The ground was uneven and irregular, and littered with large rocks and low-growing shrubs. Kane wondered if this was the way she usually took down the mountain, or if she was deliberately taking this course to add more time to their descent.

If that was the case some rocks and brush wouldn't bother him in the least. He was used to chasing wild cattle out of dense thickets.

After about fifteen minutes of riding over the rough path, Kane pulled the collar of his jacket up around his ears. The air had grown icy cold and dark, and threatening clouds had gathered in the north. He thought of the girl, with her bare feet and inadequate clothing, and imagined she was finding it very cold. He called to her to rein in.

Jade did so, but didn't look back to ask why. She sat relaxed in the saddle as Kane dismounted. Bending over, he removed one boot and heavy sock. Shoving the woolen into his jacket pocket he shoved his bare foot back into the boot. After he had done the same thing to the other foot, he took down the rolled black slicker fastened behind the cantle. After shaking out most of the wrinkles, he walked over to the stallion.

"Stick out your foot," he said gruffly to Jade. She frowned down at him. "Why?" she asked, her teeth chattering from the cold air.

"I'm going to put socks on your feet," Kane answered impatiently. Taking one of the heavy woolen socks from his pocket, he jerked her nearest foot out of the stirrup. The slender foot was almost blue, and he hurried to pull the sock over it. The sock, which came to midcalf on him, went past Jade's knee. Jade didn't demur when he did the same thing to her other foot. The heat of his body still lingered in the material and felt so good.

She didn't argue either when he told her to slip her arms into the slicker he held up for her. When she tried to button up the long garment, her fingers were too numb to manipulate the buttons. Kane knocked away her hands and swiftly did them up. The sleeves came well past her hands, and that was good, he thought. They would buffer some of the cold air. He next tucked the slicker snugly around her legs.

Jade knew good manners dictated that he should be thanked. But she was loath to do that. She told herself the only reason he had bundled her up was because he was afraid she might freeze to death, and then he would have no one to ride Satan to his ranch.

Kane hadn't expected any thanks and wasn't surprised when he didn't receive any.

He had been back in the saddle about five minutes when a snowflake landed on his hand. It was rapidly joined by others. They were large and heavy, the kind that would stick to the ground and probably stay there until spring's warm sun melted them. Within minutes the horses were moving through a white curtain of snow.

When Kane could barely make out Satan's white rump his concern grew. One false step and the stallions could go tumbling down the mountain.

"Drop the reins and let the white choose his own way," he called to Jade.

"You damn fool," she called back. "I did that twenty minutes ago."

"I should have known that," Kane muttered to himself. *She's mountain raised and has probably been caught in snowstorms many times, as has the stallion.*

The brunt of the storm, however, didn't hit them until they rode out of the foothills. Minutes later a thick mantle of snow lay on Kane's and Jade's head and shoulders.

Kane prayed that they were heading straight for Laramie. In a blizzard such as this one could easily ride around in circles. At one point he called to Jade to pull up a moment. "I want to see if I can make out anything familiar."

As he sat squinting his eyes, peering into the white world, he saw nothing but a seemingly endless stretch of snow. He sighed heavily and ordered Jade to move on.

It seemed to Kane that the stallions had been plodding along for hours when he spotted the dim lights of Laramie no more than three or four yards away. They were only a few more miles from the ranch. He debated spending the night in Laramie, to wait out the storm. He remembered then that a full-fledged blizzard like this one could go on for days and discarded the idea.

Besides, people would cast curious looks at the girl, dwarfed in his slicker, with only his socks on her feet. And he mustn't forget her dirty face and snarled hair. His friends wouldn't know what to make of her.

"I'll take the lead now." He rode up beside Jade. "Renegade can find the way home from here."

Jade made no response. Her shoulders were hunched and her head was tucked into her chest. Kane became anxious about her and took the reins from her nerveless, icy hands. He thumped Renegade with his heels, calling for more speed from the animal. But the stallion could move only a bit faster in the blinding snow.

After what seemed an eternity, Kane made out the lamplight shining through the ranch house's kitchen window.

A couple of minutes later Renegade stopped in front of the back porch. The white stallion halted also. When Kane hurried to help Jade out of the saddle she fell senseless into his arms. Her weight felt like nothing in his arms, and he jumped up on the porch, calling loudly for Maria and Jeb.

The kitchen door burst open and the house-keeper appeared. "Is that you, Kane?" she asked, staring at the white apparition holding a snow-covered bundle in his arms. "It is you!" she exclaimed, finally recognizing him. She opened the door just wide enough for him to walk through with his burden. "You look near frozen. Get in here where it's warm and thaw out."

She looked curiously at Jade as Kane walked past her and deposited the girl's limp body in a chair. "Who is that?" Maria hovered around Kane as he got the slicker and now-wet socks off Jade.

As he began vigorously to rub her narrow, dirty feet, anxious to get the blood circulating, he looked up at Maria, worry creasing his forehead. "I'll tell you all about it later. Right now, will you work on her hands? See if you can find a pulse in her wrist."

No more was said as they worked feverishly to get the blood flowing in Jade's veins. Maria finally looked up at Kane, a wide smile on her face. "I feel her pulse quickening!"

"Thank God!" Kane exclaimed, feeling weak with relief. "If anything had happened to her, I don't think I could have found the courage to tell her uncle. He'd shoot me before I finished talking. He's a tough—" Kane paused. As warmth began to move through her limbs, Jade was making little moaning sounds. He had experienced the pain of returning circulation and felt sorry for her. He knew she must be feeling as though a thousand hot needles were piercing her flesh.

But as uncomfortable as it must be, it was a good sign. By the grace of God, her feet and hands weren't frostbitten. "Do you think a warm bath would help her?" Kane asked, looking at Maria.

Maria looked down at the dirt-grimed face and said dryly, "It would certainly help her face."

"That's no lie," Kane agreed.

"Where did you find her anyway?"

As Kane filled two big kettles with water and set them on the stove to heat, he spoke briefly of buying the stallion and why the girl had ridden the animal down the mountain.

"Is it true he looks like the other white?" Maria asked as he brought a wood tub from the larder room off the kitchen.

"He's the spitting image of him. There's no doubt the wild one sired him," Kane answered, then noticed that the bathwater was beginning to steam a bit. "I guess we'll put her in Storm's old room."

Maria nodded, but there was a frown on her face. She didn't like the idea of the dirty waif using Storm's room, touching her things.

While Maria continued to steady Jade in the chair, Kane made three trips up the stairs to his sister's room: one trip to carry up the big tub, then twice more to bring up the water. Finally he carried Jade up, Maria following behind with a pail of cold water.

Maria hurried to turn down the covers of the dainty bed, and as Kane laid Jade down he said, "When you're ready, I'll lift her into the tub."

Bending over Jade's inert body, Maria gripped the neckline of her dress with both hands and ripped the thin material apart. She gasped and quickly pulled it back together again. This was no youngster lying here, as she had thought, but a young woman with full, round breasts.

She looked over her shoulder and saw Kane approaching the bed. "I'll put her in the tub," she squeaked.

"If you think so." Kane paused, then added, "I'll go tend to the horses."

When the door closed behind Kane, Maria turned her attention back to Jade and gave a start. Dark green eyes were staring up at her, full of fright as well as challenge. She was reminded of a small kitten trying to look fierce as it readied itself to do battle with a large dog. Pity for the mountain girl welled up inside her.

"Don't be frightened, Jade," she said softly. "You are at the Roemer ranch. You and Kane were caught in a blizzard. I expect you are in some pain now, but I have a nice warm bath waiting for you and you'll feel much better after you've used it."

Jade shook her head vehemently. "I want to go home."

"You can't go home now, girl. There's a blizzard going on out there. It's a miracle that you and Kane made it to the ranch. Now let's get you into the warm water and thaw out your flesh."

Jade shook her head again. "I don't want to get in a tub of water."

Her hands on her hips, Maria glared down at her. "Well, you're going to. You can get into that tub willingly or I can call Kane to put you in it."

The idea of the cold-faced rancher seeing her naked quickly changed Jade's mind. "Oh all right," she said with a half snarl, "I'll get into your damn tub." She sat up on the edge of the bed, clutching the torn dress together with dirt-stained fingers. When she stood up she cried out at the pain that shot into her feet. When she tried to walk she teetered, so Maria put an arm around her waist and helped her to the tub. Kane had placed it near the stove so that she could get the benefit of the warmth the fire sent out.

Maria thought for a moment that she'd have to take the torn dress off Jade forcibly. She continued to clutch it to her breasts as she stared fearfully down into the water. Hadn't the girl ever gotten into a tub of water and bathed herself? Maria wondered. She was getting ready to threaten her with Kane again when Jade reluctantly loosened her grip and let the dress fall to her feet.

Shock jumped into Maria's eyes. The girl wore no petticoat or bloomers. Scandalized, she helped Jade into the tub, and in doing so she was amazed at the feminine curves the sole garment had hidden. Although Jade was slender, Maria thought she had never seen a body so perfectly shaped. Even her Storm couldn't measure up to this one. And Kane's sister had a lovely body.

With an uncertain look in her eyes, Jade lowered herself into the water. As its warmth enveloped her she thought she had never felt anything so comforting. As the cold seeped out of her flesh and bones, she wanted to close her eyes and go to sleep.

That wish burst as Maria tossed a bar of pink soap and a washcloth into the tub. As water splashed into her eyes, blinding her momentarily, Maria went down on her knees, taking a brush to Jade's tangled mass of hair.

"I'll get the tangles out of your hair before I wash it."

Tears glimmered in Jade's eyes as the brush was dragged through her hair. Her long tresses had never known a brush or comb. Occasionally she combed her fingers through her hair and tied it back with a piece of rawhide. If she had her way she would cut most of it off. But Uncle John had threatened to tan her backside if she ever did. He claimed it was her crowning glory.

When Maria had removed as many tangles as she could, she laid aside the brush and stood up, shaking her head. She had found that Jade's hair was too dirty to be washed in the bathwater. "You can start soaping yourself while I go downstairs to bring up more water to wash your hair in."

Grimacing, Jade fished around for the soap, which had sunk to the bottom of the tub. Low-landers had strange ideas, in her opinion.

Her fingers found the soap and she brought it up to sniff it. Surprised, she thought it smelled like the wild roses that bloomed behind Uncle John's cabin. She picked up the washcloth that had fallen on her knee and, after an uncertain moment, rubbed the soap on the cloth and began to wash her face and throat. She was surprised at the dirt that came off on the cloth and she washed her face a second time. The rest of her body came clean with just one good swipe of the soapy washcloth. It was a different story when she came to her knees and feet. She was still scrubbing at them when Maria returned, carrying two pails of warm water.

Placing the pails on the floor next to the tub, she knelt down and said, "Hand me the soap and then lean your head back as far as you can."

It took three soapings before Maria thought

Jade's hair clean enough to be rinsed in the other pail of water. After squeezing as much water as she could from the long hair, she wrapped a towel around it and told Jade she could get out of the tub. "Dry yourself off and later you can sit beside the stove to dry your hair."

When Jade turned around to accept the towel, Maria marveled at the loveliness that had lain beneath the dirt and grime. The girl's face was as delicate-looking as her body. She had high cheekbones and a straight nose over ripe, red lips and a firm jawline. Kane had better get rid of this one as fast as he could, she thought. This wild child of the mountains just might put an end to his bachelor days.

Maria walked over to the dresser and started pulling out drawers. Jade had just finished drying her long, shapely legs when Maria returned with a white flannel gown and a blue woolen robe folded over her arm. When she had helped Jade into the garments, she pulled a chair over by the stove and said, "Let's get your hair dried and then I'll bring you something to eat."

When Maria finished toweling and combing the long tresses that hung midway down Jade's back, they were two shades lighter than before her hair was washed. It was baby soft and of a tawny color that looked like warm honey. Maria smiled at Jade and said, "Go look at yourself in the mirror."

Jade walked across the floor to the dresser and stood rooted there. Who was that person staring at her? she asked herself. She raised a hand and ran it lightly over her face, then smoothed it over her hair.

She turned her head and said to Maria in bemusement, "I'm not ugly; I'm pretty."

Maria smiled at the girl's innocent candor. "Yes, you're pretty," she said. "You're very pretty. Who said you weren't?"

"That one." Jade jerked her head toward the closed bedroom door.

"You mean Kane?" Maria looked amused.

"Yes," Jade answered sourly, then went back to studying her face.

"Jade," Maria said, "if you want to look this way from now on, you must keep yourself clean. You must wash your face every morning when you get up, and brush your hair."

"Oh, I will," Jade said gravely, continuing to gaze in the mirror.

"Good." Maria nodded. "Now why don't you get in bed and I'll bring you something to eat."

Jade took one last look at herself before climbing into bed. "It's so soft," she marveled as she stretched out on the feather mattress. "I've never felt anything like it. It's like lying on a cloud." She thought how different this bed was from the hard, straw-packed mattress she was used to sleeping on.

When Kane stepped outside after leaving Jade in Maria's care, he caught his breath at the bite of the cold air. "Damn," he muttered, "it's getting colder by the hour."

Thankful that he had made it home safely, he peered through the falling snow for the stallions. There was no sign of them. They were gone! Had he forgotten to tie them to the hitching post in his hurry to get the girl into the house? Had Satan taken off to the wilds, and had Renegade followed him?

Then he saw hoofprints leading off toward the barn, and the imprints of boots alongside them. He grinned his relief. Jeb had taken the animals to shelter. How had he managed to get Satan to follow him? Kane wondered as he clumped through snow almost past the top of his boots.

Jeb had hung a lit lantern on a peg driven into a post, and when Kane stepped inside the barn, he saw his longtime friend tossing hay into Renegade's trough. The old-timer looked up at Kane and a wide, toothless smile lit up his face.

"I see you got him," he said. "He sure is a handsome feller."

"That he is, but how did you get him in here? He never lets anyone but a slip of a girl get close to him."

Jeb shrugged. "Wasn't nothin' to it. When I started leadin' Renegade away, he just naturally followed."

"I'll be damned." Kane shook his head. "He must have known somehow that you were taking them to warm quarters."

"That's probably it. He went straight into a stall and stood there as though waitin' for me to feed him." Leaning the pitchfork against Renegade's stall, Jeb said, "I guess you found it pretty rough goin', gettin' home in this blizzard."

"I sure as hell did," Kane agreed. "I damn near froze my rod off."

"Well"—Jeb grinned—"I know how you can thaw it out."

Kane looked toward the storage room at the end of the barn. When he saw a light shining from beneath the door, his lips twisted wryly. "I see Liz has come calling," he said.

"Yeah. She rode in just before the blizzard hit. Says she's come to spend the night. But from the looks of the weather, she'll be here longer than that."

"Damn, I hope not." Kane frowned impatiently. "One night with her is enough for any man. There's no satifying the woman and tonight I'm too tired to try."

"You can sic a couple of the cowhands on her," Jeb said with a grin. "They could take turns with her."

"Now that's not a bad idea." Kane grinned, too. "If she's snowed in here for a day or so, I just might do that. I think they've had her already."

"I think all the men within thirty miles have had her." Jeb snorted.

When Kane laughingly agreed, Jeb said, "I'll see

you in the mornin'. I'm gonna go play a couple rounds of poker with the hands."

Kane remained leaning against Renegade's stall, remembering back to August. One hot day he had ridden to the Platte to take a dip in its cool waters. That was the first time he had seen Liz, and it was the first time he'd lain with her.

She was splashing around in the water naked as the day she was born. When she saw him sitting on his stallion watching her, she stood up, the water sluicing off her large breasts and wide hips. The look of invitation in her eyes was unmistakable, and he'd taken advantage of it.

They met at the river every afternoon that summer, pleasuring each other without exchanging much talk. But when autumn arrived it became too cold to lie buck naked in the grass. They couldn't go to her house. Her parents were old and very religious, and he didn't dare take Liz to the ranch house. Maria would take a broom to his head if he tried to.

So they had taken to meeting in the storage room off the barn. He had piled hay on the floor and taken a couple of blankets out of the house to make it more comfortable.

Kane pushed himself away from the stall and halfheartedly walked toward the door. What he would really like to do was climb into his bed and sleep the clock around. The thing was, no doubt Liz had heard him and Jeb talking, so she knew he was home. If he didn't go to her, he wouldn't put it past her to go to the house and knock on the door, demanding entrance. The woman just wouldn't take no for an answer, he thought sourly.

Chapter Four

Jade awakened to gray light filtering between the pretty curtains at the window. She lay in the warm cocoon of feather bed and soft comforters for several seconds before she realized that it wasn't her bed of rough sheets, scratchy blankets and hard, straw-filled mattress.

She rolled over and stared up at the ceiling as the events of yesterday came rushing back. She felt a tightening in her chest as she recalled the hateful rancher buying her beloved Satan, her rage and humiliation at having to ride him down the mountain to that man's ranch.

She shivered, remembering the blizzard that had finally overcome her, rendering her senseless. She had floated in and out of consciousness until a woman insisted she climb into a tub of warm water.

Jade grimaced, remembering the pull of the brush going through her hair. When she caught sight of the mirror across the room, Jade swept back the covers and swung her feet to the floor. She winced with pain when she stood up and took a step. Her feet were sore from being nearly frozen. She gritted her teeth and determinedly hobbled over to view herself in the mirror again.

A wide, pleased smile curved her lips. It was no dream. She was pretty. At least she was compared to the mountain women. She ran her fingers through her hair, which was now soft and silky and ever so much lighter in color. She wondered what Uncle John would think when he saw her. She couldn't wait to see his reaction.

Jade fingered the soft material of the gown, a wistful look in her eyes. It would be nice to have one of her own.

The distant sound of voices sent Jade hurrying back to bed. She had barely settled under the covers when the door opened and the kind woman stepped inside carrying a large wooden tray. The aroma coming from it made Jade's stomach grumble from hunger.

"I've brought you some breakfast." Maria smiled at her. "I bet you're hungry."

"Yes, ma'am, I am," Jade answered shyly as she sat up. "My stomach can't remember when it had food last."

"I brought you in some stew last night but you were sound asleep. I figured sleep was more important at the time than food was, so I took it away. In case you didn't hear it last night, my name is Maria," the housekeeper said, placing the tray across Jade's lap. As she poured coffee from a small, steaming pot she added, "I've fixed you some ham and scrambled eggs and hot biscuits."

"Thank you. It sure looks good." Jade's mouth was watering as she picked up the fork lying beside the plate heaped with food.

Maria walked away from the bed, giving Jade privacy as she ate. She fussed over the dresser, needlessly moving things about, an excuse to view Jade through the mirror. It reflected the girl wolfing down her breakfast like a hungry wolf cub. Goodness, she thought, the girl really is hungry.

When she saw Jade pouring herself a cup of coffee, she walked back to the bed. She was not surprised to see that every crumb had been eaten. "Feeling better?" she asked, sitting down on the edge of the bed.

"Yes, I feel fine. I'm ready to go home now."

"You won't be able to go home today, Jade," Maria said sympathetically. "It's still snowing as hard as it was yesterday. If it stops anytime soon, maybe Kane can take you home tomorrow."

"I don't need *him* to take me home," Jade said crossly. "I know the way there."

"I'm sure you do. But you don't realize how deep that snow is out there. Only a strong draft horse could make it. A slip of a girl like yourself could never handle one of them. As soon as he can, Kane will break a trail with one of the draft horses and you can follow it astride one of his sturdy little Indian ponies."

"But my uncle will be worried about me," Jade protested. "He expects me to come home today."

"Now, honey, don't worry about that," Maria coaxed. "I'm sure your uncle had faith in Kane to take care of you. He'll know you can't make it home in this kind of weather."

Maria could see that Jade wasn't fully convinced of that by the fine frown lines that had appeared between her eyes. To take her mind off her uncle, Maria gestured toward a large wardrobe, saying, "You and Kane's sister, Storm, are about the same size. I'm sure I'll find something of hers for you to put on. You can't go around in your nightclothes all day, and I'm afraid I ruined your dress getting it off you last night."

When the double doors were swung open, the clothes they revealed made Jade stare in awe. She'd never dreamed that such clothing existed. Her eyes feasted on dresses, jackets, coats—and beneath them, lined up neatly, several pairs of slippers, shoes and boots. She shook her head. This woman Storm had more clothes than the mercantile in Laramie. And they were so much fancier.

"What do you think of this one?" Maria held up a green woollen dress with a white lace collar and cuffs. "It used to be one of Storm's favorites before she had the baby and put on a little weight."

"It's awfully pretty," Jade said, unable to take her eyes off the garment. "Are you sure Storm won't mind me wearing it?"

"Not in the least. If the clothes she left behind don't fit her anymore, she'll be glad to give you any or all of them," Maria said, laying the dress across the foot of the bed. As Jade ran a callused palm over the soft material, Maria continued, "I'll see what Storm left in the way of underclothing. In the meantime, you can wash your face and hands. There's soap and a washcloth over there." She motioned toward a washstand placed next to the window.

As Jade used the scented soap and water she wondered how Maria thought that she could get dirty while sleeping. But she had to admit she felt better after washing her face, more awake and alert. She walked back to the bed just as Maria spread some white, lacy garments next to the dress.

When Maria saw Jade studying two of the articles, she explained, "That's a camisole, and lying next to it is an underwaist. And the other garment is, of course, a petticoat. Put them on; let's see how they fit."

Eager to wear the pretty underclothing, Jade whipped the nightgown over her head and stepped into her first pair of underpants. The camisole that went on next was also a first for her.

"A perfect fit," Maria said and handed her the petticoat. "Get this on and then we'll see how the dress fits you."

Excited, Jade pulled the dress over her head, and Maria tugged at it until the garment settled in all the right places. When Maria had buttoned up the pearl buttons and smoothed out the collar she stepped back and ran admiring eyes over Jade. "It fits you to a tee," she said. "Go look at yourself in the mirror."

The mountain girl couldn't believe that she was looking at Jade Farrow. Her face took on added beauty as it glowed with wonderment. Maria let Jade gaze at herself for a full minute, then said, "Put on these stockings." She held up a pair of white, sheer hose and pink, lacy garters.

Jade wondered as she pulled the stockings on how she was to keep them up. They weren't like the drab woolen ones she was used to wearing. Maria solved the problem by handing her the garters. "These will keep your hose in place." She held up a pair of black, dainty slippers. "Slip these on when you're finished with the stockings."

When Jade stood up she felt smothered with so many clothes on. But not for the world would she remove one article. She'd get used to all the material winding around her legs, she told herself.

"Brush your hair and we'll go downstairs." Maria handed her an ivory-handled brush.

When Jade's hair flowed like silk midway down her back, Maria ushered her out into a narrow hall. Before they started to descend the stairs the housekeeper motioned to a closed door next to the room where Jade had slept. "That's Kane's room," she said.

For some reason Jade didn't understand, it bothered her that the hard-hearted man had slept so near her last night.

When Jade descended to the tiled foyer and followed Maria through a large room filled with expensive furniture, she thought to herself, *No wonder Kane Roemer acts like he's a king. He lives like one.*

But I'll never treat him like royalty, she vowed to herself. *I'll treat him like the arrogant devil he is.*

"Come on into the kitchen and we can talk while I make some pies for tonight's supper," Maria said, breaking in on her sour thoughts.

The kitchen was almost half the size of her little mountain home, and Jade thought how nice it would be to fix meals in such a room. It would be wonderful not to feel cold air seeping up through the cracks between the floorboards before Uncle John put down the straw and carpet. She walked over to the red-curtained window and looked out through the shiny, clean glass. The falling snow obscured everything within a few yards of the house. She sighed, knowing and dreading the fact that she would have to spend the day and another night under the rancher's roof.

Jade started to turn away from the window, then stopped to peer outside again. The figure of a man was making its way through the the snow, coming toward the house. When he came closer she recognized Kane Roemer. She hurriedly took a seat at the table where Maria was peeling a pan of apples. She held her breath, listening to him knocking the snow off his boots before opening the door and stepping inside.

Maria looked up at him and frowned and wrinkled her nose. "There's a pitcher of hot water in your room, Kane," she said, her tone saying she wasn't pleased with him.

Kane understood what the housekeeper was hinting at. He smelled. He quickly took himself out of range of Maria and her companion. Whoever she was, he didn't want that little beauty smelling another woman on him.

As he stood in the doorway of the kitchen he studied the lovely vision who sat quietly with downcast eyes. Something about her reminded him of someone, but he couldn't place her. "Who's your company, Maria?" he asked. "A friend of Storm's from her college years?"

Jade looked at him, realizing that he hadn't recognized her. The face she saw today, smiling with twinkling eyes, was altogether different from the cold, hard face he always presented to her. She could like this man, she thought, then grew angry with herself that she was drawn to Kane Roemer. As soon as he recognized her, his face would resume its harsh lines.

The cold look she gave him made Kane's eyes

widen in surprise. He had received such a look before, but couldn't remember when or from whom. He became more confused when Maria said, "She's no friend of Storm's. She's an acquaintance of yours."

"Of mine?" Kane started to step forward but then remembered that he smelled. "It's impossible that I'd ever forget such loveliness," he said, "but for the life of me I can't remember ever seeing her before."

"Well, you have met her, and recently," Maria snapped, still put out with him. Kane wasn't aware of it, but she knew all about the time he spent in that room in the barn. She also knew who visited him there. She had realized right off that Kane was quite taken with the mountain girl, and that Jade Farrow didn't like him.

It gave Maria great pleasure to say, "Meet Miss Jade Farrow."

Maria had never seen Kane so disconcerted that he couldn't speak, but now it seemed he could only stare at Jade.

Kane's mind was racing as he tried to match this lovely young woman to the dirty-faced urchin whose horse he had taken away. Only the glittering green eyes were the same.

He felt a sharp regret that this wasn't the first time he and Jade Farrow were meeting. All the unflattering things he had said to her came to mind. He remembered the ruthless way he had bought her pet from her uncle, uncaring how much the wild stallion meant to her. He searched for words that would help undo his previous mistakes. But first he must wash up, get rid of Liz's scent.

When he turned and left them, Maria looked at Jade and said, "I see you don't like Kane."

"No, I don't," Jade answered frankly. "I detest the man."

"Oh?" Maria looked surprised. Most women loved Kane. They chased after him all the time. But she couldn't see this miss inviting his attention, and Kane would have to work doubly hard to get hers. Maria finished peeling an apple, and asked, "Do you want to tell me why you dislike him so?"

"He's a low-bellied rattlesnake. He bought my stallion when he knew I didn't want him to. He has many horses and Satan is very special to me. I tamed him, made him into the best riding horse in the mountains."

"You didn't have to sell him if you didn't want to," Maria pointed out. "I'm sure Kane didn't hold a gun to your head and force you to sell the horse."

"Of course not," Jade said testily. "Uncle John sold Satan to him."

"So you didn't own the stallion."

"Well, no, not really. Uncle John captured him. But I'm the only one who can ride Satan. If anyone else mounts him he bucks them right off." She gave a short, disparaging laugh. "The mountain people are afraid of him. They were always pressuring Uncle John to get rid of him. They claimed he was a danger to their children."

"In that case, then, your uncle would have sold your pet to someone, wouldn't he?" Maria asked.

"Maybe." Jade stood up and walked to the window again, her back held stiffly. "But it's not likely anyone else would have climbed the mountain to buy a horse. Uncle John takes a herd of the wild ones down to Laramie once a year and sells them. I could have hidden Satan the day he took the others down the mountain."

Maria could tell by the tremor in Jade's voice that she was about to break into tears. "Kane will take the best care of Satan," she said gently. "It broke him up when he had to shoot your pet's sire, so he'll do his best to make it up to the son."

Jade sat back down as Maria tried to console her. "I'm sure he'll let you visit the horse anytime you want to."

A scowl marred Jade's lovely face. "After I leave here I don't ever want to set eyes on that man again."

"I'm sorry you feel that way, Jade," Maria said gently. "I was looking forward to seeing a lot of you. Storm has her own home to run now and I miss having young people around."

"You have him." Jade nodded her head in the direction of the stairs.

"Kane's not that young." Maria chuckled. "He's thirty-five, a man grown."

Jade looked surprised, then blurted out, "He's an old man."

"He's not an old man by any means"—Maria laughed—"and you'd better not let him hear you say that he is."

"It's too late. I just heard her," Kane said abruptly from the doorway. As Maria and Jade stared at him openmouthed, he grabbed his jacket off the wall, jerked open the door and slammed it shut behind him.

Maria sighed with wry amusement. "I think you just took a large bite out of his ego, Jade. I'm sure no other woman has ever called him an old man."

Jade was silent a moment before saying quietly, "I expect he knows many women."

Maria slid her a glance from the corner of her eye. The young miss might think that Kane was an old man, but if Maria wasn't mistaken Jade was attracted to him nevertheless.

"How old are you, Jade?"

"I turned nineteen last summer."

"I guess thirty-five does sound old to you. Young girls your age wouldn't be attracted to a man that old, I suppose?"

"Some are," Jade answered quickly. "Most of the men up in the mountains have wives younger than them. Old Man Oates was forty-five when he married thirteen-year-old Jessie Moser. That was unusual, though. Uncle John said the man should be horsewhipped, marrying a child. Usually a girl is around fifteen before she gets married."

"How is it that you, at nineteen, aren't married yet? Aren't any of the men up there interested in you?"

"Oh, they're interested all right," Jade answered. "I'm just not interested in them. Besides, my uncle wouldn't let me marry a mountain man even if I wanted to. He says that mountain wives have too rough a life. They work like horses trying to grow a garden in the rocky soil and every spring they have a new baby. And if that isn't enough, most of the husbands beat their wives when they get drunk." Jade laughed softly. "Uncle John says that if any man ever lays a hand on me in anger he'll shoot him between the eyes."

"I don't imagine he means that," Maria said, laughing too.

"Oh, yes, he does. He almost knocked a friend of his right off the mountain one day when he didn't like the way the man was looking at me."

Slicing the peeled apples now, Maria wondered just how John Farrow thought Jade could meet any other kind of man where she lived. Especially if she continued to look the way she did when Kane had brought her to the ranch house.

Maria shook her head. Men! They never thought beyond their noses.

Kane was fuming as he battled his way through the blinding snow to the cookhouse. "So," he muttered, "the little witch thinks I'm an old man, does she? I'd like to get her in bed and show her just how old I am."

"What bit you in the ass this mornin'?" Cookie grinned as Kane came bursting through the door, anger plain on his lean, hard-boned face. "Wore yourself out last night, did you?"

"Hold your jaw, old man, and fix me a plate of grub."

"Who's it for, and what should I put in it?"

"You know damn well who it's for. Put anything that's handy in it."

Cookie looked down at the pieces of cubed beef he intended to put in a stew. The raw meat was handy. He lifted twinkling eyes to his boss and Kane snapped, "Don't try it."

"Don't try what?" Cookie gave him an innocent look as he broke three eggs into a bowl and started beating them together with a fork. "I was just thinkin' that your lady might like some scrambled eggs and ham."

"She's not my lady." Kane gave him a narrowed look.

Ten minutes later Kane was carrying a covered plate to the barn, cursing the snow that continued to fall. Would it never cease so that he could rid himself of the two snowbound females he had on his hands? Especially the green-eyed, sharp-tongued little witch.

Old Jeb was mending reins when Kane stepped into the barn. "Here's some breakfast for Liz," he said, placing the plate on a stool. "Take it in to her, will you?"

"I don't know if I should," Jeb said, a teasing light in his eyes. "I don't think I could perform if she jerked me down in the hay."

"I'm damn well sure that I couldn't," Kane growled as he left the barn.

Chapter Five

Jade awakened the next morning to pale sunlight shining on her face. Not used to hangings on windows, she hadn't thought to draw the drapes before she went to bed last night.

Had it really stopped snowing? She threw back the covers and scooted off the bed. Not yet adept at wearing clothes that came to her ankles, she almost tripped over the long nightgown in her hurry to get to the window.

"Glory be," she said excitedly as she looked down on the backyard and saw the towering pines there. The snow had finally stopped.

She pulled on the heavy robe lying at the foot of the bed and slipped her feet into the fur-lined house slippers. She tied the robe's belt around her waist as she half ran to the kitchen. When would the rancher take her home? she asked herself, then answered her own question: as late as possible, just to be mean.

Maria looked up from a skillet of bacon sizzling on the stove. "My, you must be hungry, walking so fast." She smiled at Jade.

"A little." Jade smiled back. "Have you noticed it has stopped snowing? I can go home today."

"Yes, it stopped snowing sometime around midnight," Maria said, removing the bacon from the fire and laying the strips on a plate. "And yes, I imagine you will be going home today."

"When do you think he will take me?"

"Not for a while. He's not even up yet. He'll want to eat breakfast first: then he'll tend to his horses."

"How long will it take him to do that?"

"I don't know, Jade." Maria was getting a little impatient at all the questions. "Kane doesn't have a set time for anything he does."

"He'll take his sweet time stirring about today," Jade complained. "It won't matter to him that I want to get home so that Uncle John can stop worrying about me."

"You're mistaken about that, Jade. Kane isn't one to hold grudges."

Jade made no response to Maria's declaration, but she was thinking that the housekeeper didn't know her boss as well as she thought she did. After a moment Jade asked, "Couldn't you knock on his door and tell him that it has stopped snowing and remind him that he's taking me home today?"

When Maria finished breaking four eggs into the hot bacon grease, she said, "Kane isn't here. He probably slept in the bunkhouse again."

"Does he do that often?"

"Often enough," Maria answered, disapproval in her voice.

"Why does he do that?"

"For heaven's sake, Jade, I don't know." Maria spoke sharply, her patience gone. "I think when he plays poker with the cowboys and it gets late, he just climbs onto one of the bunks."

As Maria sliced up half a loaf of bread Jade said, "After I've eaten and gotten dressed I'm going down to the bunkhouse and demand that he get up."

"Jade, you can't do that!" Maria looked alarmed. "You might catch some of the cowboys in their underwear. They'd be embarrassed to death."

Jade reluctantly gave in to the fact that there was nothing she could do but wait until the rancher came to the house in his own good time.

She picked up her fork and started in on her breakfast. Maria carried her own plate to the table and sat down across from her. They talked little as they ate. Jade was thinking that she'd like to get home and Maria was thinking that she'd like to get hold of Kane and lay down the law about his bringing that whore, Liz, to the ranch.

When the meal was finished Maria rose to pour the coffee. As she passed the window her gaze was drawn outside. A rider astride a very large draft horse had just reined his mount in alongside the porch. As she watched, curious, a big, burly stranger swung out of the saddle. The winter sun shone on a head of graying curly black hair and a matching short beard. Who in the world was he? she wondered as he tied the horse to the hitching post. She knew by his attire he wasn't a rancher.

"What are you looking at, Maria?" Jade asked.

"A man I don't know has just ridden up to the house."

Jade went to stand beside Maria. "Why, it's Uncle John!" she exclaimed excitedly as the big man stepped up on the porch. "He's come to take me home." She hurried to fling open the door. When John Farrow stepped inside the kitchen he looked even larger than he had seemed outside. Not fat, just big. When he grabbed his niece in a bear hug Maria thought that surely he was going to crack some of the girl's ribs.

But Jade only laughed joyfully and hugged him back. "So you're all right," the man said, holding Jade away from him and searching her face. "I near to killed my horse gettin' here through the snow. I was right concerned about you, girl."

"I know you were, Uncle John, but it snowed so hard there wasn't any way I could get home. I was planning on doing it today, though."

"And who is the pretty lady?" Big John's eyes glowed warmly as his gaze frankly took in Maria's plump, though shapely figure. Anyone watching could easily read the thoughts going through his mind.

Maria knew quite well what he was thinking, and she grew angry with herself for responding to the message in his eyes. It had been a long time since she had been attracted to a man. She asked herself why it had to be this big, wild mountain man whom she'd never see again.

When Jade said, "This is Maria, Uncle John, that man's housekeeper," John raised a quizzical eyebrow at her.

"Do you have a hard time remembering the rancher's name, girl?"

When Jade only shrugged indifferently, the big man held out his hand to Maria. "I expect you're the one who dressed my niece up in the pretty clothes she's wearin'."

Upset with herself for the way her pulse leaped at the clasp of his hand, Maria said sharply, "I also cleaned her up. You should feel ashamed to let her run around like that, and practically wearing rags. She's a very pretty young woman."

"Hell, I know that, woman," John said gruffly. "She looks like her mother, my deceased sister-in-law. I let her run around dirty and ragged on purpose. I don't want her attractin' the notice of them yahoos up where we live any more than she already has. My brother would haunt me if I let her get hooked up with one of them. I've got plans for her when she gets older. I expect you've noticed

88

she speaks real good, not like me and the rest of the mountain folks."

Maria nodded. "I noticed and I wondered about it."

"I bought her a lot of school-learnin' books. When she was little we used to play a game. Ever' time she didn't say a word right she lost a day of ridin' her pony around."

Maria's opinion of the big man rose a bit. In his own rough way he had his niece's best interests at heart. She wondered what his plans for Jade were.

"Have you had breakfast, John?" she asked, her tone softening somewhat. "Jade and I just finished eating. I can fry you up some bacon and eggs."

"That sounds right good, Maria." John gave her his rakish smile.

"Well, sit down at the table," Maria said, her heart all aflutter. "In the meantime, Jade, pour your uncle a cup of coffee."

"Where's Roemer?" John asked after taking a long swallow of the strong brew.

"He's, uh . . . down at the barn, I expect," Maria answered. "He'll be along any time now."

Kane had come awake hours earlier at the creaking of the bunkhouse door. He looked at the uncurtained window. The east was gray with coming daylight. In the dimness of the room he recognized his new drover, Pete Harding, moving quietly to his bunk. Kane's lips curved in a crooked smile and he raised himself up on his elbow and said over the sound of snoring, "You're up early, Pete."

The drover gave a start, then answered gruffly, "I had to go relieve myself."

Kane waited a moment, and then asked with amusement, "Did she relieve you real good?"

There was a tight silence as Harding sat down on his bed and pulled off his boots. When the second boot hit the floor, he said, "I guess you know I've been with Liz." Before Kane could answer he went on, "It wasn't all my fault. Last night after we finished playin' cards and you all had gone to bed, I really did go out to relieve myself. First thing I knew, she was standin' beside me, watchin'. When I was buttonin' up my fly she asked if you had gone to bed. When I said yes, she asked me if I'd like to keep her company for a while.

"I knew what she really wanted, and without thinking of the consequences, I let my pecker think for me."

When Kane didn't say anything right away, Pete said, "I guess you'll be wantin' me to move on now."

"Because you had Liz?" Kane snorted. "I'm not about to lose a good hand over her. I see it's stopped snowing, so after you've slept and rested for a while, I'd like for you to take her home."

"I'll see to it," Pete said as he stretched out his tired body beneath the blankets.

Kane pulled his covers over his head to shut out

most of the snoring. He would like to catch a few more hours' sleep.

The long-legged, green-eyed mountain girl teased at his mind as sleep overtook him.

Jade's image was still with him when Kane awakened three hours later with a hard arousal. The bunkhouse was empty except for himself and the drover. He imagined the others were at the cookhouse eating breakfast.

As Kane drew on his clothes he decided he'd eat breakfast at the house. He told himself that it was Maria's cooking he wanted, but deep down what he really wanted was to see Jade again.

Back at the ranch house, Big John's eyes followed every move Maria made as she went about the kitchen, her body swaying sensuously. The housekeeper stirred an excitement inside him he hadn't felt in years. He was wondering if it was possible she would let a rough mountain man court her when the kitchen door opened and Kane stepped inside.

Both men wore friendly smiles when they greeted each other. "I was wondering who the big draft horse belonged to," Kane said, and added as he sat down at the table, "I planned to take your niece home right after I had breakfast. I knew you would be worried about her."

"I admit I didn't get much sleep the last two nights, frettin' about her. We ain't had a blizzard like this one for ten years or more. On my way here I had to dismount a couple times and shovel my way through snowdrifts too high for my big horse to get through."

Kane nodded, a glum look on his face. "I'm worried about how my cattle have fared."

"They'll be all right if they had sense enough to go up into the foothills. I saw several head there on my way down. Most likely they're all up there. How many did you keep back after your fall roundup?"

"A few hundred for breeding. But even if they find shelter, I'm afraid they'll starve to death. Cattle are too dumb to dig under the snow and find the dry grass there."

"Them longhorns are tough," John said. "They may be skin and bones by spring, but I bet most of them will survive."

"I hope so. I'm sure glad I thought to keep the new breed I bought last year penned up behind the barn. They're heavy and have short legs. At least I can feed them."

"Well, son, there's no use frettin' about the longhorns. There ain't a thing you can do about it," John said.

As Kane and Big John talked Jade shot Kane frowning glances. Why did this man she hated stir such intense feelings inside her?

From beneath lowered lids Kane had been watching Jade, feeling confused in the same way. Never before had he felt the contemptuous slice of a woman's tongue as he had from Jade, yet he wanted to reach out and gently stroke the sleep-tumbled hair that trailed over her shoulders and down her back. He wanted to scoop her up in his arms, carry her to his room and make slow love to her for the rest of the day.

He remembered then that she thought him an old man and forced himself to look away. He wasn't going to tease himself.

Big John's thoughts about Maria ran in the same vein as Kane's about Jade. But where Kane dreamed of making slow, careful love to Jade, her uncle wanted to get the housekeeper in bed and ride her fast and hard. He visualized her naked beneath him, her wide hips cradling him as he thrust in and out of her, while she responded just as wildly as he. He had sensed right off that there was a fire beneath her calm exterior, a fire that could scorch a man.

The mountain man vowed to himself that one day he would make his wish come true. For now, he glanced at Jade and said, "Well, girl, get your duds on and let's get goin'. It's gonna take a while to get through the snow."

Jade looked at Maria as if willing her to speak, to explain the disappearance of her worn-out clothing. Maria was equal to telling the big man what had become of them, for she still became riled every time she remembered the rags Jade had been wearing the night of the blizzard.

"In my hurry to get Jade's wet clothing off, I'm afraid I tore her dress too badly to be mended," she said curtly.

"Well, now, that poses a problem, don't it?" Big John's eyebrows drew together.

"No, it doesn't." Maria softened her tone as she continued, remembering mountain people's pride. "When Kane's sister got married and moved to a home of her own, she left a few of her clothes here. I hate waste and it pains me to see those clothes just hanging in the wardrobe when somebody could be using them. Jade and Storm are the same size and it would please me greatly to give them to your niece."

"I'm not sure I like that," John said at once, his brow darkening. "I'm able to buy the girl anything she needs." He looked at Jade for confirmation of his statement and saw the yearning in her eyes. After a moment he cleared his throat and said gruffly, "But I reckon you're right about wastin' things. I'm of the same mind. Me and Jade will be much obliged."

"Thank you, Uncle John!" Jade jumped up and ran around the table to give her uncle a fierce hug.

"Now don't go gettin' mushy on me, girl." The big man's voice was rough, but the softening of his features gave away how pleased he was at his niece's show of affection. Kane realized again just how much Jade meant to the big man. God save the man who ever did her wrong, for certainly Big John Farrow wouldn't.

"She always was an affectionate little soul," John said, a little pink faced. "Most younguns are afraid of me because I'm rough-lookin', but Jade never feared me, even the first time she seen me. When the woman who brung her to me stood her on the floor, that little thing came right up to me, a big smile on her pretty little face."

"How old was she when she came to live with you, and what happened to her parents, if you don't mind my asking?" Maria looked at John.

"I'm originally from the East. When our elderly parents died, my brother Luke got married and I came west. Jade was almost four when Luke and his wife caught typhoid fever from drinking bad water. To make sure the little one didn't catch it, too, Luke's mother-in-law only let Jade drink milk, and she kept her away from her parents. After they passed on, the grandmother sent Jade to me in care of a cousin."

Big John paused to laugh and slap his thigh. "Boy," he said, "you should have seen the look on that old maid's puckered-up face when she found out I was the uncle. And my cabin wasn't much to look at either. 'I think I'll be taking the child back east with me,' she said, her lips drawn so thin a person could hardly see them."

"What did you say to that?" Kane grinned.

"Not much. I just took her by one scrawny arm and marched her to the door. While she was splutterin', her face all red, I pushed her through the door and told her to have a nice time on her way back east."

Jade and Maria interrupted the male laughter to go pack, but when they returned, the men were still talking. Maria followed Jade, a leather-bound satchel in her hands. Though Kane could only stare at how beautiful Jade looked as she stood uncertainly before her uncle, Big John looked thunderstruck.

"What kind of dress is that?" he demanded in a roar. "It almost shows her knees."

"Don't take on so, Mr. Farrow," Maria said sharply. "She's not wearing a dress. It's a riding skirt she has on. It enables a woman to sit in a saddle without having to be bothered with cumbersome skirts blowing around. Showing a few inches of leg isn't going to make the world come to an end. And the boots she's wearing cover more of her legs than the dress she was wearing when she arrived here."

By God, John thought, I'm half-afraid of that woman. After a long scrutiny of his niece's new attire, he looked at Kane and asked, "What do you think, Roemer?"

While John had been studying Jade from the waist down, Kane had been feasting his eyes on Jade's new attire from the waist up. More precisely, his eyes were glued on her full breasts, which pushed proudly against the material of her shirt.

He was visualizing cupping them in his hands, lowering his head to taste them. He had a glazed look in his eyes when John's question penetrated his mind. "She's uh . . . uh . . . it looks fine to me, John," he finally stammered.

"All right then, that's settled." John nodded his head. "Do you happen to have a sturdy little Indian pony she can ride?"

"Yes, every rancher around here keeps two or three of them for just such times as this. They can't be beat for stamina. I'll go saddle one."

"Will you have another cup of coffee while you're waiting, Mr. Farrow?" Maria asked.

"That sounds right welcome." Big John smiled at Maria, then added, "I wish you'd stop callin' me mister. I ain't never been called mister in all my fifty-two years."

"It does sound funny, doesn't it, Uncle John?" Jade grinned at him. "The word doesn't suit you somehow."

"Why not?" John bristled. "I'm just as much a mister as any other man. I just don't care for the handle."

"I didn't mean that you don't deserve being called mister," Jade said, hurrying to smooth her uncle's ruffled feathers. "I just never heard the word applied to you before."

"That's true," John agreed as he watched Maria refill his cup. When she carried the pot back to the stove, he asked, "Maria, do you think you might come visit Jade sometime? I'd like to show you some things up there on my mountain."

Maria looked at him, and the wicked twinkle in his eyes told her exactly what he would like to show her. She blushed and said shortly, "I doubt that I'll ever get up that way."

"Oh, Maria, I wish that you would," Jade exclaimed, innocent of the message her uncle had sent to the housekeeper. "The mountains are so beautiful. I'd like to show you some things, too. The waterfalls, the quiet pools and the wildflowers."

"We'll see," Maria said, giving in to her pleading. "And I expect you to come visit me. Often."

"I'd like that." Jade looked at her uncle for permission.

Big John nodded after a while. "I reckon you can. I'll try to find time to bring you down now and again."

"I thought you might," Maria said derisively, reading the lazy, slumberous look in his eyes.

Kane's arrival put an end to the innuendos passing between Maria and John. Maria softly sighed her relief. The big man would be hard to resist if he ever got her alone. And she was afraid that he would manage to do that. She'd best keep herself off that mountain.

"All set," Kane said. "Anytime you're ready."

John stood up and pushed his chair back under the table. "Put your coat on, Jadie, and let's hit the trail."

"Did you bring a blanket up from the barn to wrap around Jade's legs?" Maria asked Kane as she helped Jade into a sheepskin-lined jacket.

"Yes, I remembered to do that," Kane answered as though it was a foregone conclusion.

"Now don't go mollycoddlin' the girl," Big John

grumbled. She's gonna expect that from me. I don't want her gettin' soft. Women are tough where we come from."

"Oh, hush up, John," Maria said impatiently. "A woman can be tough without freezing to death to prove it."

"You've got a sassy tongue in your mouth, don't you, woman?" John growled, but the twinkle in his eyes said that he approved.

They were leaving then and Maria hugged Jade and kissed her on the cheek. The way Jade's body grew still for a moment told Maria that it was probably the first kiss she had ever received. "Don't forget to come visit me," she said with a smile.

"I will, Maria, every time I can talk Uncle John into bringing me." I wish she could come alone, Maria thought as she closed the door behind Jade.

Outside, Kane said, "I'll be coming up your way one of these days, John. I saw a couple other of your horses that interested me."

"Come on up, Roemer. I'll be glad to see you."

When Kane saw that John wasn't going to help Jade mount the little Indian pony, he stepped up to her side and, placing his hands on either side of her waist, lifted her into the saddle.

She looked down at him in surprise. Not since she was a very young child had she been helped to climb onto a horse. She was even more surprised when, instead of handing her the blanket to wrap around her legs, he unfolded it and tucked the warm wool around her waist and legs.

"There," he said, "that will keep you warm."

A tremor ran through Jade. The softness of Kane's voice stirred something in the pit of her stomach, something she didn't understand. Her mind in confusion, she reacted in her usual sharp way with him. She scowled down at him as she picked up the reins. When he stepped back, she jabbed her heels into the pony and without a word followed her uncle, who was already several yards ahead of her.

Kane stared after her until she was a black dot against the snow-covered land. "You're going to change your mind about me, Jade Farrow," he said. "Sooner or later I'm going to put my brand on you."

Chapter Six

As the little mustang plodded along behind the big draft horse, carefully keeping in the tracks the large farm animal had made, Jade looked around at the landscape. There was nothing to see, just a seemingly endless stretch of snow. There was no movement of any living thing.

But how beautiful it is, she thought as her uncle reined in the draft horse. The animal was breathing hard, snorting great clouds of vapor into the cold air. Big John had rested him every hour since they'd left the Roemer ranch. The little mustang seemed thankful for the rest as well.

Both humans and animals were relieved when they reached the foothills where the snow wasn't so deep and the tall pines blocked some of the icy wind.

It was early afternoon when Jade and her uncle drew rein and dismounted in front of the cabin. The old hound, Jelly, scrambled from under the porch, greeting Jade with much enthusiasm, his hard tail whipping across her legs as he jumped around her.

"Uncle John, why didn't you put him inside before you left?" Jade scolded the big man. "He could have frozen to death."

"I meant to," John answered as he took the mustang's reins along with the draft horse's to lead them to the barn. "But when I called him a couple times and he didn't come, I rode off. I was more worried about finding you."

"Come along, fellow." She patted the rough head as they both climbed the two steps to the porch. "You can thaw out in front of the fireplace."

She pushed open the door and for the first time took a good look at the cabin's interior, seeing it with new eyes. How different its messy state was from the Roemer ranch house, which Maria kept so clean and neat.

When she took off her jacket and started to toss it onto a chair, she paused, remembering that there had been no clothing strewn about the Roemer home. She looked for a place to hang the heavy garment, but only bare walls met her gaze. In her mind's eye she saw a row of pegs in the kitchen at the ranch house, where everyone hung their coats and jackets as soon as they took them off.

She carried the jacket into her bedroom and found the walls the same as in the kitchen. They were completely bare, not even a picture hanging on them, as there was in the room of Roemer's sister. All the clothes she owned were piled on the foot of the bed. She carefully hung the jacket on a bedpost. In her mind's eye she saw the bed she had slept in for the past two nights, all nicely made up with a colorful quilt.

Tears glimmered in Jade's eyes as she began to yearn for some beauty in her home. When she tripped over her broken boots where she had left them last May, the month she started going bare-foot until freezing weather, she told herself that things were going to change in this old cabin. She grew determined when she thought of the nice clothes Maria had given her and realized she had no place to put them.

When Big John came in a few minutes later, carrying the leather-bound satchel, Jade was wielding a broom, making the dust fly as she swept years of debris toward the door.

"What are you doin', girl?" John said at the end of a loud sneeze. Jade paused and leaned on the broom as she answered almost defensively, "I'm getting rid of all the dirt and trash in the cabin. We're not going to live like pigs anymore, Uncle John."

"So, you think to live like the Roemer people,

do you?" John placed the satchel on the floor and shrugged out of his jacket. As he tossed the garment on the floor, he said, "I can't give you the things Kane Roemer has. He's rich; he can afford all them nice things."

"Uncle John, I don't want their nice furniture," Jade said softly. "I just want our home to be clean. Just a few little things would help cozy it up a lot. How much would it cost to have some pegs driven into the walls to hang our clothes on instead of littering the floor with them? And how much time and money would it cost for you to build a few shelves—some in the kitchen to hold my dishes and cooking utensils instead of keeping them in wooden crates under the window. And I'd like some shelves in the bedroom to put our clothes on and some pegs to hang the nice dresses that Maria gave me. Also, I'd like some hangings on my window in the bedroom."

As Jade resumed sweeping she added, "I'm tired of men peeping through my window at night, trying to see me getting ready to go to bed. On bright, full-moon nights my room is lit up almost like daylight."

"Who's been peering in your room?" Big John roared. "Why didn't you tell me?"

"Half the men on the mountain, I think, and I didn't tell you for fear of what you might do."

"I'd beat the hell out of them, that's what I'd do."

"Don't you think it would be simpler to hang something over my window? They'd stop coming around if they couldn't see into my room."

Big John didn't say anything for several minutes as he watched Jade diligently making wide sweeps with the broom. He was remembering an almost forgotten time when he had watched his mother do the same thing. The difference being that the farmhouse was always neat and spotlessly clean. He came to the conclusion that although he hadn't raised Jade to clean and scrub, it was her nature to be like her grandmother. Even if she had not spent time in the ranch house, he imagined that sooner or later Jade would have become like the other Farrow women.

"I guess a little fixin' up wouldn't hurt anything," he finally said, looking around at the walls, measuring with his eyes how many feet of lumber he would need for shelves, then doubling the amount so he'd have enough for the bedrooms.

"Thank you, Uncle John." Jade gave him a wide smile, her face streaked with dirt from her vigorous cleaning.

Kane had lingered on the porch, watching the Farrows ride away, wondering how long a time he should wait before making a trip up the mountain. If he went too soon Big John might think that he was more interested in his niece than he was in his horses. If that happened Kane Roemer might not ever see the little green-eyed witch again.

And he did want to see her again. He wanted to hold her in his arms, kiss her red lips and— His attention was drawn to the barn when feminine laughter rang out. Two horses had emerged from the barn. Liz and Pete, his drover, were astride them. Thank God, he was finally getting rid of Liz. He wondered with a wry grin how many times the drover had had to satisfy her before she consented to put on her clothes and climb onto the mount.

Kane hurried into the house before Liz could see him. He didn't plan on ever bedding her again and she would probably raise a ruckus about it. But as far as he was concerned, if she made any more trips to the ranch, it would be the cowhands who would make her welcome.

When Kane went back inside, Maria was sitting at the table, a cup of coffee in front of her. The look on her face said that her thoughts were far removed from what was usually on her mind: what to make for supper, ironing to be done. Kane suspected he knew what had brought that faraway look to her eyes. He hadn't missed the way Big John watched her, the calculating glint in his eyes. The mountain man was very interested in Maria. And judging by the way she had blushed on a couple of occasions, she was drawn to Jade's uncle.

Kane wondered if he should warn Maria about the big man, tell her that he wanted only one thing from her. After thinking about it a moment, he decided that he'd best keep his advice to himself. Maria might clobber him over the head. After all, she was a mature, sensible woman, capable of making her own decisions.

He poured himself a cup of coffee and sat down across from Maria. The attractive woman started and came back to the present when he said, "Well, what do you make of our mountain neighbors?"

Maria blinked a couple of times, then answered, "Jade is a lovely young woman, inside and out. She is remarkably innocent, considering her environment and the man who raised her."

"Big John is very protective of her," Kane said, defending the man he had gotten to know and like.

"Yes, he is," Maria agreed with some reluctance. "He has plans for her that don't involve any of the young men up on the mountain."

His interest aroused, Kane asked, "What kind of plans?"

"He didn't say, but he has relatives back east. He might be planning to send Jade for a visit, to see if she can attract a husband there."

Maria's answer didn't sit well with Kane. He asked himself what man in his right mind wouldn't be interested in the beautiful Jade. She would be able to pick and choose the best among them.

The thought of another man intimately knowing the girl gripped him hard. It was his intention to be the first with Jade, to teach her what pleased him, to learn what pleased her in bed.

Maria saw the dark frown on Kane's face and secretly smiled. She thought to herself that maybe the handsome rancher's bachelor days were numbered. She wondered why it was that a man chased every loose woman in sight, wallowed around with whores, and then had the nerve to expect the woman he married to be a virgin.

She looked at Kane and posed that question to him.

"Hell, Maria, I don't know," Kane answered, squirming a bit. "I guess it's just natural that a man wants to be the first and the last with the woman he marries. He wants a decent woman to be the mother of his children."

"What about love? Would he necessarily have to love the woman?"

"Of course, if he was going to marry her." Kane gave Maria a sharp look. They had never had such a serious talk before. Was she leading up to something?

"You know"—Maria wasn't finished yet—"it always struck me as strange how a man can profess his love for his wife and still fool around with whores. What do you make of that?"

Kane squirmed some more before saying a little sharply, "Maybe because his wife is stingy in bed. She won't do for him what a whore will."

"What about his vow for better or for worse? Shouldn't he be faithful to the woman he married regardless of whether she pleases him in bed?"

"Hell, Maria," Kane said scraping his chair away from the table and standing up. "You sound like a preacher this morning. Why don't you ask

Big John Farrow his opinion on some of these things?"

Maria felt the heat rising to her face and was thankful that Kane had left the kitchen before he could notice it. Evidently John's flirting with her hadn't gone unnoticed by her employer.

A few minutes later, as she washed the breakfast dishes, she wondered what John's answer to her questions would be if she put them to him. He is a virile, lusty man, she thought, probably one woman wouldn't be enough for him.

Unless, of course, his wife made it her business to keep him satisfied. Maria's lips curved in a small smile as she stared into the dishwater. She could do that, and enjoy every minute of it.

Chapter Seven

A pale noonday sun shone through the sparkling-clean window, spilling its light into the cabin kitchen. It shone on the top of Jade's head as she sat at the table, chewing on the stub of a pencil. Had she forgotten to add anything else to the list she was making for the trip to Laramie?

She scanned what she had already written. Two irons. Maria had shown her how to heat them on top of the stove, and how to use them in pressing wrinkles out of clothing. A washboard to scrub out the dirt in the clothing. Stove black. Uncle John had said that his mother used to rub it on their cookstove once a year to keep it shiny. A new broom. The old one was mostly all handle with only a few straws left in it.

Jade paused and took a sip of coffee from the cup sitting at her elbow. Would Uncle John allow her to buy a few towels like the ones she had used at the Roemer ranch? she wondered. They had felt so soft on her skin, not like the rough fustian ones she had used all her life.

And would he part with enough money to purchase some white goods that she could tear into lengths to dry her dishes and cooking utensils with? She'd be ashamed for Maria to see what she dried those items with now.

After all, she thought as she wrote the last two items on her list, Uncle John was saving a lot of money by not having to buy her new clothes. She rashly added two bars of rose-scented soap, the kind she had used at the Roemer ranch. Maria had put one bar, along with a toothbrush, in a small bag for her, but it wouldn't last forever, and she seldom went to Laramie where she could purchase more.

The toothbrush reminded Jade to add baking soda to the growing list. Maria had said to use it when brushing her teeth, that the soda would keep them white and shiny.

Jade was about to lay the pencil down, sure that she hadn't forgotten anything, when her gaze fell on the brush and comb Maria had also given her. Hardly daring to hope, she wrote down in big, bold letters LOOKING GLASS. She would fight Uncle John tooth and nail for that. A woman needed one to see if her face was clean and whether all the tangles were brushed out of her hair.

This time Jade did lay down her pencil. She gazed out the window. It had taken her an hour to get the years of grime off it. The cabin still didn't look like much, but in the week she had been home she had used the stub of a broom on the floors, made up the beds every morning and kept the dishes and pots and skillets in the crates, not piled on the table and stove as used to be her habit.

And she had remembered to clean the lamp chimneys every morning, and to trim the lamps' wicks. It was remarkable how much more light they now put out.

Jade looked forward to going into Laramie. She hadn't been there for three years. The last time she was in town it had been too hard having people stare at her, whisper among themselves. But now, realizing how she had looked then, she really couldn't blame the women for gawking at her.

She looked different these days, though, and she felt that she wouldn't be given a second look. She could walk the streets of Laramie with her head held as high as any wealthy ranch woman. If Uncle John was willing, they might even go into the cafe and have a piece of pie and a cup of coffee.

When Jade heard her uncle's heavy tread on the porch, she drank the last of her coffee and stood up. John opened the door and carefully wiped his feet on the buffalo hide she had placed there for that purpose, and she gave him a warm, approving smile. She still couldn't believe that he did this for her. Also that he had finally stopped muttering in his beard that a man couldn't relax with all the sweeping and cleaning that went on these days.

"Are you ready to get started?" Big John asked, keeping his jacket on. "I've got the horses saddled and waiting."

"I only have to put my jacket on," Jade answered, folding the piece of paper she had been writing on.

"I'll take a look at your list while you do that." John held out his hand.

Jade hesitated but a moment before handing over the neatly written list. Actually she would rather argue about it here than later in the store in front of a bunch of people. It would be humiliating to have him declare in his loud voice that she didn't need some of the "frippery" she had written down.

With her jacket on, and a scarf tied over her head, Jade waited nervously for her uncle to finish reading the list. Relief whooshed through her lips when he handed back the white slip of paper without any comment. As she followed him out the door she asked, "Did you remember to feed Pansy his cracked corn?"

"Yes, I fed that damned rooster," the big man grumbled. "If he ever ruffles his feathers and flies at me again, he's gonna end up in your stew pot."

"I'll speak to him about that," Jade said, a sparkle in her eyes.

"You're just full of funnies this mornin', ain't you?"

Jade made no response, only grinned as she climbed onto the mustang he'd saddled for her. When John kicked a heel into the draft horse and it moved out, the little mustang followed him down the path through the snow. The air was cold and Jade was tucking her chin into her collar when they arrived at the spot where other paths ran into the main one that led to Laramie. She looked up when John swore under his breath.

Jessie Oates and three of her sons were just emerging from a patch of scrub pine. Each boy had a string of furs slung over his shoulder. "That lazy bastard has sent his wife and younguns out to run his traps," John said to Jade from the corner of his mouth.

Jessie made no eye contact with them, only nodded and hurried up the path that would take her to the old cabin that looked like the roof might cave in at any time.

The poor woman was embarrassed at being caught doing her husband's work, Jade knew. He was always embarrassing and humiliating her in the most base ways.

No one ever said anything or objected to the treatment Jessie received from her vulgar husband. It was the law of the mountain that there was never to be any interference between a husband and his wife. But there were many dark looks turned on the despicable man.

Jade's lips curled scornfully. If Old Man Oates had a teaspoon of brains he'd have learned a long time ago that shortly after he caused Jessie shame in front of her neighbors, bad luck always visited him: his horse would disappear for several weeks, his whiskey still got turned over somehow, his traps would come up empty. That was mountain justice.

Jade smiled at her uncle's broad back. Before the week was over Oates would pay for sending his wife out to run his trapline.

Against her will, Jade's thoughts turned next to Kane. What was he doing today? she wondered. Giving someone trouble, she had no doubt.

"I wonder what Roemer is doin' today," Big John said, echoing Jade's thoughts.

"Something ornery, I imagine."

John caught the bitterness in Jade's tone and said, "You sure don't like him, do you?"

"No, I don't."

"You've got to quit holdin' it against him that he bought Satan. Like I told you before, he'll be good to the stallion. I might have sold him to someone who would have broken his spirit."

"I don't think you'd have ever sold him if that one hadn't come nosing around."

"You're wrong, girl. My mind was made up to the fact that I had to get rid of him. If I didn't, one of our neighbors would have shot him." After a short pause John continued, "And don't think that you could have hidden the stallion away. I'd have taken him down to Laramie at night while you were sleeping."

Jade's green eyes bored into her uncle's back. She knew he was speaking the truth. But she had other reasons for not liking Kane Roemer. She still boiled inside every time she remembered the cutting words he'd flung at her, the sneering way he looked at her.

"I think he likes you," John said.

"Ha! You must be blind, Uncle John."

"No, I'm not. I could see the way he looked at you when I rode down to his ranch to fetch you home. He'd make you a fine husband, girl."

"Husband! The cold air must have frozen your brain if you think for one minute I'd ever marry that one."

"Don't you ever think about gettin' married someday?"

"No, I don't. I'm perfectly happy living with you, Uncle John."

"What if I decided to get married someday and my wife didn't want you underfoot?"

Jade's amused laughter hung in the air. "Who would marry you?"

When John didn't challenge her statement, only stiffened in the saddle, Jade realized she had hurt the big man's feelings. "What I meant to say, Uncle, was who in these mountains would you want to marry?"

"Maybe I wouldn't marry a mountain woman," he answered, seemingly satisfied with Jade's explanation.

"Who then? You don't know any other women."

"I could always meet one," John said, picturing Maria in his mind.

He had thought of the attractive, curvaceous housekeeper often in the past week, something he had never done with another woman. He would like to court her, but was afraid she wouldn't have anything to do with a rough mountain man.

Deep in thought, Jade and Big John rode into Laramie without being fully aware that they had reached the town. People were coming in and out of the stores, picking their way over the narrow paths that had appeared from the many feet traveling from store to store. Only around the hitching posts had any attempt been made to remove the snow.

Big John drew rein in front of Shane's Mercantile. As he and Jade dismounted and wound the reins over the post, he said, "While you get the things on your list, I'm goin' across the street to the Longhorn and have a drink with my old friend, Magallen. Ain't seen him lately." He handed Jade a roll of bills. "Here's the money to pay for your purchases."

Jade grew nervous at the thought of being left alone. What if the women she could see through the window still stared and whispered about her?

What if she didn't look as nice as she thought she did?

"What should I do when I've finished trading?" she asked. "Should I go to the saloon?"

"No, you can't come in the Longhorn." John frowned at her. "You're never to go into any saloon. Only loose women go into them. I'll be keepin' an eye on the store. When you've finished just step outside and I'll come get you." He was slogging through the snow then, walking to the other side of the street. Jade looked after him until he entered the saloon; then she squared her shoulders and, stepping up onto the narrow porch, went inside the mercantile.

The store owner and three women looked Jade's way as she closed the door. She relaxed when she saw there was only curiosity in their eyes. They did not recognize her. When she walked up to the counter, Mr. Shane, the store owner, said politely, "How can I help you, Miss . . . ?"

From her peripheral vision Jade saw the women listening intently for her to provide her last name. She didn't want to give it. If they learned that she was Big John Farrow's niece they might start whispering about her again.

She ignored the opening Mr. Shane had given her and handed him her list. He ran a fast glance over the items she had written down and said with a friendly smile, "It will take me a while to fill your order. Why don't you look around the store while you're waiting?"

Jade nodded and stepped away from the counter, turning her back on the women, who were full of questions. They weren't apt to talk to her back, she figured. She remembered them. They were three of the women who had always looked down on her.

As she moved about the store, ignoring the women, they finally accepted the fact that they weren't going to learn anything from the beautiful stranger. They picked up their packages and left the store.

Mr. Shane chuckled. "I can just hear them jabbering away, trying to find out who you are."

Jade walked back to the counter and returned Shane's friendly smile. She remembered he had always spoken kindly to her the few times she had visited his store.

"Are you sure you don't recognize me, Mr. Shane?" she asked.

"I'm afraid not. Your eyes look familiar, though."

Jade hesitated a moment before saying, "I'm Jade Farrow, Mr. Shane."

Mr. Shane was not a man easily startled. He had dealt with the public for twenty years and had seen and heard many things. But he couldn't believe that this young woman could be the same half-wild girl he had last seen three years before.

"My goodness, Jade, I can't get over how you've changed. You've grown into the prettiest young woman in all the territory."

Pleased laughter bubbled from between Jade's lips. "I'm the same as I always was, Mr. Shane. I'm just scrubbed up and wearing some decent clothes for a change."

"Well, all I can say is that all that dirt was hiding a very lovely face. The storekeeper shook his head in amusement. "What's Big John going to say when the bachelors around here start climbing the mountain to court you?"

Jade's laughter pealed out again. "He won't say anything. He'll just put some buckshot in their rear ends."

Shane shared her laughter a moment, then said on a more serious note, "He's got to hand you over to a husband someday. It would be a shame for you to become an old maid."

All levity left Jade's face. "That wouldn't bother me in the least," she said sharply. "I like my life with Uncle John just fine."

"Maybe you haven't met the right man yet," Mr. Shane teased.

When the hard face of Kane Roemer flashed before her eyes, Jade's answer was short and almost angry. "I haven't been looking for one and I don't intend to."

Shane said no more on the subject, but inside he was grinning. Miss Jade Farrow didn't know what she was talking about. He'd be willing to bet his store that before another winter rolled around she would be married.

"Well," he said, as he laid a framed mirror on

the counter, "here's everything you had on your list. This is the only looking glass I had on hand. It's about twenty inches wide and thirty inches long. Do you think it will suit?"

"It's just fine, Mr. Shane." Jade's eyes sparkled. She would have been pleased with one half that size.

"I'll wrap it up real good so it won't get broken on the trip back up the mountain."

"Thank you," Jade said and waited while he totaled up her bill. When it was handed to her and she saw what she owed, she worried that Uncle John had not given her enough money to pay it. But as she counted out the money, she found that she had more than enough to cover her expenses.

"Is Big John going to pick this up for you?" Shane asked as he placed Jade's other purchases in a fustian sack.

"No, he said that I should walk outside and he'd see me and come get my packages. He's in the Longhorn."

"I'll carry them out for you then."

They had barely stepped outside when the saloon door opened and Big John stepped outside. Coming up to them, he greeted and shook hands with the storekeeper, whom he had known and liked ever since the store opened. Shane commented that his niece had grown into a beautiful young woman.

"She'll do, I guess," John said gruffly as he tied the mirror and sack onto the strong draft horse.

When everything was secured to his satisfaction, he said, "Come on, girl; let's get goin'."

"I was wondering, Uncle John," Jade began cautiously, "if we might stop at the café and have a cup of coffee and a slice of pie."

"We don't have time today, Jade." John swung onto the back of his mount and picked up the reins. "I've got to stop at the lumberyard and pick up some boards for them shelves you've been yammerin' about."

Jade's shoulders slumped in disappointment, but she said no more on the subject. Her shelves were more important than a piece of pie.

The lumberyard was at the end of the street, and Jade followed her uncle into the big room full of boards of all lengths and different kinds of wood. It was too cold to wait outside.

But as soon as she stepped through the door, she was sorry she had chosen to enter the place. At the far end of the building Kane Roemer stood talking to the bald-headed man who owned the mill. She felt an odd tightness grip her chest and her pulse began to race. She quickly looked away from him.

Her eyes then encountered two young men across the room staring at her. She didn't know where to look next.

Her gaze fell on the stove in the center of the room. It glowed red from the flames leaping inside it. She walked over to it and stretched her hands out over its heat just as her uncle was greeting Kane.

"Hiya, John." Kane straightened up from the small counter, a genial smile on his lips. "What brought you down from your mountain?"

"The girl has been botherin' me to make her some shelves, so I'm lookin' at lumber."

"How is Jade?" Kane leaned his elbow on the rough surface of the counter. "Is she still mad at me?"

"She's standin' over there by the stove. Why don't you go over and ask her?"

"I don't know if I should." Kane looked quickly to where Jade continued to hold her hands out to the heat. "She wasn't talking to me the last time I saw her."

"Suit yourself," John said and turned his attention to the lumberyard owner. While they were involved in conversation about some pine boards, Kane gazed at Jade through smoldering eyes half-concealed by lowered lids. His mind was busy stripping away her clothes and laying her on his bed. He would kiss every inch of her lovely body before climbing between her long legs.

As he pictured himself entering her, an arousal strained against his fly. Damn! he thought, I can't go talk to her with this bulge in my pants.

Kane frowned and swore under his breath when he spotted the two young men staring at Jade hungrily. Tom Fredrick and Paul Callen. They were ranchers' sons, good-looking and at least ten years younger than himself. Their youth would appeal to Jade. She thought him an old man.

Anger gave Kane control of his body, if not of his mind, when he saw the two young men starting toward Jade. His long strides covered the distance to the stove, outdistancing the uncertain steps of Paul and Tom. From the corner of his eye he saw them draw back as he said, "How are you, Jade?"

He knew from the scowl on her face that she would rather spit in his eye than talk to him. Consequently he was a little surprised when she answered stiffly, "I'm fine, thank you."

Yes, you're fine all right, Kane thought. Fine as silk. "You should take your jacket off," he said. "You're gonna get all heated up, and once you go back outside, you're gonna freeze."

Jade admitted reluctantly that he was right and unbuttoned the heavy jacket and pulled it off.

Kane wanted immediately to order her to put it back on. The blue dress she wore today was slightly snug across her breasts, emphasizing her cleavage. While he ached to free a breast and ravish it with his mouth and tongue, his gaze dropped to her trim waist, then on down to her gently rounded hips.

God! he thought, I've got to have her, and soon.

Kane became aware that Jade was looking past his shoulder, smiling at someone. He turned his head and was surprised to see that the two young men had gotten up the nerve to approach Jade after all. They probably thought that there would be no competition from a man fifteen years older than the young woman at his side.

When Tom and Paul waited for him to introduce them to Jade, he ignored their silent request. Finally Tom, the more forward of the two, spoke up. "I'm Tom Fredrick and this is my buddy, Paul Callen. We'd be right pleased to meet you."

Jade glanced over at her uncle, who stood watching them. When he didn't frown at her she knew it was all right to talk to the two attractive young men.

"I'm Jade Farrow," she said, holding out her hand, "from off the mountain."

"They sure grow them pretty up there," Tom said, shaking her hand.

"They sure do." Paul smiled shyly, taking his time to release her hand.

Kane stood rigidly disapproving beside Jade. But no one was paying any attention to him and the three young people chatted on.

Finally they were interrupted by Paul's father. He smiled at Jade as he said, "You fellows ready to go?"

They nodded, though reluctantly, and before they took their leave Tom said, "We'd like to call on you when the weather permits."

Jade smiled and answered, "That would be nice." Kane's breath made a soft hissing sound as he drew it in. He hoped they'd get another blizzard that would seal the mountain off from civilization until next June.

Big John walked up to Jade and Kane as Paul and Tom walked outside, giving Jade one last, lingering look before closing the door behind them. "You ready to go, girl?" he asked, a bundle of smooth pine planks under each arm.

Before Jade could answer, Kane said stiffly, "It seems that Jade has met a couple of admirers."

"Yeah, I noticed that," Big John said, a wide grin on his face. "They seemed quite smitten with her."

Before Kane could make some scathing remark about the young men, Big John asked, "How's that housekeeper of yours? She sure is a fiesty one."

Kane was so deep in thoughts of what he'd like to do to his young neighbors, it took a moment for him to realize what the big man had said. "Ah, Maria's fine. Still bossing everyone around."

"I'll bet she's good at that." John laughed. "Tell her I'll be comin' down the mountain to visit her one of these days."

Stunned by John's frankness that he intended to court Maria, Kane could only watch them leave. He had wanted to hint to the uncle that Paul and Tom were kind of on the wild side, that maybe they weren't really the sort Jade should keep company with.

He immediately felt ashamed of himself. His young neighbors weren't wild exactly, no more than any other young men of their age. Maybe they drank a little too much on a Saturday night, shot up the town a little. But they worked hard all week and deserved to let off a little steam at the end of the week. He had to admit that either one of the young men would make a fine husband for some lucky girl.

Kane also had to admit that he didn't want Jade to be that lucky young woman. Not for a while, at least. Like maybe for a year or two. He figured that would be enough time for him to get her out of his system. Although no other woman had kept his interest more than two or three months, he felt sure that it would be different with Jade. A man wouldn't tire of her easily.

While Kane was thinking his lustful thoughts of Jade, she was thinking about the two young men she had just met as the little mustang plodded behind the strong draft horse.

"Uncle John," she called to him, "why don't you object that Tom and Paul plan on coming to visit me?"

"Because they're the sort of men I want you to marry someday. Get you off the mountain."

She didn't ever want to get married, but if she did someday, she thought it would be fine to be a rancher's wife. She didn't understand why Kane Roemer's image flashed before her eyes.

Chapter Eight

Jade stood looking out the window at the falling snow. It had started early this morning, heavy and wet, falling straight down. She hoped that some neighbor women would be able to come visit today.

The past week had been a busy one. She and her uncle had been busy changing the appearance of the cabin. When her uncle had finally finished sawing and hammering, swearing when he hit his thumb instead of a nail, she had three decent-looking shelves in the kitchen and two each in the bedrooms.

Jade turned from the window to survey her kitchen area. It didn't look like the Roemer kitchen but it didn't resemble her old one anymore either. Uncle John had nailed one shelf on the wall next to the door and hung the mirror over it. In the daytime the winter sun shone on her brush and comb, her scented bars of soap and neatly folded washcloths and towels. Squeezed in beside them was her uncle's comb and the small scissors he trimmed his beard with.

In the corner where the old stove stood, all the rust spots now covered with stove black, John had placed a shelf on each wall. The one closest to the table held her few dishes, glasses and flatware. On the other shelf she had placed her two skillets, the three battered pans she used for baking biscuits and sourdough bread and occasionally sugar cookies. A long-handled fork and a butcher knife were kept there, too.

To brighten up the kitchen area more, John had gone to the nearby Indian village and traded some honey, which he had collected in the summer, for some lengths of cured doeskin. They were soft and pliable, and the Indian women had painted pictures of wildflowers on them. She had carefully taken her scissors to the skins and from them she had cut a pair of drapes each for the kitchen, the two bedrooms and the living area. Her uncle had judged correctly how many skins it would take for all four windows, for there was only a narrow strip left over.

The window hangings were not only very pretty, but when drawn at night, they kept out a lot of cold air.

Jade's lips curved into a crooked grin as she remembered that it had taken two days of pleading to talk her uncle into taking more of his precious honey to the village to barter for a woven cover for her bed. When she had hinted that it would be nice to have one for his bed also, he had told her that if she dared fuss with his room he would take a switch to her.

She had laughed at his idle threat but had dropped the subject. She still couldn't believe that she had gotten as much as she had from him. It was so out of character for him to allow any "fancyin' up" of the cabin.

But on second thought, she could be mistaken, Jade told herself. Only since her short stay at the Roemer ranch had she shown any interest in her home. Had she done that earlier, Uncle John might have gone along with her.

Her thoughts lingered on her gruff but kind relative. For all of his great strength he was going to be tired after running his trapline today, fighting the blinding snow while tramping over the mountain. She would make sure that she had a pot of hearty venison stew waiting for him when he got home late this afternoon. Sometimes it was almost dark before she saw him plodding toward the cabin.

Jade went back to the window and peered through the snow. Her neighbors were late. It looked as though they weren't coming. Was it because of the weather? she wondered. Or were they jealous of the clothes Maria had given her, or that she had prettied up the cabin a little?

If that was the case, it wasn't fair. Most of them had more and better furniture than she.

Jade had about given up on her expected visitors when through the curtain of snow she saw three of them making their way to the cabin, their shawl-covered heads bent against the cold wind. When they stepped up on the porch she opened the door wide, laughing as she exclaimed, "My, my, you look like snowmen. Come get close to the fireplace."

She tried to hide her grimace of dismay as the women trooped into the kitchen without making an effort to wipe the snow off their feet. In her mind she was envisioning what the dirt they dragged in would do to her nice clean carpet.

She helped the women out of their jackets and coats and spread them before the fire to dry out. "Martha, you sit here," she said to the oldest woman in the group, as she dragged her only rocker up close to the fire.

Martha Graham was in her mid-fifties, but her careworn face looked much older. She had borne and buried four children, losing them at an early age from pneumonia. Her husband, Calendar, had knocked out her three front teeth in one of the drunken beatings he had given her.

Jade seated redheaded, rail-thin Virginia Henderson next to Martha. Virginia was thirty-five years old and had ten children. As Jade helped her off with her coat she saw that another baby was on the way.

Kathy Greene was the last to wearily sit down. She was twenty-seven years old. She had married Boris Greene when she was fifteen and he forty. She'd had twelve pregnancies but only seven had reached full term, due to Boris insisting on having relations with her every night, right up until the time she went into labor.

"Do you know if Jessie is coming?" Jade asked, sitting down on the hearth.

"Jessie won't be comin'," Martha said in knowing tones.

Jade sighed and said, "I guess Carter has beaten Jessie again."

"Yeah," Martha answered. "He beat her real bad yesterday. Somebody broke up his still again and he took out his anger on Jessie. Threw her up against the wall and dislocated her shoulder and broke three of her ribs."

Jade shook her head sadly. She understood fully for the first time her uncle's determination that she never marry a mountain man.

Kane swore soundly as he squinted his eyes, trying to see through the heavy fall of snow.

When he had left the ranch early this morning the sky was clear and a bright sun was shining. Then, just before he reached the foothills, the sky had become overcast and threatening. Ten minutes later, as he began to climb the mountain, the snow blew in. In a very short time it was hard to make out the faint trail.

Leaning forward, keeping his eyes glued to the ground, Kane cursed himself for a fool. He was caught in a damn blizzard all because of his over-powering desire for the mountain girl.

Half an hour later Kane knew he was lost. Should he return to the ranch? He directed a derisive laugh at himself. How was he going to find his way there?

He reined the weary stallion in and sat in the white silence trying to get his bearings. "You jack-ass," he muttered, "how can you do that when you can't see more than two feet ahead of you?"

His only chance was to keep moving, very slowly, and hope that maybe he would stumble onto a cave. Then he could at least find shelter until the storm passed. He prayed that he would, for it was growing late. Once darkness came, it could very well mean the end of Kane Roemer.

Kane gathered up the reins again. Renegade had taken no more than half a dozen steps when something whizzed past Kane's head and thudded into a tree trunk. "What the hell?" he grated, leaning forward and straining to see through the snow.

A split second later he drew his Colt and snapped off a shot at a running Indian. He missed and the shadowy figure disappeared into the black and white of the gathering dusk. His searching gaze found the embedded arrow. He touched Renegade lightly with his heels and as the stallion moved out, Kane wondered why the Indian had shot at him. As far as he knew the whites and the tribe whose village was situated in the foothills were on friendly terms.

Kane ceased thinking about it when there drifted to him a loud voice calling in response to his shot, "Anybody out there needin' help?"

Relief was in Kane's voice when he recognized Big John Farrow's gruff tones. "It's Kane Roemer," he called back. "A damn Indian just shot an arrow at me and I took a shot at him. I'm also lost."

"Start walkin' toward my voice. We're about a mile from my cabin."

"How in the hell do you know that?" Kane slid out of the saddle and started leading the stallion forward. "I'm sure you can't see any better than I can in this damnable snow."

"I've tramped these mountains for thirty years. I could find my way home blindfolded."

Kane opened his mouth to respond but almost walked into Big John. "I sure am glad to see you." He grinned at the big man. "I'd just about decided that if I couldn't find a cave to crawl into I'd freeze to death and not be found until spring."

"You wouldn't be the first man to do that." Big John shifted a string of furs to his other shoulder as he struck off walking. "Over the years we've lost at least a dozen men and two women in blizzards. The men were drunk and the women weren't strong enough to fight the elements. When I've been drinkin' I don't set foot outdoors. Moonshine muddles your brain, keeps you from thinkin' straight."

"I sure as hell could use a drink when we get to your place," Kane said. With darkness settling in, the air had become several degrees colder.

"So could I." John laughed, then pointed up ahead. "See that bobbin' light? That's Jade comin' to look for me. I'm usually home before dark."

"Isn't she afraid of getting lost?" Kane asked, his heart leaping at the prospect of seeing Jade again.

"Naw, she wouldn't be afraid of that. I learned her from a little tyke how to travel in the dark with the wind. She knows that as soon as she steps outside she's to test the direction it's blowin'. Does she find it against her, or behind her? Is it comin' from her right side or her left? Determinin' all that she will know which direction to go when she wants to find her way home. She knows where I laid my line."

Jade was upon them then, a wide, relieved smile on her face. "I was beginning to think that something had happened to you, Uncle John," she said. "I was afraid you'd been attacked by wolves."

"No, I didn't come up against any of them. I did hear them though, a distance away. I'm late because I caught more animals than usual. They sure do like my new apple bait."

Jade had made out the dim figures of Kane and Renegade by now. She peered through the snow, and when she recognized Kane, she gave him her usual scowl and asked ungraciously, "Where did you find him?"

"He found me," Big John said, but didn't go on to embarrass Kane by saying that he had become lost.

Her only greeting to Kane was to say as she turned and led the way, "You pick a strange time to come visiting."

Kane ground his teeth in helpless anger. The anger was mostly directed at himself. He couldn't wait to see her, and she didn't care if she ever saw him again.

Kane's face was numb from the stinging snow that blew against it when finally lamplight was spotted shining from the kitchen window. When they reached the low, sturdily built cabin, John took the reins from Kane's hand, saying, "I'll take care of your horse when I drop off my furs at the shed."

Kane said, "Thank you, John," and followed Jade inside the building, stopping first, as she had, to wipe his feet carefully on the buffalo hide. The delicious aroma of simmering meat, herbs and vegetables made his mouth water. He hadn't eaten since early this morning.

Kane's first sight of the inside of the cabin was a total surprise. He had dreaded seeing the sort of home that could have produced the half-wild girl Jade had been the first time he saw her. But the big combination kitchen and living area was warm and cozy, making him feel welcome.

He didn't get the same feeling from the mistress of the cabin, however. She went about stirring the stew, checking on the biscuits. Her demeanor told him that as far as she was concerned she was alone.

The dark frown on his face showed his irritation. Kane took off his jacket, hung it on the wall next to hers and stalked over to the fireplace. He sat down in the rocker, pulled off his boots and crossed his feet on the hearth. He could play the this game, too.

Nevertheless he was glad when Big John entered the cabin shortly. As his host rolled up his sleeves and began to scrub his hands in a basin of warm water Jade poured for him, he called to Kane, "Did the girl pour you a snort of corn squeezin's?"

"Not yet," Kane answered, then with a devilish grin he added, "I expect she's getting ready to."

"There's no time for whiskey now," Jade said crossly. "Supper is on the table."

As John dried his hands he gave his niece an amused look, although there was a hint of irritation in it. He knew she didn't like their guest and spoke out of pure cussedness. But damn it, he needed the bite of whiskey to warm him up a bit.

John decided he'd let her have her way this one time and called, "Come have a seat, Roemer. I guess we'll have our drink after we eat."

Kane walked to the table in his stocking feet and pulled out a chair. Saliva gathered in his mouth as he waited for John to dip into the bowl of stew, to fill his plate. But when the big man only sat staring hard at Jade, Kane looked at her and realized that she didn't intend to join them.

At the same moment it seemed that she became aware of the storm cloud gathering on her uncle's brow. She shot him a stubborn look but slid into the chair across from him. Only then did John fill his plate.

"Dig in, Roemer," he invited, passing him the steaming bowl.

Kane wanted to say, "No thank you, I'm not hungry," but he was. Terribly so.

The stew was the best Kane had ever eaten, but he was damned if he'd say so. He was fed up to his eyes with Jade's churlish behavior. When John asked how he was coming along with the white stallion, he answered, "Just fine. We've become good friends." He slid a sly glance at Jade, who had a death grip on her fork as she stared into her plate of stew. "I'm happy to say he's forgotten all about the mountains," he continued, "and the people living on it."

Big John hadn't missed the calculating look Kane sent his niece. The way she was acting, she deserved to hear that Satan had taken to his new owner so well . . . if that was really so. He suspected that Kane wasn't being entirely truthful about the stallion.

"How's that housekeeper of yours, Roemer?" John asked, steering the conversation in another direction. "She's a fine-lookin' woman. A man wouldn't have to shake the sheets to find her."

"You'd better not let Maria hear you describing her that way." Kane laughed. "She'd clobber you upside the head."

"Yeah, she would." John laughed also. "She's a high-spirited woman."

After a short pause, John said, "I expect a lot of men came callin' on her."

"No," Kane answered with a crooked grin. "I think they're all afraid of her. She's been a widow for a long time and she claims she likes it that way. She's never said so, but I don't believe her marriage was all that good. She's let drop a few things, like her husband was lazy, that he was drunk more often than he was sober."

"She got any younguns?"

Kane shook his head. "But she has a bunch of nieces and nephews she thinks highly of."

The rest of the meal was eaten in silence. When Jade was pouring coffee, Kane looked at John and asked, "Do you have any idea who shot that arrow at me, and why?"

"Yeah, I have a pretty good idea who it was and why. There's this young buck, Long Feather, who's got a yen for Jade. He probably thought you was on your way to court her."

"Does he shoot at all the young men who come around?"

"There ain't none that comes around," Big John said, grinning. "They know I'd kick their rumps off the mountain. They're probably afraid of Long Feather as well."

Kane frowned into his coffee. "Doesn't it bother you that the Indian has his eye on Jade? That he might harm her in some way?"

Big John shook his head. "He knows he'd have to deal with me if she ever came to harm at his hands." He stuck out his broad chest and declared with a grin, "Every man jack on this mountain is afraid of me."

Kane thought John was probably right and wondered if he and the big man would ever tangle.

John pushed away his empty cup and said, "We'll have that whiskey now, Jade."

Jade rose and slapped two glasses on the table, and then, her movements stiff, she took a jug from the shelf that held her cooking utensils. Kane grinned wryly when she filled her uncle's glass to the rim, but barely half filled his.

Big John had taken note of her action also, and, with a dark look at her, he took the jug and thumped it down in front of Kane. "Help yourself, Roemer," he said as he stood up. "I'm gonna go skin those furs now. If you get sleepy before I get back Jade will make you up a pallet in my room."

In his room, Kane thought, amused, as the big man relit the lantern and left the cabin. *He wants me where he can keep an eye on me.* The crusty mountain man was no fool. He knew what drove a man. The same thing that was driving him with regard to Maria.

"I'll go make up your pallet now," Jade said stiffly. "You'll probably want to go to bed soon."

Kane watched the gentle sway of her hips as she left the room and thought to himself, But not soon enough to please you, you little vixen. He sat on at the table because he knew it would aggravate her to return and find him still sitting there.

He wasn't mistaken. When Jade walked back into the room she gave him a look that would curl most men's toes. She began noisily gathering up the dirty dishes. When she grabbed for the jug, his hand shot out and clamped around her wrist.

"I'm not finished with it yet," he growled, flinging her hand away. He was getting pretty well fed up with her rude behavior.

"Go ahead," she said with a sneer, "drink yourself into a stupor like you're used to doing."

Kane jumped to his feet, his eyes flashing. "I've had just about enough of your sharp tongue, young lady." He grabbed her by the shoulders. "You're rude and ill-mannered and you need to have your backside tanned."

"I'm sure you know better than to try it." Jade glared up at him as she tried to free herself from his viselike grip.

"Don't be too sure about that." Kane glared back at her. "I don't know if I can resist turning you across my knee and flipping your skirt up over your head."

Kane became aware then of how soft Jade felt in his hands. His voice was raspy when he added,

141

"But then again, I could never bring myself to hurt that lovely little bottom."

And while Jade glared at him in openmouthed indignation, he put an arm around her waist and drew her up against his body. His head lowered and he captured her lips with his own.

The pressure of Kane's mouth on hers took Jade's breath away. It was the first kiss she had ever experienced. When his tongue began slowly to trace her trembling lips, a pulsing pleasure flooded her lower body, leaving her weak and bewildered. She was only vaguely aware that he was undoing the buttons on her blouse as his kiss seemed to plunder her very being.

She gave a soft little gasp when Kane slid a hand inside her bodice and cupped the heavy weight of her breast.

"Oh, God, you feel so good," he whispered huskily against her lips as he brushed a thumb across the passion-hard nipple, then teased it with his fingers.

Jade held her breath when he freed her breast from its confinement, then left her lips to fasten his mouth over it. As his lips drew and suckled her she became so weak she fell against him. Kane grasped her hips and spread his legs enough to pull her in tight against his throbbing arousal. He returned to her mouth and began bucking his hips against her in rhythm with his tongue thrusting in and out of her mouth.

Minutes passed in which Jade could only cling

to Kane. She was in the grip of overwhelming sensations caused by his thrusting hardness. In her innocence she didn't understand when suddenly Kane's body shuddered and he hoarsely whispered her name.

Her eyes silently questioned him as he gently rearranged her blouse and redid the small buttons. He dropped a tender kiss on her swollen lips then and said in confusion, "I think I'll go to bed now."

Chapter Nine

The crowing of Jade's rooster awakened Kane. He lay on his hard pallet and gazed into the gray darkness.

He was still as confused as when he'd retired last night. Never had he received satisfaction in such a way before.

But he had with Jade, and it had been exceptionally pleasurable. What would it be like, he wondered, to hold her slender, bare body in his arms and slowly penetrate her? He had no doubt that she was still a virgin. Big John would have seen to that. Yes, he said mentally, he would have to be gentle with her the first time. But once she was accustomed to his size . . . He didn't dare think further. He could feel an arousal growing.

Kane became aware of John puttering around in the kitchen, preparing to brave the elements. The big man evidently trusted him to be around his niece, and he felt a twinge of guilt at what had happened between him and Jade the night before.

And worse yet, he knew that if he had the chance he would take Jade to bed today with no thought that he was breaking John's faith in him. The sharp-tongued mountain girl was a fire in his blood that would give him no rest until he possessed her.

Was she awake also, he wondered, soft and warm in her bed? If so, what was she thinking about? Were her thoughts on him? Was she going over in her mind what had happened in the kitchen? She had been just as confused as he, only in a different way. He was sure that everything that had happened was new to her.

A throbbing began in his loins. He had set a fire in her, and he knew he could do it again. She didn't know it, but he could make her as randy as her uncle was.

Pansy had awakened Jade also, and she, too, lay staring into the gloom, reliving the events of last night. What in the world had happened to her? How could a man whom she despised make her lose all control, revel in passion brought on by his lips on her breast, wish for more of what she couldn't describe?

Jade's face blushed a deep red. She was as much

a wanton as the Indian women who came to visit Uncle John.

A frown creased her forehead. Why had Kane's large body shivered just before he took his arms from around her? And why had he then covered up her breast as though he didn't want to see it anymore? Didn't he like how it looked? He certainly seemed to like the taste of it.

She imagined that he had known a lot of women and that her endowments didn't measure up to theirs. Well, he wouldn't be seeing that part of her body again, she vowed. All he was ever going to see of her was her face and hands.

Pansy crowed again and Jade tossed back the covers and sat up on the edge of the bed, her feet dangling to the floor. The room was icy cold because she had closed the door when she went to bed. None of the heat from the fireplace had been able to drift into her room.

She grabbed her robe from the foot of the bed and hurriedly pulled it on, then felt with her feet to find the warm house slippers she had kicked off before retiring. As she walked into the main living area, she hoped that Kane wasn't up yet.

The room was empty and, thankful for that, Jade went and stood close to the leaping flames in the fireplace. She knew that her uncle hadn't been gone long. The fire had barely eaten into two large logs placed recently on the grate. She prayed it had stopped snowing for Big John's sake. It would make running his line doubly hard if he had to fight the elements also.

She walked into the kitchen area and pulled aside the doeskin drapes at the window. To the east a watery sun was trying to penetrate the gray sky, and, best of all, the snow had stopped falling.

"Just as soon as you've eaten breakfast, you can leave my mountain, Mr. Kane Roemer," she said to the empty room. "And never come up here again. I just might shoot you."

Jade put off making a trip to the privy as long as she could. Shoving her feet into the boots she had left next to the buffalo hide, she threw a heavy shawl around her shoulders and stepped outside.

Her visit to the tall, narrow building was quick, as was her trip afterward to the shed to feed her raggedy rooster. She hurried back to the cabin, then stepped inside and stiffened.

Kane stood at the stove pouring himself a cup of coffee. His hair was sleep rumpled and his un-buttoned shirt hung out of his trousers. She glimpsed the short, dark curls that covered his chest, running in a narrow strip down to his waist, and then disappearing into his trousers. A stubble of whiskers covered his strong jaw, which only made him all the more handsome.

Kane gave her a slow, knowing smile. Blushing, she looked away from him and busied herself with taking off her boots and hanging up her shawl.

"Shall I pour you a cup of coffee?" Kane asked, trying to put Jade at ease. How was he ever to get her into his arms again if she returned to her usual cool self?

"I'll get it," Jade said and started to brush past him to reach the coffeepot.

Kane's long arm reached out and curled around her waist. "I'll get it for you," he said, pulling her around until she was snug against him, her hands resting on his warm chest.

"I said I'd get it." Jade strained against him, her fingers pushing at his chest.

"Don't do that!" Kane said sharply.

"Don't do what?" Jade's green eyes glittered at him.

"You know what." Kane growled and ground his hips into hers. "You know what happened last night when we got this close to each other."

"I know and I don't want it to happen again." Jade was panting from her useless struggle. "So turn me loose."

"I will in a minute." Kane moved a hand to cup and fondle an unfettered breast.

"Don't do that." Jade gasped, holding her body still, finally realizing that her squirming was getting him aroused.

"Why not? You let me do it last night." His fingers had been busy all the while working at the tiny buttons of her nightgown. Jade gave a surprised gasp when he slowly slid the soft flannel off her shoulders, baring both breasts to his view. When she grabbed at the gown to pull it back in place, he took hold of her wrists and held her hands down at her sides.

As she stood there, helpless to cover herself up, there was a hungry look in Kane's eyes as he gazed at her breasts. "God," he said softly, "they are so beautiful. So perky, teasing me to taste them, suck their honey."

"They're doing no such thing." Jade shook her head, trying to sound firm but knowing that her hardening nipples were saying something else. "Anyway, you didn't think they were so special last night."

"Why do you say that?" Kane asked in surprise. "I damn near devoured this one." He ran a gentle finger across the nipple he had spent so much time on.

Jade looked up at him and demanded, "Why then did you give a great shiver and hurry to cover me up?"

Kane's lips curved in tender amusement. "Ah, my little innocent," he whispered. "You really don't know what the shuddering of my body meant, do you?"

"I thought my breasts were distasteful to you."

"Ah, Jade, what am I going to do with you?" Kane pressed her head down on his shoulder. "I have so much to teach you. I want to make your body convulse with almost unbearable pleasure."

"No!" Jade drew away from him, pulling her gown back in place. "You make me feel all mixed up."

"That's because you know nothing about love-making, honey. Your body is taking over your mind. Your brain tells you, 'Don't do this' while your body is telling you what it wants. Just relax and do what feels right."

Kane took hold of her arms and coaxed softly, "Let me teach you, Jade. Right now."

Jade gazed up at Kane, her body and mind warring. She wanted to do as her body urged her, but something held her back. Kane hadn't even courted her. The only thing on his mind was having his way with her. When it was over, she would probably never see him again. He would go back to his big ranch and never give her another thought. As for herself, she would never forget him once she surrendered to his pleas.

Tightening the belt around her waist, she shook her head. "No," she said. "Maybe I'll marry some-day—Uncle John says that I must. I'll let my husband teach me all about the mystery of lovemaking."

"Jade." Kane almost groaned the word. "You don't want one of these mountain men to teach you about that. They don't make love. They just climb on a woman, grunt and sweat for a minute or so and then roll off her. Within another couple minutes they're snoring beside her."

"Maybe you're right and maybe you're wrong." Jade moved, putting the table between them. "I've never been invited into my neighbors' cabins to watch what goes on between husband and wife."

While Kane glared at her Jade added, "Anyway, I won't be marrying a mountain man."

"Who then? One of those wet-behind-the-ears young ranchers you met in Laramie?" Kane sneered. "They don't know any more about love-making than the men around here. The only women they've ever slept with are whores at the Pleasure House."

Her hands on her hips, Jade demanded, "Are you saying that you're the only man in the area that knows how to make love?"

"Of course not," Kane snapped, angry that he had been drawn into a trap. "I was only general-izing."

"I see. Mountain men are insensitive and young men are ignorant in the art of lovemaking. It makes me wonder how you came to know all about loving a woman, how as a young man you developed all your skills." Jade's scathing words bit into Kane.

"Never mind how I learned," Kane snapped back, angry that Jade had led him into another trap.

When he said no more Jade added, "This is a useless discussion. When the time comes, Uncle John will choose my husband, and he's said many times that he would never let me marry a moun-tain man."

"Who else does he know?" There was a sarcastic tone in Kane's voice.

"He knows other people," Jade declared, her

voice sharp. "He has relatives back east. He might send me there to find a husband. He has hinted at it."

While Kane glared at Jade, unable to argue about that, she asked, "What would you like for breakfast?"

"I don't care," Kane said with a growl and stamped to the other end of the room and plopped down into the rocker.

As Jade placed a skillet on the stove she told herself that she should feel elated that she'd had the last word in their confrontation. But she didn't feel at all happy about it. With all the talk of Kane saying whom she shouldn't marry, he hadn't once hinted that he would like to be her husband. His only wish was to be the first with her; then he would let another man have his leavings.

An anger rose inside her, so strong it almost choked her. When she called to Kane that breakfast was ready she served him half-raw bacon and eggs so hard he was afraid he'd chip a tooth on them. A glance at her plate showed him crisp bacon and lightly scrambled eggs. His eyes narrowed. The little hellion was back to her old tricks. Thank God the coffee was good, he thought, picking up his cup and walking back to the fireplace. He ground his teeth in frustration as Jade went about straightening up the kitchen, softly humming a tune he had never heard before.

When she walked past him on her way to her bedroom, she said sweetly, "The wood supply is getting low in here. Maybe you should bring some in from the porch."

Kane glowered at her. He knew that the wood-box was empty and had been on the point of pulling on his boots and bringing in some split logs. He made no response, however, to what amounted to an order. Let the little witch bring in her own wood. He'd be leaving here when the sun warmed up a little, and, by hell, he wouldn't be coming back.

Jade stayed but a short time in her bedroom, and when she returned from making up her bed, she looked at the woodbox. It was still empty. She paused but a moment, then walked into the kitchen area muttering to herself, "Let the big oaf freeze." There was enough wood stacked beside the stove to keep it going all day. And if he dared try to sit beside its warmth when his fire gave out, she'd break the broom handle over his head.

Jade discovered that she was getting low on bread. There was only half a loaf wrapped up in a white cloth to keep it from drying out. She decided that this was as good a time as any to start a new batch of sourdough. As she reached for her dough bowl on the shelf next to the window she noticed dark clouds gathering in the north.

Was it going to snow again? she asked herself, frowning. She didn't want that arrogant man to be stuck here another night.

She broke her self-imposed ruling never to speak to him again. "It's clouding up to snow again," she said to Kane's back. "If you don't want to get stuck up here for another night you'd better get on your horse and ride back down the mountain."

Mixed feelings tugged at Kane. On one hand he didn't want to do anything that would please the wildcat, but on the other hand, he was anxious to get home and put her out of his mind for all time.

He pulled on his boots and looked out the kitchen window. The clouds did look threatening, he thought. He wordlessly took his jacket off the wall and shrugged into it. If he hurried he could beat the storm home. Besides, he knew the mountain trails pretty well by now. He wasn't apt to get lost again in a blizzard. If it came to that, he would do as Big John and his ornery niece did: direct himself by the wind.

His hand was on the doorknob, ready to give it a twist, when he released it and moved to the window to have a better look at what he had glimpsed from the corner of his eye.

"Damn, I don't believe it." He groaned disgustedly.

Jade spread a towel over the bowl of dough and went to the window, wondering what had upset the rancher so.

"It's Maria," she exclaimed excitedly, "with your drover, Pete Harding."

"I know who it is." Kane growled, not at all happy to see his housekeeper and Pete Harding.

"What I don't know is what in the hell they are doing up here."

"She's come visiting." Jade's eyes sparkled.

"She picked a hell of a time to do that," Kane grumbled, removing his jacket and hanging it back up. "She's not going to like it one bit if she gets stuck up here overnight . . . maybe two or three nights."

"Oh, I wish that would happen," Jade said as she continued to peer around Kane's broad shoulders. "She's so nice."

"Ha." Kane grunted. "She's not always so nice. She can be mean as a polecat when she gets mad."

"She's not alone when it comes to that," Jade muttered with a sideways glance at Kane.

They stood in front of the window until the riders reached the porch and Pete was helping Maria to dismount. Jade ran to the door and flung it open.

"Maria," she cried, "I'm so happy to see you. But you look half-frozen. Hurry inside and get thawed out."

"I don't think I'll ever be warm again." Maria's teeth were chattering as she embraced Jade.

"Why ever did you come out in this weather?" Kane demanded as he helped his housekeeper off with her heavy riding coat. He turned on Pete. "You shouldn't have let her come."

"Let her?" Pete shot back. "Have you ever been able to stop her from doing something she's set her mind on?"

"Hush up, both of you." Maria took off the shawl that covered her head and most of her face. "I made that awful trip up here because I was afraid that something had happened to you, Kane Roemer, what with the blizzard and all. And then you didn't come home last night."

"Aw, Maria, I'm sorry you had to worry about me." Kane put his arm around her and led her to the fireplace. "Sit here in the rocker and warm up."

"Warm up by this?" Maria pointed to the bed of glowing coals. "Are you short of wood?"

"Pete, go fetch some wood from the porch. I was just about to bring some in when I saw you two coming up the mountain."

"Ha!" Jade snorted. "You were on the point of leaving when you saw them."

"No, I wasn't."

"Yes, you were."

Kane shook his head. "Was not."

Jade nodded her head. "Were too."

"I wish you two could hear yourselves," Maria broke in. "You sound like a couple of five-year-olds. Now stop your squabbling and help me get the chill out of my bones. Jade, honey, I sure would appreciate a cup of coffee." When Jade hurried toward the kitchen area, she called after her, "Put a splash of your uncle's moonshine in it; then bring the bottle for Pete."

As if on cue the foreman entered the kitchen, his arms loaded with split logs. Kane hurried to take them from him so that he wouldn't leave dirty footprints on Jade's carpet. "Don't tell me that it's snowing already." He brushed at Pete's shoulder.

"Yeah, damn it, it just started."

"I'm not gonna have one head of stock left by the time spring arrives," Kane said dispiritedly as he dumped the small logs into the woodbox.

As he carefully crisscrossed the wood on the red coals, Maria said soothingly, "Try not to worry too much, Kane. We saw at least half your herd in the shelter of the foothills on our way up here. I'm sure the other half are scattered about in the same area."

"I hope so," Kane said, straightening up and brushing off his hands. "The thing is, even if they can survive the cold, what are they going to eat? Last year they found spots of dry grass where the wind had swept it clear of snow. That carried them through the winter, but this year the snow is too deep."

"They'll eat the foliage off the fir trees if they have to," Pete said. "I've even heard of them chewin' the bark off trees, too."

"I've made up my mind about one thing," Kane said. "Come spring I'm gonna have three or four acres plowed up and seeded with rye. Next winter we'll have hay to spread around for the animals."

"Now that's good thinkin'," Pete said, and while he and Kane discussed the idea Maria and Jade chatted away.

"You're a good little housekeeper, Jade," Maria

said. "Everything is so clean and cozy-like. I confess that your home is not at all what I expected to find."

Jade smiled wryly. "It's not like it used to be. After seeing how nice your home was I made Uncle John help me fix things up."

"Where is that uncle of yours?" Maria asked.

"He's out running his trapline. He'll come home around dusk unless the weather gets really bad. It takes him longer to gather his furs then."

"I'm sorry I won't get to see him," Maria said, trying to hide her disappointment.

"You'll get to see the ol' renegade." Kane had overheard his housekeeper's remark. "Take a look outside the window. That snow means business. You're gonna be spending the night here. Maybe longer."

"Oh no!" Maria exclaimed in dismay. "Old Jeb is down with a bad cold. Who'll take care of him?"

"The hands will," Pete spoke up. "They may complain about his long tales and constant jabbering and sticking his nose in everybody's business, but they're awfully fond of the old geezer. He'll be all right."

"I hope so," Maria said, doubt in her tone.

It was around lunchtime when Jade excused herself and went into the kitchen to punch down the round piece of dough that had risen to double its size. She formed it into three loaves and shoved it into the hot oven. Next she went into the larder room and brought out a large piece of beef she had roasted the day before. Cut into good-sized slices it would make hearty sandwiches.

Maria joined her shortly, a pair of Big John's socks on her feet and her empty cup in her hand. Before she sat down at the table she refilled her cup from the big coffeepot warming on a back burner. As Jade sliced the beef they picked up their conversation.

Time passed swiftly, and before Jade knew it she could smell that it was time to take her bread from the oven. She set the loaves aside to cool a bit, then amassed in the center of the table a small crock of butter, a jar of blackberry jelly and a small wooden bowl of pickles.

Maria picked up one of the pickles and bit the end off. When she had chewed and swallowed it she said, "These are the best pickles I've ever eaten, Jade. I'd like to have your recipe."

"I didn't make them, Maria. Old Tillie Clark, back of the waterfall, makes them every summer and gives me some. She made the jelly, too. I pick the berries and supply the sugar and get half of what she makes."

"Do you think she would share her recipe with me?"

"I doubt it. I think every woman on this mountain has asked her how she makes her pickles and she always refuses to tell them."

Jade laughed lightly. "She promised me that she was going to leave me the recipe in her will."

"How old is she?" Maria asked, amused. "How

long do you think you'll have to wait for it?"

Jade's eyes crinkled at the corners. "Uncle John claims she's as old as the mountains, but she says she's ninety-three."

Maria shook her head in wonder. "I'd like to meet her, learn the secret of her long life."

"She boasts that it's the bark-and-herb tea she drinks every day." Jade's face grew somber. "It will be a sad day here in the mountains when old Tillie passes on. She's the only person up here who passes for a doctor. She's delivered most of the people living here, set broken bones, brought them through pneumonia, and all the other ills that can strike a person."

"Does she have a husband and children?"

Jade shook her head. "She's never been married." Jade added then with a grin, "She says that there's not a man alive she'd let boss her, or worse, knock her around when it pleased him to do so. One time after she had patched up Martha Graham after a brutal beating from her husband, Calendar, the old woman said that if she had her way she'd gather up all the men over thirteen and set fire to them." After a pause, Jade added, "All except Uncle John. She likes him. I expect it's because he keeps her supplied with fresh game."

Jade stood up and remarked, "I guess the bread has cooled enough so that I can slice it."

After lunch was eaten and the kitchen was put back to its neat state, Maria asked Pete where he had put her reed bag. He stood up and brought it from the corner, where he had placed it on entering the cabin. Maria untied its drawstring and brought out a ball of gray yarn with two knitting needles stuck in it, and a half-finished sweater she was making for Kane.

Jade watched in awe as Maria's flying fingers manipulated the needles. "I wish I knew how to do that," she said wistfully.

"There's nothing to it once you learn how to handle the needles." Maria reached into the bag again and brought out a ball of red yarn and two more needles. "Pull your chair over here beside me and I'll teach you how."

At first it seemed to Jade that she had ten fingers on each hand, she handled the needles so awkwardly. Then gradually she got the feel of the needles and was painstakingly knitting one, purling two. The stitches were uneven, some tight, some loose, but the scarf she intended to make for Big John was taking shape.

Kane and Pete dozed beside the fire, and the only sound in the room was the ticking of the clock and the clicking of knitting needles. Outside it continued to snow.

When the clock struck three times Maria looked at Jade, whose attention was on her creation, and asked, "Shouldn't you be starting supper pretty soon? Dusk will be arriving in another hour."

"Yes, I suppose so." Jade sighed, reluctant to leave off her newly learned craft.

"What did you plan to make for us to eat?"

"I thought I'd put a ham in the oven and roast some sweet potatoes along with it."

"Why don't you keep on with your knitting and I'll make supper?" Maria suggested.

"Are you sure? You're company and it doesn't seem right for you to make supper."

"I'm not company," Maria protested as she put away her knitting and stood up. "Besides, I'm tired of sitting."

It was a little after dusk and Maria had lit the lamp in the center of the table, when the kitchen door opened and Big John walked in, covered with snow.

His eyes, warm and glowing, went straight to Maria, who was setting the table.

Chapter Ten

Maria blushed at the message in the big man's eyes. She hoped that those by the fire hadn't looked their way.

"I must be dreaming," John said, bending over and removing his snow-encrusted boots. "I've been thinkin' about you all day." He straightened up and, taking off his gloves, fumbled at the buttons on his jacket. "How about givin' me a hand here. My fingers are numb from the cold."

A little voice inside Maria warned, "Don't get that close to him. He's as wily as a wolf."

Maria considered the advice a moment, then ignored it. After all, what could John do with three other people in the cabin?

She walked over to him, and as she raised her

hands to help with the buttons, he took hold of them and pinned them between their bodies. In the process, he managed to rub the backs of his hands against her breasts. She looked up at him, her eyes widening. When her nipples grew hard beneath the rubbing of his hands he gave her a knowing smile before he lowered his head and caught her parted mouth with his.

The kiss was hot and fast. When John released Maria's hands and stepped back, her legs felt so weak she was afraid she might fall. As she gazed up at him she saw by the pleased smile on his lips that he was fully aware of the effect the kiss had had on her.

Angry that he had unnerved her so, had made her react like a young girl receiving her first kiss, Maria opened her mouth to give the big man a tongue-lashing. But before she could utter a word he gently laid a finger across her lips.

"Don't fight this thing between us, Maria," he said softly. "It is good and will go further than a quick kiss . . . just as soon as I can get you alone."

"No!" Maria shook her head.

"Yes," John said softly, "and it will be good between us."

Before Maria could protest again, John was walking away from her, calling a greeting to Kane.

Kane roused from his sleep and grinned when Big John joked, "Do you purposely come up here to get snowed in for a spell?"

"It would seem that way, wouldn't it?" Kane grinned ruefully.

Big John moved to stand in front of the fire, soaking up its heat. When he turned around to warm his back, he smiled down at Jade. "What you doin' there, girl?"

Jade proudly held up the beginning of his scarf, about five inches long now. "Maria taught me how to knit, and I'm making you a scarf."

"Well, now, ain't that somethin', Roemer?"

Kane ignored the question and said instead, "I don't believe you've met my foreman, Pete Harding. He brought Maria up here looking for me."

"And here I thought the lady had climbed the mountain to see me." John slid a sly look at Maria, who had regained enough composure to finish setting the table.

Maria pretended not to have heard him, but the heat that rose to her cheeks said that she hadn't missed one word.

"I'll not shake hands, Pete. My hands are dirty and grimed with dried blood from taking animals out of my traps. But welcome to my home."

Pete nodded his thanks and John turned his attention back on Jade. "Is there water in my room, girl?" When Jade absently nodded, he said, "I'm gonna go wash up and change my clothes now. It smells like Maria has supper about ready."

There was much talk and laughter among the five crowded around the table as the evening meal was eaten. When everyone sat back, their hunger sated, John said on a more serious note, "I learned a bit of news that will make our womenfolk happy." When everyone looked at him expectantly, he went on, "Just before the storm struck I stopped by the Oates place for a snort of whiskey and to warm up a bit. Accordin' to Carter, a nephew of old Tillie Clark's is comin' up here to teach their younguns."

"My land, I can't believe it," Jade cried excitedly. "We've tried for years to get a teacher up here. I never knew old Tillie had any relatives."

"Nobody knew it, and they're just as surprised as you are," John said. "You know how close-mouthed the old woman is about herself. I expect there's a lot of things we don't know about her."

"When is he coming?" Jade asked.

"Any day now. Course this latest snowstorm may hold back his arrival a few days."

Jade nodded agreement, then asked, "How is Jessie?"

"She's still pretty much banged up. That bastard Carter almost killed her this time."

When Jade explained to their company the beating Carter Oates had given his wife, Maria was outraged. "A man might beat me once, but by all that's holy, he'd never do it a second time."

"What would you do about it?" John asked with gentle humor.

"After I'd laid him out with a poker upside his head, I'd leave him."

"What if you had no place to go?"

"I'd find a place, even if it was only a cave."

"And how would you care for yourself, feed yourself?"

Maria gave John a speculative look. After a moment she said, "I understand what you're getting at. The beaten wives have nowhere to go, no way of making their own living."

Big John nodded. "Sadly, that's right. They have to take whatever their husbands hand out."

Silenced by that knowledge, Maria sat staring into her coffee, wishing that she were a man for about an hour. She'd teach those wife beaters a hard lesson.

John looked at her bent head, admiration in his eyes. Here was a woman who would give back as good as she received. He had given up hope of ever finding a woman like her, and, by God, he wasn't going to lose her.

Chairs scraped as the men stood up and left the table. "Go with them, Jade. I know you're dying to get back to your knitting."

"Oh, Maria, I feel so guilty leaving you to clean up the kitchen, especially since you made supper."

"Don't fret about it, honey. It will only take me a jiffy to wash things up."

"If you're sure, Maria, I appreciate it."

Maria wanted to be alone, to mull over everything John had said, to try to decide just what the big man had meant by his words. He had made it clear that he wanted to take her to bed, but was that the extent of it? She hoped not. She had waited for ten years for such a man to come into her life, and she would be devastated if lust was the driving factor in his attention to her.

When Maria joined the others at the fire, she was careful not to look at John. She intended to hold herself aloof from him until he came right out and said what his intentions toward her were.

As the men talked of trapping and ranching, Big John sent Maria many puzzled looks. What had made her sunny face turn solemn in such a short time?

Around ten o'clock Kane yawned and said he was about ready to turn in. Pete echoed his words, and Jade laid aside her knitting and stood up.

"I'll go make up the pallet for the two of you," she said.

As she walked toward her uncle's bedroom, Kane spoke the first words he had uttered to her since early morning. "I'd like a couple more blankets added to my pallet. My bones still ache from practically lying on the bare floor."

Big John frowned at Jade. "Didn't you lay our extra straw mattress on the floor for Kane to sleep on last night?"

Jade blushed to the roots of her hair. "I didn't think about it," she muttered, her sullen tone telling everyone that she was lying.

"Well, think about it tonight, missy."

Jade felt Kane's pleased gaze boring into her back as she stalked out of the room. When she had dragged the mattress from under her uncle's bed, she spread the sheet and blankets over it. Then, unlike last night, she reached under the bed again and pulled out two pillows. She returned to the main room then and smiled at Maria.

"I hope you won't mind sleeping with me tonight."

"Of course not, Jade." Maria grinned and added, "I'll try not to kick you in my sleep."

"I hope I don't kick you," Jade said, grinning back. "I'll say good night now. Come to bed when you please and don't worry about waking me up. I'm a very sound sleeper."

Jade hurried into her room then. Kane and Pete had gone outside to use the privy, she imagined, and she didn't want to be up when they returned.

She had barely changed into her gown and crawled between the covers when she heard the two men return, stomping the snow off their boots.

"Good news, folks," Kane announced. "It's stopped snowing. You'll be rid of us tomorrow, John."

"Well now, I don't know as that will make me happy." The big man looked at Maria.

Maria lifted her gaze to him, read the message in his eyes, then quickly looked down at her knitting. Would she be safe from this big man's charm once Kane and Pete went to bed? Maybe she should retire before they did.

She had come to that conclusion too late. Pete

and Kane were saying good night just as she was about to put her knitting away. She'd look like a scared little schoolgirl if she jumped up now and hurried to bed.

Maria swallowed convulsively when John scooted his chair up close to hers and laid his hand on her nervous fingers.

"What's wrong, Maria? Why this sudden change in you? Was it something I said? I would never intentionally insult you."

Maria sighed and let the knitting needles lie idle in her lap. Here was the chance to speak out, to say what was on her mind. But could she be that bold? she asked herself. Yes, she had every right to know what he had in mind for her.

Looking straight into John's warm brown eyes, she said bluntly, "It's not what you said, but what you didn't say."

"I don't know what you mean, Maria." John leaned closer to her. "Surely you know how I feel about you."

"I know that you want to take me to bed, but I would never knowingly let a man make love to me once and then forget that I exist."

"Maria, Maria." Big John stroked gentle fingers down her cheek. "Do you think that's all I want from you? I admit that wanting you is a gnawing pain in my gut, but I want more than that from you. I want you to be here when I come home from running my traps. I want to sit with you in front of my fire when blizzards howl around the cabin."

He squeezed Maria's hand. "The first time I saw you, I said to myself, I'm goin' to marry that woman."

"Did you really, John? You're not just saying what you think I want to hear?"

"I swear on Jade's life, I mean every word."

Maria gave him a watery smile and reached her arms out to him. John pulled her onto his lap. Between kisses and fondling they made their plans. They would get married in the spring. They would live in John's cabin, and Maria laughingly said that she would be a mountain woman then. "But no beatings." She playfully shook a finger at John.

"I'd be afraid to try." Big John chuckled. "I don't want a poker laid upside my head."

When Maria would have thrown her arms around his neck, John held her away. "Woman," he said, "you'd better get off my lap and go to bed. I'm in danger of bustin', I want you so bad."

Maria gave him a quick kiss and said with a pained smile, "I know exactly what you're talking about."

"Do you think we dare . . ." John looked suggestively at the fur piece spread in front of the hearth.

"My goodness, no." Maria shook her head. "Sure as shooting, someone would come in and catch us."

"Yeah, I guess so," John agreed dejectedly, then added more brightly, "One little fast comin' together would only be a teaser. Besides, I don't want to have to worry if we're makin' too much noise, or be afraid to cry aloud the pleasure we're going to give each other."

Lying next to Jade a little later, Maria smiled into the darkness. She had never been happier in her life.

A bright sun shone on Kane's head the following morning as he followed Jade's footsteps in the snow. They led to the shed where the horses were stabled. He had offered to saddle all three mounts, and Pete hadn't objected. His foreman was back in the cabin talking with Big John while they drank another cup of coffee. John had delayed his start on the trapline until after they had left.

Maria, of course, was the reason. Kane was still reeling from John's announcement that he and Maria would wed come spring. He couldn't visualize his housekeeper living in that little cabin.

Arriving at the shed, he pushed open the door. When his eyes became accustomed to the dim light he saw Jade pitching hay into the horse's troughs. "I'll do that," he said curtly, taking hold of the pitchfork.

"You'll do no such thing." Jade tightened her hold on the long handle.

"Why are you so damn stubborn?" Kane yanked at the pitchfork.

"I'm not being stubborn." Jade yanked back.

"The hell you're not," Kane said, determined

that he would take the pitchfork away from her.

In their struggle, which had nothing to do with who tossed hay to the horses, Jade lost her balance and fell flat on her back, bringing Kane down with her.

Winded, Jade glared up at Kane, unaware that in their tussle the three top buttons of her bodice had popped off and that her breasts were spilling over the top of her camisole. When she saw where Kane's eyes were fastened she grabbed at her jacket, which she had loosened on arriving at the shed.

"No," Kane ordered, his voice husky as he caught her wrists in one hand and held them over her head.

"Don't do that," Jade said in a small voice when Kane tugged down her camisole, freeing her breasts to his view.

"Why not?" Kane questioned huskily. "You want me to."

"I do not," Jade protested weakly, but too late. Kane had fastened his mouth over a pouting nipple. As he suckled it, his fingers teasing the other one, she moaned in a mixture of passion and frustration. His drawing lips were sending sensations from her breasts all the way down to the core of her womanhood.

Hating herself for it, she raised her hips, searching for the bulge she was sure was striving to be set free. Kane groaned deep in his throat at her action and freed her hands so that he could rip his fly apart. Jade's hands instinctively moved down his body to curl around his thickness.

When she merely held him, Kane wrapped his fingers around hers and moved them up and down in a slow rhythm.

So soft, yet hard as a rock, Jade thought, then stopped thinking when Kane took possession of her breasts again. She gasped aloud her pleasure as he slid a hand up her skirts and settled it in the vee of her thighs. She moaned aloud when he found the little nub of her femininity and began to rub it.

But all the stroking wasn't enough for Jade. She wanted that throbbing part of him inside her. She sensed that only it could bring her relief.

Kane had reached the same conclusion. He tore off his boots and trousers and, slipping off her drawers, positioned himself between her legs. When he felt her stiffen, he reached down and began to rub the place that set her on fire.

When once again she strained her body into his he gently and slowly entered her. She let out one little whimper of pain as he broke through her maidenhead. Kane held himself still until he felt the walls of her femininity closing around him, actually sucking at his manhood.

God, that feels good, he thought. *I bet I could lie perfectly still and she could bring me release.*

But he wanted Jade to reach that crest of small death also. He began moving in and out of her, each stroke bringing him pleasure he had never known before.

They reached the crest together, Jade's soft cry of elation followed by Kane's hoarse moan of satisfaction. They lay side by side then, willing their breathing to return to normal. When Jade began to push her skirts down over her nakedness, Kane did it for her. Before he sat up and reached for his trousers, he brushed a light kiss across her eyes.

He had stood up and was pulling on his trousers when the shed door opened and Big John and Maria stepped inside. He knew exactly when the mountain man saw him and Jade by the roar John let out. While Jade sat up, Kane barely had time to yank his trousers up around his waist before the outraged man was upon him.

John's ham-sized fist lashed out and caught Kane on the point of his chin, snapping his head back. As he tried to get away from the man who was determined to beat him to death, John hit him again, right between the eyes. He staggered, dizzy beyond belief. He could dimly hear Maria and Jade pleading with the almost demented man to stop, that he was going to kill Kane.

The women's voices finally penetrated the big man's rage. He dropped his fists to his sides, his breath coming in short gasps. Kane sat down on the keg that held the rooster's feed, his hands dangling between his knees, his head hanging and blood trickling out of his nose. Both Jade and Maria wanted to go to him, but they were afraid that if they showed any sympathy for the bloodied man it might set John off again.

When John could speak, he said, "I'll not hit the bastard again." Maria and Jade breathed their relief, then stared at him in disbelief when he said, "I want him to be able to stand beside Jade when Preacher Hart reads the weddin' vows over them."

"Are you crazy?" Kane jumped to his feet, his battered face twisted in rage. "I didn't rape her. She was quite willing."

The big man flinched at the slur cast on his niece, but let it pass. "I'm not crazy," he said, "but you are if you don't think there's a possibility that you'll be a father nine months from now."

A startled look came into Jade's eyes at her uncle's charge. There was a chance that she and Kane could become parents. She had felt Kane's release and had thought nothing of it. At the time she hadn't been able to think logically about anything.

"Uncle John," she pleaded, "couldn't we wait and see if I'm in a family way first?"

"No, we'll not wait," John declared loudly. "Whether you have a babe or not, he's ruined you for any other decent man who might want to marry you. Now get yourself straightened up while I go get the preacher."

Stabbing a hard look at Kane, he threatened, "If you try to get off this mountain before I return I'll come after you and shoot you in both knees. I'll hate for Jade to be wed to a cripple, but that's the way it will be if you're gone when I get back."

Kane glared back at the cold-eyed man, knowing that he would do exactly as he threatened. He jerked his jacket up off the floor where he had discarded it and strode out of the shed, slamming the door behind him so loudly, Pansy started squawking.

When John left only moments behind Kane, Maria put an arm around the stricken Jade. "Are you all right, honey?" she asked gently.

"I'm all right physically"—Jade dabbed at her eyes with a crumpled handkerchief—"but mentally I'm all torn up. I feel like I'm living a nightmare."

"I know," Maria said angrily. "I could just beat Kane until he can't stand up."

"No, Maria, don't lay all the blame on him. As he said, I was willing."

"Of course you were. Kane's an expert at getting what he wants from a woman. It was no problem for him to make you willing. If he'd kept his hands off you, we wouldn't be in this predicament."

"We, Maria?" Jade asked, puzzled. "How will all this affect you?"

Maria sighed. "John and I won't be getting married."

"Why not? You had nothing to do with what happened between Kane and me."

"I have been with Kane so long, he's like family to me. Now that there's bad blood between him and John, I don't know who I should side with. I'm caught in the middle."

"But what about Uncle John's feelings? It's clear he loves you very much."

"I know he does, but he'll let that mountain pride of his override his feeling for me."

"Then he's not worth having."

"Most men aren't, honey. Let's get on up to the cabin and get you straightened up."

Chapter Eleven

Kane strode into the cabin, purposely not removing his boots first. As he left a trail of snowy footprints on Jade's clean carpet, he gloried in the dirty puddles he was leaving behind him. That he was acting like a vengeful schoolboy didn't enter his mind. To him he was striking back at the people who had put him in this plight.

He ignored Pete, who gave him a startled look, and walked on into John's bedroom. When he heard Maria speak briefly to Pete and heard Jade's bedroom door close, he said with a sneer, "Gonna get all prettied up for your wedding, huh?" Well, damned if he was going to do anything about his appearance. He wasn't even going to wash the blood off his face.

The bedroom was growing quite chilly by the time Kane heard Big John return. He could hear Jade's uncle introduce the preacher to Pete, then to Maria. Jade, of course, would already know Reverend Hart. His body jerked when the door was flung open and John stood glaring at him.

"The preacher is here," he said in a voice cold as ice. "Wash your face and get your ass into the livin' quarters." He turned and left then, as though knowing his order would be obeyed.

Kane swore long and fluently. Never before had he been in a squeeze he couldn't get out of. He couldn't shoot the man he had dishonored, nor could he fight him if he wanted his face to remain whole. He pushed himself to his feet and walked over to the crudely built washstand. He filled the basin sitting there with water from the matching pitcher. He bent his head over the basin of water and began scrubbing his face with his hands, splashing as much water as possible on the floor.

"Clean that up, too, Miss Priss," he jeered to himself. After he had dabbed at his face with a towel he found hanging on a peg, he ran careless fingers through his hair, then left the room, a scowl on his face.

They were waiting for him, gathered around the hearth. Pete, John, Maria, Jade and the preacher. Big John looked at his rebellious face, noted that hay still clung to his trousers and jacket. He clenched his fists, but hung on to his temper. Things had a way of making a full circle. A day would come when Kane Roemer would regret how he had acted this day.

The preacher motioned Kane to take his place beside Jade. As he did so he slid her a hard look and was surprised that she hadn't made an effort to get herself all fancied up.

Jade had been forced to change her dress because of the buttons she had lost from the one she had worn in the shed. But she had changed into one that matched her mood. Gray in color, very plain, with sleeves that reached to her wrists and a neckline going all the way up to her chin. She had pulled her beautiful hair back into a loose knot at her nape. She was pale, but looked composed.

Kane was wishing he felt that way when Pete stepped up and stood beside him. Maria moved to stand beside Jade, the preacher opened his Bible and the ceremony began.

When the reverend asked him, "Do you take this woman to love and to honor, forsaking all others?" Big John had to give Kane a hard poke in the back to bring him back to the present.

The preacher was looking at him expectantly and he imagined this was when he was supposed to say, "I do." He almost choked on the two words as he uttered them.

A moment later Jade said in a low voice, "I do."

When Hart saw that no wedding band was forthcoming, he said, "I now pronounce you man and wife." He smiled at Kane and said, "You may kiss the bride."

Kane made a growling sound in his throat and, taking Jade by the elbow, said, "Let's get the hell out of here."

"Hold on there, mister," John ordered. "You have a paper to sign here."

Kane snatched the paper from him, scrawled his name on it, then waited impatiently for Jade to write her name on the certificate. When she had finished and handed the pen back to the reverend, Kane took hold of her arm again. "Come on."

"Take your hands off her, Roemer," Big John ordered, the chill in his voice slicing the air. "She's not going with you."

"What do you mean, she's not going with me?" Kane demanded. "She's my wife, isn't she?"

John took a step toward him, his big hands clenched as though he'd like to wrap them around Kane's throat. "Do you think for one moment that I'd let you take her away from my protection, where you could treat her like an Indian whore, insult her at every turn, break her spirit while venting your spleen on her?"

He took another step toward Kane, his fingers working, and said through gritted teeth, "Now get on your horse and ride out of here. And don't let me ever again see you on this mountain."

Jade couldn't believe it when Kane said aggressively, "She's my wife and it's her duty to go with me."

"And it's my duty as her uncle to do what's best for her," John answered just as forcefully.

"What if she has a child?" Kane demanded. "A son? Am I never to see it?"

"Not if I have anything to say about it."

"We'll see about that," Kane challenged, and then said to the waiting Maria and Pete, "Let's get the hell out of here."

When Pete and Kane had left, Big John walked up to Maria, his harsh features soft now. "It grieves me, Maria, that we can't go on with our plans," he said gently, "but you must know that it would be impossible for us to wed now."

Tears glittered in Maria's eyes as she nodded her understanding. She embraced the sobbing Jade and whispered in her ear, "Things are going to work out, honey. You'll see." She tightened the scarf around her head, gave John one last, lingering look, and left the cabin.

The news of Jade Farrow's sudden, early morning wedding spread like a stampeding herd of longhorns. Her neighbors asked each other why Big John had allowed his niece to marry a lowlander. Opinions were offered. Some said with a sniff that John always thought his niece was too good to wed one of them. And when they learned that Jade still lived with her uncle it was hinted among some that the big man had caught Jade and the rancher in bed together. If that was the case, it was a shotgun wedding.

It was all speculation on the part of the Farrows' neighbors, for none dared ask the easily aroused uncle. They all feared his rage. His answer might be a fist in the mouth. They hadn't hesitated to ask the preacher, but he had been very tight-mouthed about the marriage. All he would admit to was that yes, he had married the couple.

The question then was whether he had been warned to say no more than that. A few protested that John wouldn't do that to a man of the cloth.

The conclusion the mountain people finally reached was that Preacher Hart didn't know any more than they did. The women marked the date, then waited to count the months before Jade's body changed its shape. If her body grew large, then all their questions would be answered.

At the end of the week the mountain people had something new to talk about. Old Tillie's nephew, the new teacher, arrived in the mountains.

Virgil was slightly built, had light brown hair and wore thick spectacles. He lost no time in climbing on his mule and visiting the members of the community. The evening that he visited the Farrows, Carter Oates was there. Virgil's attitude toward Oates was cool and he stayed but a short time. As soon as the door closed behind him, Carter snickered. "He's a little feller, ain't he, John?"

"He is that," John agreed with a thoughtful frown. "Most of his students could beat him up if he tried to punish them."

"Ain't that the truth? Why, my oldest girl could whip him."

"That could be." John nodded. "But it's gonna be up to you fathers to make sure that none of your younguns give him any trouble. We've waited too long to get a teacher up here. We don't want to scare him off." John bent a dark look on Oates. "You spread the word that I said so."

Jade had immediately liked the gentle little man, and two days after meeting him she bundled up and climbed the half mile to Tillie's little cabin. As she and the old woman and Virgil sat before the fire sipping herbal tea, she found that they had much in common. They both loved poetry and had read many of the same books. When they said good-bye near dusk, she invited Virgil to visit her, to look at her supply of books in case she had some he would like to borrow.

As the fathers worked to make a schoolhouse of an old cabin that had stood empty since the death of its owner three years before, Jade and the teacher spent many hours together, taking turns reading poetry out loud and discussing books they had read. It took but a couple of days for eyebrows to be lifted and tongues to wag.

Why did John allow Jade to spend so much time alone with the teacher? the mountain people asked each other. Of course, no one dared to ask him.

Within a couple of weeks' time the schoolhouse had been weatherproofed and benches had been made for the students to sit on. The big stove that old Tillie had donated was installed. The fathers would take turns keeping the woodbox filled. Tillie gave her nephew a cowbell to call his students in, and Jade loaned him the books she had learned from.

School started the following Monday. Sixteen children, ranging in age from six to fifteen, made their way to the schoolhouse.

School had been in session a week when one morning Jade awoke to find that her menses had started overnight. She wanted to shout aloud her relief. The fear that she might be expecting had hung over her like a heavy shroud ever since her wedding day.

Wedding day, she scoffed, reaching up to take a clean strip of white cloth from one of the shelves newly erected in her bedroom. What a farce that had been, she thought, folding the white material into a thick pad, then pinning it inside a pair of underwear. She was surprised that God hadn't struck her and Kane dead, making vows that neither meant to keep.

As Jade went about making breakfast, drinking a cup of coffee as she turned the bacon strips in the frying pan, she reminded herself that although she wasn't going to have Kane Roemer's baby, she was still married to him. For how long she had no idea. It could be years, or maybe just a few months. It would depend on Kane. Marriage was a sacred thing with Uncle John and he would never allow her to file for a divorce.

Kane, however, was bound to fall in love with some woman one day and would want her for his wife. The woman would be from his world, of course. Someone with the same background as he.

Whatever happened, Jade thought as she sat down to bacon and eggs, it made no difference to her one way or the other.

She did wish, however, that she could stop dreaming of her husband, reliving the time they made love in the hay.

No one wanted to be around Kane these days, and everyone avoided him as much as possible. He never had a genial word for anybody and was curt and sharp when issuing orders to the cowhands. His face was always set in grim lines.

Only old Jeb felt secure enough to demand one morning, "What in the blue blazes is botherin' you, Kane? For the past month you've been goin' 'round like a bear with a sore foot. What happened to you on your last visit to the mountains?"

"Nothing happened to me." Kane glared at the old man. "I'm just sick and tired of snow and cold, and worrying about my cattle."

"Yeah, that could get a man down, but you've weathered these winters all your life and it never bothered you before."

"Well, it bothers me this winter," Kane said curtly, and walked away to the barn.

He would visit Satan. He always found comfort with the stallion. It had taken him all winter—visiting him every day, talking softly to him as he fed him an apple—but the big white had finally accepted him. Kane had been taking him for short rides for a couple of weeks now.

He grinned wryly. Jade wouldn't like that if she knew.

Much to his chagrin Jade seemed always to be on his mind these days. The last thing he saw at night before falling asleep and the first thing that came to him on awakening was the vision of her lovely face. During the day he was able to get a few hours' respite from her by keeping himself busy. But at night, when he was asleep and vulnerable, she came to him, her naked body shining in the moonlight as she slipped into his bed.

Did Jade ever think of him? he had asked himself many times. Did she ever recall how sweet the lovemaking between them had been that day in the shed? It had been her first time, though, and maybe it hadn't been all that special to her, considering that she had no other experience to compare it to.

Chapter Twelve

On the evening of February fourteenth, disbelief gripped those living on the mountain. Carter Oates had been found strangled to death in one of the snares he had set to catch animals.

The men of the mountain were crowded into the Farrow cabin to discuss suspicions and opinions. The women and children had gone to the Oates place for his widow's sake.

"Is everyone here?" Big John asked, looking around the room.

"Everyone but the schoolteacher," Calendar Graham said.

"You're not going to be seeing that one after dark anymore." John chuckled. "When the little feller knocked on my door to tell me how he had found Carter, I think every bone in his body was shakin', he was so scared."

"Well then, let's get down to business," Boris Greene said, his eyes shifting over everyone but making eye contact with none of them.

"To my way of thinkin' it seems unlikely that Carter would be careless enough to try to bait his snare after the noose had been set," Elisha Collins said, "and that's the onlyest way it could have happened."

The men were divided on that remark. Some said that yes, Carter was dumb enough to do that, while others argued he wasn't that ignorant. Carter had been a trapper all his life and would know better than to do a crazy thing like that.

"Unless he was drunk," Big John said. "I saw him this mornin' where our traplines cross, up there by that lightnin'-blasted tree. He could barely stand on his feet he was so drunk. It's possible he could have fallen headfirst into the snare. The jerk of the released saplin' could have easily broken his neck."

That made sense to everyone, who really didn't care how the man had met his death.

The talk then turned to the matter of a coffin.

Boris Greene looked up at Jade's shelves and said, "You're the handiest with a hammer and nails, Big John. I think you ought to do it."

Everyone agreed and John reluctantly said that he would do it. He privately thought that if he had his way, Carter Oates would be rolled down a canyon and left there for the buzzards and wolves to feast on.

Everything was settled to the men's satisfaction and they prepared to join their womenfolk.

Jade had barely glanced at the dead man lying stiffly on four rough boards placed on two saw-horses, but it had been long enough to see the cruelty on his features. She imagined he'd looked that way the night before, when he'd beaten poor Jessie again. The poor soul had lain on the sagging bed in the corner, unable to move without experiencing extreme pain.

One of the children had slipped out of the cabin and gone to old Tillie, begging her to please come and take care of his maw. At least Jessie would be able to stay in bed after this beating until she mended. There would be no Carter to order her to get up and take care of her wifely duties.

Jade knew that her children would see to it that she didn't stir until she was healed. And though Jessie was in much pain, there was such a look of relief on her face, Jade wanted to cry. What kind of hell had the woman lived through all these years?

Jade silently thanked God that her uncle would never make her marry a man from around here. She gave a bitter little laugh. He had made her marry a man she detested, a man who felt the same way about her. She had the consolation, however, of not having to live with her husband. She had hoped that evening when she informed

Uncle John that there would be no baby, he would give her permission to have her marriage set aside.

His answer had been a firm no. "You stood in front of a preacher and promised to be Kane Roemer's wife until death do you part, and that's the way it's gonna be."

She hadn't bothered to argue. When her uncle made up his mind about something, nothing but death could jar it loose.

Jade left off thinking about her marriage and her husband when the door opened and her uncle and Calendar Graham stepped inside. They carried a pine box between them.

The Oates children, stony faced, watched closely as their father was lifted inside his final resting place. Only when Big John placed a lid over the coffin and nailed it shut did their features relax. It was as though it took that action to assure them they were free of the man who had beaten them so often.

The oldest boy, Johnny, knelt down and dragged a whiskey jug from under the bed where his mother lay, and it was passed around among the men who had arrived later. One of them said in an aside to Big John, "Carter was a mean bastard, but he sure knew how to make good likker."

"Yeah," John agreed, "but that ain't much for a man to be remembered by." He walked over to where Jessie lay, said a few words to her, then motioned to Jade that it was time to leave.

As Jade and Big John walked the quarter mile to their cabin, their feet crunching on the frozen snow, Jade asked, "Did you and the men decide if Carter's death was an accident?"

John shook his head. "Naw, we didn't come to any conclusion, so we just left it that he was dead."

His indifferent answer didn't surprise Jade. No one really cared what had brought about the death of the most hated man in the mountains.

"Do you think Jessie and the children can get by without him?"

"Ha." John snorted. "The lad, Johnny, has provided meat for the family ever since he learned how to shoot a rifle. It was Jessie and the younguns who managed to scratch out a garden every spring. They're much better off without him."

As their cabin came in sight Jade couldn't help wondering if her big uncle had had anything to do with the death of Carter Oates. He had always detested the man and had provoked many fights with him just so he could give him a good beating.

The big white horse stepped along the clearly defined path in the snow. Kane, his shoulders hunched, his eyes red rimmed, had given Satan his head. He had a blinding headache and his stomach was rebelling against the whiskey that had been poured into it the evening before.

When he had ridden into Laramie yesterday his intentions were to get the supplies that Maria had requested and then go straight home. He avoided his friends as much as possible these days. He was tired of hearing about having the loveliest wife in all of Wyoming Territory and fielding questions about why he didn't live with her. His friends stopped short of expressing what they thought he was missing by not sleeping with the green-eyed beauty. He remembered that one man who had made a suggestive remark had received a hard fist in his mouth.

On arriving in Laramie, Kane had stopped at the mercantile and purchased the items on Maria's list. Then, following the impulse of a moment, he'd stopped in at the jeweler's to buy a plain gold wedding band. Feeling suddenly foolish, he'd thrust it angrily into his pocket and crossed the street to the Longhorn Saloon. There were only two horses tied to the hitching post, both belonging to older ranchers who weren't apt to rag him about Jade.

Kane was right about the two ranchers. Both were in their early sixties. After nodding a greeting to him, they returned to whatever they had been talking about.

He'd already finished one drink when Reverend Hart entered the saloon and walked over to stand beside him. After they had exchanged greetings, Kane asked, "Can I buy you a drink, Preacher?"

"That would sit right well with me, Kane," the genial Hart said. "I'm near frozen to death." As the bartender poured his drink Hart said, "Carter

Oates, up on the mountain, accidentally got himself hanged by one of his snares."

"Is that a fact? I don't imagine there were too many tears shed over him. From what I heard he beat his wife all the time."

"You're right. No tears were shed at his passing. He was an evil man."

"How are the folks up there?" Kane asked cautiously. He didn't want the preacher to know he was fishing for news of Jade.

"About the same as always, I reckon. Folks are tired of the snow and cold. They're looking forward to spring. There's a schoolteacher now. He's old Tillie's nephew. He lives with her."

"What type of man is he? How old is he?"

"I'd say around your age. Mild mannered, polite, very intelligent. He can talk on any subject brought up."

Preacher Hart slid Kane a sly look, and, lowering his voice, he said, "The teacher asked me if Jade was really married, seeing how the two of you don't live together. And he's not the only man who's wondering if she's available."

Kane's hand shook slightly as he lifted the glass of whiskey to his lips. When he set the empty glass back on the bar he said tightly, "You know my marriage was no love match, Preacher. For all I care Jade can see as many men as she wants to."

Reverend Hart sighed. "I had hoped that things would work out for you two. You seem like a perfect match, to my way of thinking."

Kane's answer was to order another drink.

In quick succession Kane downed two glasses of whiskey. He wasn't aware when the preacher left, was barely cognizant of the bartender and the two ranchers. He was trying to sort out why the possibility of Jade's seeing another man had affected him so. He didn't love her, so why should he care what she did?

The afternoon passed and darkness set in. Kane's bottle was half-empty and he was still telling himself that he didn't care what his wife did. To prove it, when one of the saloon whores sidled up to him and asked if he would like to go to her room and have a little fun, he agreed to it. The last he could remember was sprawling across her bed and passing out. An hour ago the whore had shaken him awake.

"You owe me five dollars," she'd announced. "Since you took over my bed all night, I lost several customers because of it."

Kane had laid the money on her pillow, said that he was sorry and gone hunting for his stallion. He'd found him at the livery, where some kind soul had taken the animal.

And now, feeling more dead than alive, he had to face Maria.

Kane was right in thinking he would get a tongue-lashing from his housekeeper. She railed at him for being inconsiderate, unconcerned about those around him.

"It's about time you take stock of yourself, Kane

Roemer, and think of others for a change," she scolded.

When Kane thought that surely his throbbing head would split wide open, Maria ran out of breath. He ventured over to the stove and poured himself a cup of coffee. He took one long swallow of the invigorating brew and then Maria spoke again, this time in a more controlled voice.

"John Farrow stopped by yesterday afternoon."

Kane gave a start, almost spilling the coffee that was halfway to his lips. He carefully set the cup back down. "What did he want?"

"It wasn't a neighborly call, if that's what you're thinking. He said he came because he thought you had the right to know that there would be no baby for you to support."

There was an almost accusing ring in Maria's tone, and for the first time Kane realized that, although she had never said so, Maria blamed him for the break between her and Big John.

He stared into his coffee, guilt washing over him. Because of his driving need to possess Jade, he had disrupted the lives of three people, as well as his own. And there wasn't a thing he could do to correct it. Unless he managed to talk Jade into living with him at the ranch . . . If he could dispel the animosity between them, Maria and Big John could get married.

Maria was speaking again. "Now that you know there will be no babe, will you want to divorce Jade?"

Kane looked up at Maria, his heart skipping a beat. "Did Big John say that was what Jade wanted?"

"No, he didn't say that."

Kane stared blindly into his coffee cup again, confused thoughts running through his mind. Why had he felt that little pang of disappointment that he wasn't to become a father? Why the jolt of anger that Jade might want a divorce?

"Well, do you?" Maria's voice broke in on his troublesome thoughts.

"Do I what?" he asked distractedly.

"Do you want to divorce Jade?" Maria said impatiently.

Kane knew that Maria was watching him as she waited for his answer. He didn't like this feeling of being penned in. It was the same way he had felt when being forced to marry Jade. Willing his face not to show any emotion, he answered, "I'll have to think about it."

When Maria only made a snorting sound in response to his somewhat haughty answer, he asked, "How did you and Big John get along? Does he want to get back together with you?"

"If he does, he didn't mention it," Maria said shortly.

"I'm sorry I caused the break-up between you and Big John, Maria," Kane said earnestly.

Maria shrugged her shoulders and said, "You lost as much as I did."

Chapter Thirteen

Jade awakened to a watery dawn. She lay still a moment and then her face lit up with a smile. Sometime during the night it had started to rain, a prelude to the coming of spring. After all, the ides of March had passed and rain was expected.

How nice it would be to see the wild mountain flowers bloom again, to see the moss turn green on the north side of trees and rocks along the many streams created by meltwater rushing down the mountain. Frogs would croak again in the evenings and birds would mate and nest in the trees.

Once more the sleeping mountains would come alive.

Jade sat up, scooted off the bed and reached for her robe. When she had slipped on her fur-lined slippers, she walked into the kitchen area. As was her habit she poured herself a cup of coffee, then walked to the window and pushed aside the curtains she was so proud of.

As she gazed outside, the rain slashed onto the roof, running down in streams onto the ground. She ran her gaze over the area around the cabin, a satisfied smile lifting the corners of her lips. The snow had begun melting. A few spots even showed patches of gravelly soil. If it rained all day and tomorrow, most of the ground would no longer wear a coat of white.

But it would still be cold the rest of this month and a good part of April. It wouldn't be freezing cold, but a chill wind would blow, making everyone bundle up before going outside for any length of time.

Jade smiled and waved her hand at Big John, whom she spotted coming toward the cabin. His left shoulder was weighed down with lines of traps. He would put them in the shed until the first frost in late autumn. They would be dragged out then and reset in their usual spots.

Her uncle carried a rifle in his right hand, and she knew there was a handgun shoved into the waistband of his trousers. All the mountain men had armed themselves in this manner lately. Another of their neighbors had met with a curious death. It appeared that Boris Greene had slipped in the snow, and in falling forward had hit his forehead on a large rock. What his neighbors couldn't understand was how he had come by the wound at the base of his skull.

Neighbors were beginning to look at each other suspiciously. Who among them was causing the mysterious deaths?

Jade turned from the window and set about making breakfast. Uncle John would be hungry.

She had the table set and a stack of flapjacks warming on the stove when the big man entered the kitchen. He grinned at Jade and said, "This rain is giving the snow a kick in the rump."

"Yes, thank goodness," Jade agreed and helped him take off his water-soaked jacket. As John removed his boots she carried the wet garment over to the fireplace and spread it on the hearth to dry. When she returned to the kitchen area John had washed his hands and placed the flapjacks on the table.

"Well, girl," he said as he spread butter on one, "I'll be goin' to the rendezvous in a couple weeks. Meet up with old friends again, have a rousin' good time."

"I always worry when you go to one of those," Jade said, reaching for the butter crock. "Promise me that you'll not get into any fights."

Big John gave her a look that said she was asking the impossible. When she pressed him for an answer all he would promise was that he wouldn't be picking any fights. "But if some pumped-up drunk insists on brawlin' a little, I'll not disappoint him."

I'm sure you won't, Jade thought to herself, then said, "I get lonesome when you're gone so long. And with those two suspicious deaths, I confess I'm a little nervous."

John gave her a crooked grin. "You could always ask the teacher to come stay with you. I trust him to behave himself."

"Virgil, the little fellow, protect me?" Jade laughed. "If anyone tried to break into the cabin I'd have to protect him."

"That's no lie." John laughed with her. "Old Tillie was tellin' Martha Graham that if wood wasn't brought in before dark she had to tote it in herself, 'cause her nephew wouldn't leave the cabin after dark."

"I agree that he's not the bravest man in the world," Jade said, "but he's sweet and a fine teacher."

"Yes, evidently he's good at teachin'." John nodded. "Everyone I've talked to says the younguns are learnin'. Folks are real proud that the older ones can read now. The mothers like for them to read from the Bible at night. Before, all they knew about the Good Book was what they could remember their parents tellin' them. They can hardly take in the new things they're learnin'."

"I hope the men learn that it's a deadly sin to kill. One of them, at least," she added.

"I doubt that will penetrate their thick skulls," John said as he stood up to bring the coffeepot to the table. "They've been killin' each other for years."

When he had filled both their cups and returned the pot to the stove, Jade asked, "Have you come to a conclusion yet which man might have killed Carter and Boris?"

"Hell, I haven't even decided if it was a man or a woman."

"A woman! What woman around here is big and strong enough to have killed two big men?"

"Ha! How much strength does it take to slip up on a man and give him a hard push? The same goes for whacking a man on the back of the head. You forget that circumstances have made the mountain women as tough as a piece of rawhide."

That does make sense, Jade thought, and fell to wondering which of the women in their small community was capable of murder. There were so many with a motive, she left off thinking about it.

"How are you goin' to pass the day?" John asked as he finished his coffee and pushed his chair away from the table.

"I don't know." Jade looked at the window, where water was running down the panes. "What about you? Will you be staying home today?"

"No, I'm goin' to ride into Laramie as soon as I load my furs on our draft horse. I'll probably be there half the day, arguin' with that fur buyer. Why don't you dig out your slicker and come along with me? You've been cooped up in the cabin all winter. It will do you good to get off the mountain for a while, buy yourself that string of beads I saw you eyein' at the mercantile."

"I don't know." Jade was ready to turn down his invitation, but then she decided that maybe a trip to town would break the monotony of her routine of cleaning the cabin and cooking meals.

But then, what if she ran into Kane? Would he speak to her, or give her one of his hard looks and pretend he didn't even see her?

Jade's own eyes hardened. She wasn't going to let the overbearing man control what she did. And she wasn't going to spend the rest of her life trying to avoid him.

She looked at John and said before she could change her mind, "I think I'll go with you. Give me a minute to brush my hair."

The rain had slackened somewhat when Jade and Big John started the descent to the valley below. The big draft horse plodded along behind them, John's winter catch strapped on his broad back.

When they rode out of the foothills they startled a herd of a dozen or more wild mustangs. "They're beautiful little animals, aren't they?" Jade said, watching them trying to run in the snow.

"They're good, sturdy little animals, too," John said, watching to see in what direction they were going. As he expected, they soon veered into the foothills. That was where they probably stayed most of the time. "When I come back from the rendezvous I'll know where to catch them. They'll make fine mounts once I've tamed them."

"You've made a fine mount, after all," Kane crooned to the white stallion as he saddled Satan. He was preparing for a trip to Laramie. Where once he wouldn't have minded being stuck in the house all day with Maria, these days he stayed out of her way as much as possible. She wasn't the same laughing and joking woman she used to be. She went around with a long face, talking to him only when forced to do so. Guilt wore at him all the time, for he knew she was missing Big John.

And it was out of the question to spend another day in the bunkhouse listening to the cowhands argue over a hand of poker, and to sit through one of old Jeb's tales that went on and on.

He was thankful for the rain as he climbed into the saddle. It would begin melting the snow. He hoped that he and the hands could ride the range and foothills tomorrow, discover how many head of cattle he had lost. Being busy again would keep his mind from straying to Jade so often.

The first person Kane saw when he entered Laramie and rode down its muddy main street was his boyhood friend, Wade Magallen. His relationship with Wade and his sister, Storm, had been strained since Kane's marriage to Jade.

It was understandable that Storm would be upset at his hasty marriage. She had nagged him for years to get married, to settle down and have a family. But she had learned of his marriage through gossip. He had been too cowardly to go tell her himself.

Storm would like Jade, he thought as he came abreast of Wade Magallen. They were both mule-headed and willful, but both women were very honest.

"Hey, stranger." Wade grinned as he reined his mount in. "Your sister has been raising Cain that you haven't been over to see your nephew all winter."

"I know. I should have dropped in. But after she took my head off the last time I saw her, I didn't know if I would be welcome."

"She's still mad as hell at you," Wade said wryly, "but she misses you." After a slight pause Wade said, "I suppose you and your wife are still living separate lives."

"Her uncle would shoot me if I showed up there and tried to talk her into coming home with me. Not that I want to," Kane hurriedly added.

"I've heard about Big John Farrow," Wade said. "They say he's a crusty devil."

"Crusty doesn't begin to describe him. He's hell-ish mean when he's riled. Everybody but Jade is afraid of him. She'd spit in the devil's eye if he angered her enough."

Wade slid Kane a curious look, but didn't voice what he was thinking. There had been pride in Kane's tone when he spoke of his wife. Maybe he didn't realize it, but he had tender feelings for his wife.

"What about going to the Longhorn for a drink?" Wade asked, picking up the reins. "I haven't seen much of Pa since winter set in."

"Sounds good. I'd like to see Jake." Kane turned the big white stallion so that he rode alongside Wade.

The two men had been in the Longhorn about half an hour when Jade and Big John rode into Laramie. As Jade pulled up in front of the mercantile and swung to the ground, Big John said, "I'll meet you at the restaurant in about an hour." He stood up in the stirrups and, digging into his trouser pocket, he pulled out a bill and handed it to Jade. "Buy yourself some purties. Some ribbons or somethin'."

Jade smiled her thanks and the big trapper rode on down the street, pulling up in front of a small building whose crudely painted sign read FUR BUYER. Ten months of the year it was closed. A week ago it had been opened for business. The trappers would be bringing in their furs in a steady stream for the next two months.

After John had haggled over price for half an hour, a deal was struck and payment for his furs was handed over. Outside again, he crossed the street to the Longhorn Saloon. He and Jake Magallen were old friends.

John frowned as he stepped up on the narrow

porch. He recognized the big white stallion tied up at the hitching rail.

There were several men lined up before the bar, and when a fast glance showed Kane and Wade standing at the end of the bar close to the door, John walked to the other end. Kane hadn't missed the entrance of his relative by marriage, and his body stiffened. He wanted to walk up to Big John and smash his fist into the face of the man who had disrupted his life. Because of him, things could never be the same again.

"Are you going to buy your new relative a drink?" Wade joked as they watched John and Jake shake hands.

"Are you out of your mind? I'd only get it dashed in my face. That one has no love for me."

"You never know. It might soften some of the hostility he feels for you."

"Ha." Kane snorted. "There's nothing on God's green earth that would soften the hard feelings he has toward the man who robbed his precious niece of her virginity."

Wade gave him a frowning, startled look. "The girl was still a virgin when you took her?"

Kane nodded, avoiding his brother-in-law's eyes.

"That does paint another picture," Wade said stiffly. "Did you know she was still pure when you made love to her?"

Kane sighed. "Yes, I did."

Puzzled, Wade said, "It's not like you to play fast and loose with an innocent."

"You've never seen her," Kane said, trying to defend himself. "She's wildly seductive and doesn't even know it. I could have no more stopped myself than I could keep the sun from rising."

Wade's anger softened a bit as he remembered how his desire for innocent Storm had made him lose control a couple of times before they got married. But he had loved Storm. Evidently Kane didn't have that feeling for the mountain girl.

He wondered about that, though, when a little later he saw pain flash in Kane's eyes as Big John stopped beside Kane on his way out. "Jade is doin' just fine without you," he announced. "Don't even think about comin' up the mountain."

Kane's hand trembled when he lifted the whiskey bottle and filled his glass again. Knowing Kane so well, Wade sensed that his longtime friend wanted to be alone. He pushed himself away from the bar, laid an understanding hand on Kane's shoulder and left the Longhorn.

Chapter Fourteen

Night had fallen and the rain had become a drizzle when Kane staggered out of the Longhorn. After two tries he managed to mount the white stallion. He turned Satan's head in the direction of home and then let the reins lie loose on the horse's neck. He didn't know whether the animal would go to the ranch, or travel up the mountain.

Although Satan had grown to trust him, Kane knew he still missed Jade. "Everybody misses that one," he slurred, his head hanging, his chin almost on his chest.

There crept into his mind a bit of information Jake had let slip after talking to that old scoundrel, Jade's uncle. Big John would be leaving for the rendezvous in a couple of weeks. Kane's lips lifted in a lopsided grin. "And that's when I'll make a trip to visit my little wife."

Satan went to the ranch. Perhaps he was cold and he remembered the warmth of the barn and the mash that would be given to him.

Jeb had just left the ranch house when Kane rode up. Seeing the difficulty Kane was having in dismounting, the old man hurried to help him. "Can't get my limbs to work right, old friend," the bleary-eyed rancher complained as Jeb grabbed hold of his waist to pull him out of the saddle.

"I can see that." Jeb grinned but the next thing he knew, he was lying on the ground with Kane's heavy weight on top of him. "Dadblast it, Kane, get the hell off me." He struggled against the body holding him down.

"I will in just a minute, you old renegade. Just let me rest awhile."

"Rest, hell, you're squashin' me. You damn well better not pass out."

The cookhouse door was suddenly jerked open. Cookie, having heard all the commotion, hurried to tug his boss off the bony old man. Together, he and Jeb got Kane to his feet and half carried him into the house.

"What in the world!" Maria exclaimed, rushing into the kitchen. "Is he hurt?"

"He ain't hurtin' now"—Cookie grinned—"but he sure will be tomorrow."

"He's drunk!" Maria said in disbelief.

"He is that," Jeb said, panting, "drunk as a skunk."

"Well, get him into his room and put him to bed."

Jeb nodded and he and Cookie half carried the muttering Kane out of the kitchen.

Ten minutes later they were back in the kitchen. When Maria raised a questioning eyebrow, Jeb said, "He's snorin' away. The whiskey fumes comin' out of his mouth could almost knock a man down."

"Boy"—Cookie grinned—"I wouldn't want to be him in the mornin'. He's gonna be sicker than a mangy dog."

"I've never known Kane to drink like that." Maria shook her head. "I wonder what set him off."

"He was mutterin' somethin' about missin' her and that the old devil was goin' to a rendezvous. I guess he was talkin' about his wife and her uncle."

When the men left the house Maria went into the family room and sat down in one of the rockers. With a push of her foot she set it into slow, creaking motion. She stared into the fire, thinking.

John had no right keeping Kane and Jade apart, she thought. Although they'd had a rocky start, if left alone, she felt that the newlyweds could have worked things out. She had learned tonight that Kane, although he would deny it, cared deeply for Jade.

The big fool probably doesn't even know it, Maria

thought. *He's never loved a woman before and doesn't understand this new emotion, which gives him no peace.*

"Men are the stubbornest, dumbest animals that walk the face of the earth." She was still muttering to herself when she rose and went to her room behind the kitchen.

Up on the mountain Jade and Big John were sitting in front of their fire, having a last cup of coffee before retiring. They hadn't talked at all on the way home, and very little afterward. Jade had known from experience that her uncle was pondering something and imagined it pertained to his upcoming trip.

Jade looked over at John and said, "I forgot to ask you the price of furs this year. Did you do well?"

"Yeah, pretty much. Especially with the mink pieces. Seems that mink coats are in demand."

Jade was thinking how many pelts it would take to make a coat and was feeling sorry for the little animals when John spoke again.

"I saw Kane in the Longhorn today."

Jade's heart skipped a beat, then raced. Even so, she managed to affect a careless shrug and to ask sarcastically, "What did my dear husband have to say? I'm sure he asked about my welfare."

Big John laughed at her caustic remark before saying, "I'm afraid not. He was on one end of the bar talkin' to his brother-in-law and I was at the other end."

John was asking himself if he should tell Jade what he had said to her husband, but just then she stood up and announced that she was going to bed. Her face looked so pale, he was sorry he had even mentioned the rancher. He didn't want to admit it, but he feared that his niece cared for the man.

The big man sat before the fire, wondering if Jade missed Roemer the same way he did Maria. Had losing his temper that day messed up the lives of four people? Why hadn't he just made the rancher marry Jade and then left it up to them to do whatever they wanted to do?

I'm a meddlesome old fool, he thought as he stood up and made his way to his bedroom.

Chapter Fifteen

Big John made little preparation for his trip to the rendezvous forty miles away in a deep valley. It was not quite daylight and the lamp Jade had lit shed its wan light on the items her uncle was shoving into a small grub bag: a handful of pemmican, strips of dried beef and two wrinkled apples that had survived the winter in the larder.

"Don't forget your slicker and a heavy jacket," Jade said. "We could get more rain, and the March wind is sometimes as cold as the winter ones."

Big John gave her an amused grin. "I bet you think I couldn't get along without you directing me."

"Since you have no *wife*"—she stressed the

word, thinking of Maria—"somebody has to look after you."

"That's what you think," John retorted. He gave her a sly look, knowing that his next words were going to rile her. "Man only needs a woman for one thing."

"I won't bother to rise to that." Jade sniffed. "You just said it to rile me up. But I will point out to you one good reason a man needs a wife. Married men live much longer than crusty old bachelors who have no woman to look after them. That should tell you something."

"But wives outlive their husbands. How do you figure that?"

Jade shrugged and gave him a twinkling grin. "I guess it's all in God's plan. He gives the long-suffering wives a few years to live in peace, to enjoy life for a change."

"Hogwash." Big John growled. "Why don't you go back to bed. You're still half asleep, spoutin' such nonsense." He picked up his bag of provisions and said, "Daylight is comin', so I'll be on my way. Now you know to keep the door barred all the time and check the shutters before you go to bed. I spoke to the little feller about checkin' on you in the daytime." John grinned. "I knew it was useless to ask him to drop in on you at night."

Jade chuckled and followed her uncle to the door. "Have a good time with all your friends, and don't get into fights with anyone," she said as he picked up the rifle leaning beside the door.

"Now don't go worryin' about me for the next two weeks. You should know by now that I can take care of myself." John leaned over and kissed the top of her head as he took the rifle. He opened the door then and stepped out into the gray light of approaching dawn.

The range had been clear of snow for a week, and the brown, dry grass that had been buried all winter was beginning to turn green. The cattle, in small groups, grazed from sunup to sundown. For two days Kane rode around, checking how many head he had lost to the winter weather. He found the bones of fifty steers that wolves had fed on. He had no way of knowing whether the wolves had attacked them while they were still alive or if they had frozen or starved to death before the wolves had come upon them. He consoled himself with the thought that he could have lost his whole herd.

Kane had let the cattle feed on the new green growth for a couple of days, to let them regain some strength. But starting today he and his men would ride the range, bringing them into one herd.

It was a cold, blustery morning when he walked to the cookhouse, where the cowhands waited for him. They were still half-asleep, but they had dressed themselves for the rough day ahead. Heavy gloves hung from their waistbands; sheepskin-lined vests were pulled over flannel shirts; spurs, a cowboy's most prized possession, had been fastened to boot heels; chaps of heavy leather covered their legs.

Kane greeted his men and then said, "Come on, let's get started."

As they climbed up on the horses waiting for them, Kane said, "I want you men to fan out, check the foothills, the basin, and especially the thickets."

With nods of their heads the cowboys rode out in a wide, sweeping circle to rout the cattle. After a while there carried on the wind the sound of cracking whips and shouting voices as groups of cattle were spotted.

The longhorns were sullen and dangerous-looking as they were herded together, and the men were careful to keep a safe distance as they popped their ropes at them. The half-wild cattle could rip a horse's belly open with one sweep of their long horns.

When the sun was straight overhead Kane and his men rode up to the chuckwagon, where Cookie had their lunch ready. By now vests had been discarded. The sun had warmed them up considerably and there were sweat stains on their backs and under their arms.

They lined up and Cookie passed out bowls of chili and thick slabs of sourdough bread. Sitting Indian-fashion on the ground, the men wolfed down the hot chili and went to stand in line again for second helpings.

When finally stomachs were full the men sat

back, drinking coffee and rolling cigarettes. Sitting apart from the cowhands, Kane gave them a leisurely hour to rest sore arms and legs. They had worked hard all morning. He had worked just as hard, and he relaxed against the trunk of a cottonwood that was just beginning to show new green growth. He frowned slightly when he saw his drover, Pete Harding, coming toward him. He didn't feel like talking to anybody today.

Nevertheless, when Pete hunkered down beside him, none of Kane's displeasure showed.

"It turned out to be a nice day, didn't it, Kane?"

"Yes, it did."

"Maybe we ain't gonna get any more rain for a while."

"Look, Pete," Kane said impatiently, "I know you didn't come over here to discuss the weather. What's on your mind?"

"Well"—Pete looked uncomfortable, as though he was sorry he had even come within a yard of his boss—"the thing is, I don't know if you'll care about what I overheard in the whorehouse last night, but I feel you ought to know about it."

Kane's body went still. Instinct told him that he wasn't going to like what he was about to hear. He looked at Pete and said coolly, "Out with it, Harding. I'll decide how I feel about whatever it is you want to tell me."

Pete picked up a brittle twig lying at his feet and, nervously snapping it into pieces, blurted out, "Your wife is bein' seen a lot with the schoolteacher up there on the mountain. Like they was courtin'."

Kane sucked in his breath. He hadn't expected to hear that, nor that hearing it would affect him so. He felt as if he'd been kicked in the stomach by a horse.

However, he managed to keep his features bland as he said in a harsh voice, "You shouldn't listen to whore's gossip, Harding."

"Yeah, I reckon." Pete stood up, knowing by the tone of his boss's voice that he'd been dismissed.

As the well-meaning cowboy walked back to the chuckwagon, Kane stared unseeingly before him. He hadn't really worried about any of the mountain men coming around Jade. They would know better. Not only would she rebuff them, but Big John might take a club to them.

But with the schoolteacher it could be altogether different. He wasn't from the mountains. He would be well educated and wouldn't be clumsy.

Kane stood up and called out, "Mount up, men. It's time to get back to work."

As he trailed along behind the cowboys, his mind wasn't on chasing cattle. He was thinking that Big John would have left for the rendezvous three or four days before. As soon as the cattle had been gathered into one herd, he was going to ride up the mountain and take a look at the schoolteacher who was stepping into territory that was forbidden to him. Maybe it was time to give Jade that wedding band, so other men would see that she belonged to him.

Usually evening on the mountain was Jade's favorite time of the day. But today as she hurried along in the near twilight it was spooky somehow. The shadows among the trees seemed ominous, sometimes taking on the shape of a man, sometimes a wolf or a cougar.

The sudden snapping of a twig made her heart race. When a groundhog scurried across her path she chastised herself for acting like a scared child. She wished that she hadn't stayed so long at old Tillie's place. She and Virgil had been discussing books they had read, and before she knew it, the sun was a red ball in the west, ready to dip behind the mountain. Old Tillie had offered to walk her home, for of course Virgil wouldn't stick his nose out with nighttime so near.

There had been another killing—or accident—last night. This morning Elisha Collins had been found trampled to death by his horse. It was well known among his neighbors how cruelly he treated the poor animal.

The old nag had been found standing meekly several yards from Elisha's body, and strangely there were no fresh cuts on his hide. The men asked each other what it was that had sent him into such a rage that he would attack his owner.

Everyone said openly now that something strange was going on, that there was one among them who had set himself up as judge and jury, killing those he thought unfit to live any longer. Jade imagined with a curl of her lips that the wife abusers were quaking in their boots, wondering if they would be next.

She thought with satisfaction that long-suffering wives would benefit from the killings. Husbands were going to think twice before taking their fists to their mates from now on.

Strangely, though, Elisha Collins had never beaten his wife. She remembered then that he was guilty of something much worse. It was whispered that he'd abused his daughters.

Jade relaxed when she heard the high-pitched voices of children laughing and calling out to each other in play. She rounded a bend in the path and saw her home only yards away. It was a welcome sight, with smoke rising from the cabin chimney.

She hurried inside her home and barred the door behind her. After lighting the kitchen lamp she took off her shawl and went to the fireplace to lay more wood on the fire. A rising wind found its way down the chimney, making the flames jump and cast wavering shadows on the walls.

Jade sighed. It looked as if it was going to rain again.

By the time she heated a bowl of stew for her supper, the first drops of rain were splattering on the roof.

Jade had just sat down at the table and dipped her fork into the meat and vegetables when a heavy knock sounded on the door. Fear gripped her and the fork made a clanging sound as it fell from her nerveless fingers and hit the bowl. She slowly rose from the table and took down the rifle hanging above the fireplace. There was a calmness in her voice that belied the panicky quickening of her pulse when she called out, "Who's there?"

Chapter Sixteen

"It's me, Jade," came a well-remembered voice. "Kane."

Surprise held Jade speechless for a moment. What did he want? she asked herself. Well, she knew what she didn't want, and that was to see *him*.

"Uncle John will be here any minute. You know what he said about your coming up here."

"Tell me another lie, Jade. I happen to know he's gone to a rendezvous and won't be back for at least another week. Come on, now, open the door. The rain is really getting heavy."

Jade stood undecided. Outside that door was a man very dangerous to her emotions. Although she thoroughly disliked him, his slightest touch weakened her knees.

When Kane again demanded entry, she sighed and unbarred the door. She opened it just a few inches. Wordlessly she stared up at her husband. She had forgotten how very handsome he was.

"Are you planning on shooting me?" Kane grinned as he looked at the rifle in her hand.

Leaning the rifle against the wall, Jade scowled at him and asked, "What do you want?"

Kane ran a slow, slumberous look down her body and said huskily, "What do you think I want?"

"I have no idea what you're talking about," Jade said tartly, swift color flooding her face.

"Yes, you do. But we'll let that pass for the moment. Are you going to let me in? I brought you something."

She looked down at the gunnysack Kane held in his hand and asked cynically, "What? Some potatoes?"

"Let me in and I'll show you."

"You can show me out here."

"No, damn it, I can't," Kane said impatiently. "Are you afraid I'm going to rape you?"

"Of course not," Jade answered stiffly. However, as she opened the door wider she was thinking that he could very easily seduce her.

Kane brushed past her and walked over to the fireplace. He set the sack on the hearth and, reaching inside it, brought out a pure white hen. He looked up at Jade with a wide grin. "This is Elmer."

"Elmer?" Jade scoffed. "That's no rooster. That's a hen."

"So? What about that rooster you call Pansy?"

Jade saw the humor in his remark and couldn't help laughing. She sobered up quickly and said, "She can't stay in the cabin, so take her out to the shed and put her in with Pansy."

As Kane shoved the bird back into the sack he said sorrowfully, "I bet Elmer will get a warmer welcome than I have."

"No doubt," Jade agreed as she followed him to the door. "Thank you for the hen, and don't get too wet on the way home."

"Are you crazy, woman?" Kane wheeled around and gave her a challenging look. "I'm not about to try riding down this mountain in pitch dark with rain coming down in buckets. Especially when I can spend the night in a warm cabin and sleep in a soft bed."

"Uncle John won't like it if you spend the night with me—" Jade began, but then Kane was cutting across her words.

"I don't give a damn if he likes it or not. I'm not going to chance a broken neck to please him." He was gone then, he and the horse and the squawking chicken, lost from sight in the dark and rain.

Jade closed the door against the slashing rain that reached onto the porch. She wondered wryly if any other woman had ever received a chicken for a gift.

"He'll probably want to eat, too," she muttered and walked to the stove to shove another stick of wood into the firebox. While the pot of stew reheated, she placed a bowl, cup and eating utensils on the table, then brought out half a loaf of bread.

She was slicing it when Kane returned. As he removed his boots he sniffed the air. "Something smells awfully good." He smiled at Jade. "I'm hungry enough to eat one of my steers."

When Jade made no response he said, "I'm soaked through. I'd like to get out of these wet clothes. Maybe I can change into something of Big John's."

"His clothes wouldn't fit you." Jade recalled the feel of his flat waist and narrow hips as they made love. "His trousers would be too big at the waist and the legs would be too short."

"At least they would be dry. I'm catching a chill." He gave her a teasing grin. "You wouldn't want me to catch pneumonia, would you? Just think, you'd have to nurse me back to health."

"God forbid," Jade snapped. "I'll go see what I can find."

Jade walked into her uncle's bedroom and lifted the lid of the trunk at the foot of the bed. After going through the neatly folded clothes, she took out a much-faded flannel shirt and a pair of trousers that had known many washings.

When she straightened up and turned around

she found Kane standing right behind her. She grew flustered at his nearness, and, shoving the clothes at him, she hurried from the room. Kane's mocking laughter followed her.

She was ladling stew into his bowl when Kane walked out of the bedroom, his wet clothes folded over his arm. As he spread them on the hearth to dry she looked at him from the corner of her eye and repressed a giggle. The shirt strained a bit across his broad shoulders and he had cinched a belt around his waist to keep the trousers from falling down. The legs ended above his ankles. He had helped himself to a pair of her uncle's woolen socks.

"That sure looks good," Kane said, pulling a chair away from the table and sitting down. He said no more as he picked up his fork and began to eat with the appetite of a larger man.

Jade stood beside the stove, watching him shovel the stew into his mouth. When finally he shoved his empty bowl aside and rubbed a full stomach, she picked up the coffeepot and carried it to the table. Her pulse started pounding at being so close to him, and her hand trembled slightly as she tilted the pot over his cup.

Kane watched her from beneath lowered lashes, and a knowing smile curved his lips. When she set the pot on the table and started to walk away, he stretched out an arm and clamped it around her waist. He pulled her down on his lap, but she put her hands against his chest and strained against his grip on her. When his clasp didn't lessen in the least, she looked at him with beseeching eyes.

"Please let me go," she pleaded.

"I will in just a minute. I only want to hold you awhile. You feel so good. Sometimes I dream of how soft and satiny your body is."

"I'm sure you do." Jade's lips curled, and her tone said that she doubted it.

In her desperation to get away from him, Jade had been unaware of Kane's fingers working at the buttons of her bodice. She started to protest when she felt his hand on her bare breast, but her words were shut off by his mouth descending on hers.

His lips were firm and strong as they moved against hers, demanding a response. A flood of unwanted desire flooded through Jade's body, and she again tried to push herself away from him. This time she was determined that she would not give in to him.

She gasped, then wilted when he left her mouth and lowered his head to settle his lips on her breast. He had her stripped bare to the waist. She looked down at his golden head lying on her white flesh, his lips moving on her nipple, and she moaned low in her throat. Unconsciously, she raised a hand and pressed his head closer to her breast.

Kane answered with a moan of his own and slid a hand up her skirt. It closed over the thatch of soft, curly hair, his middle finger searching for, and finding, the hard little nub hidden there. He switched his mouth to her other breast and suckled her in rhythm with his stroking finger.

Jade whimpered and thrashed her head about at the passion that was overwhelming her. When Kane removed his hand and stood up with her body cradled in his arms, she moaned a little protest, afraid that he was going to leave her with the awful ache in her loins.

She smiled and relaxed when he carried her into her bedroom and set her on the bed. He came down beside her and they tore at each other's clothes, tossing them onto the floor in their hurry to come together.

As though she were another person in another world, Jade stretched out on her back, her arms lifted to Kane. He came to her, his face tight with the need to join her body with his. She felt his large maleness throbbing against her stomach and she reached down to take it eagerly into both hands.

As she lovingly squeezed and stroked him, Kane braced himself on his hands over her. He gazed down at her flushed face bathed in the light from the fireplace and whispered huskily, "Take me home, honey. Open wide and make me feel welcome."

When Jade had sheathed him deep inside her, Kane lowered himself to his elbows and kissed her deeply.

He had suspected once that she could bring him satisfaction without his even moving, and now he found that it was true. She wrapped her legs around his waist and, lying perfectly still, used her muscles to stroke and squeeze him.

Kane gave a soft moan of pleasure. Never in his life had he ever felt anything so satisfying. He wanted it to go on forever. Twice he almost gave in to the demanding climax but managed to hold himself back.

Finally, he could hold off no longer. He cried out Jade's name as he released his passion. He dropped his weight on top of Jade, too drained to crawl off her.

Then, incredibly, even before his hard breathing had calmed down, Kane felt his manhood growing inside Jade, strong and hard. He gathered her slim body into his arms, and, holding her slightly off the bed, he began a slow, deep thrusting. She whispered huskily, "More, Kane, faster."

The bed began to creak and the headboard to bang against the wall when Kane slid his hands under her rear and drove fast and hard inside her.

They climbed skyward together, their bodies shuddering with the strength of their climaxes.

Twice more, before dawn lighted the window, Jade and Kane satisfied each other. Weak and completely sated, Jade lay sprawled on her back.

Kane, equally depleted, leaned up on an elbow and traced a finger over her eyebrows. "What's this I hear about you being seen with the schoolteacher all the time? Is it true?"

Jade yawned widely, then said, "We see each other often, but not all the time."

"What are your feelings for him?"

"I don't know." Jade yawned again. "He's a very nice man, has a good sense of humor. He makes me laugh a lot."

"What about here?" Kane laid a possessive hand between her thighs. "Does he please you as much as I do?"

"I wouldn't know," Jade answered sleepily. "I haven't slept with him . . . yet."

"What do you mean, yet?" Kane demanded roughly.

Jade mumbled an answer he couldn't make out. When he asked her to repeat herself and she made no answer, he discovered that she was sound asleep.

Kane lay back down and stared up at the raftered ceiling. Jade turned over on her side, and in her sleep curled her body alongside his. Feeling one firm breast against his chest and a silky smooth leg flung across his thigh, Kane felt himself growing hard again.

He swore softly under his breath, and, turning Jade onto her other side, he slid out of bed. He walked naked into the main room, where he had spread his wet clothes to dry. His wife could become a habit with him, one that would be hard to break. He must never make love to her again, because there was no future for them.

It had stopped raining when Kane stepped outside in the dim dawn, the shapes of trees and the shed beginning to be visible. He saddled Renegade and led him out of the shed. As he climbed onto the stallion's broad back, he took a long last look at the sturdy little cabin, visualizing Jade as he had last seen her: curled on her side, her hands tucked under her chin like a small girl.

That was the way he would always remember her, for he wouldn't be climbing the mountain again. If he continued to see her, it wouldn't be long until he lost his own identity. His carefree days would be gone forever. He would become one of those whipped husbands the bachelors snickered about.

Kane nudged Renegade in the sides and they started down the mountain. "Let her have her schoolteacher," he muttered, patting the band of gold that still rested in his pocket. There was no point in giving it to Jade after all.

Chapter Seventeen

The hungry squawking of Pansy and Elmer awakened Jade. She lay curled on her side thinking how sweet it was of Kane to have brought her the hen. Maybe Pansy wouldn't be so ornery anymore now that he had a mate. And maybe Elmer would produce some little chicks later on.

Jade gave a long, lazy stretch. Never had she felt so good, even though her legs were a little sore for having had them wrapped around Kane's waist for most of the night. She remembered with a soft smile and a stirring in her loins how wonderful their lovemaking had been. A mischievous light twinkled in her eyes. She would wake him up and make him pay in advance for his breakfast.

Turning over, she reached for Kane. Her hand

found only an empty space. Where was he? she wondered. When the clock over the mantel in the family room chimed nine times, Jade sat up, thinking that he had probably been up for a while. Most likely he was in the shed taking care of the horses.

She pulled on her robe and slippers and hurried into the kitchen area. Kane was probably hungry for his breakfast. Her lips curved in a grin. He'd had a good workout last night.

"He could have at least built a fire," she muttered, feeling the top of the stove and finding it stone cold. In a short time she had flames dancing in the firebox and a pot of coffee beginning to brew.

Half an hour passed, the coffee was done and Elmer and Pansy were making a terrible racket. *Why doesn't Kane toss them some corn?* she thought impatiently. *And what is keeping him in the shed so long?*

A feeling of unease formed inside Jade. What if Kane wasn't in the shed? What if he had left and was now at his ranch?

"No," she scolded herself, "he wouldn't leave me after what we shared last night." Their lovemaking had been perfect. He had wanted her again and again.

When another ten minutes passed and Kane still hadn't made an appearance Jade exchanged her slippers for a pair of boots and pulled on her jacket. As she sloshed through mud and water she had a gut feeling that she wouldn't find her husband in the shed.

When she pushed open the shed door, the first thing she saw was the empty stall where Kane's stallion had spent the night. For a moment she couldn't breathe, the pain in her heart hurt so. How could he be so cruel, so uncaring that he hadn't even bothered to tell her good-bye?

A black, bitter anger engulfed Jade. The cur had used her again. Used her in the same way he would use a whore. The only difference was that he hadn't left money on her pillow before sneaking off. If he ever dared show his face on the mountain again she would shoot him between the legs. He would never again play fast and loose with another woman after she gelded him.

She fed the two complaining chickens, tempted to wring the white hen's neck. The blasted bird had helped weaken her determination not ever to have anything to do with Kane Roemer. Jade pitched some hay to her mare and the big workhorse. As she walked back to the cabin, she was a different woman from the one who had left it a short time before.

By rote Jade made her breakfast and went into her room to make up her bed. Bitter memories rushed over her when she saw the jumble of clothing scattered about on the floor. How eager she and Kane had been to get rid of them.

Kicking the clothes into a pile, she next stripped the bed. The linens held his scent and for a moment she wanted to burn them. The only thing that stopped her was the fact the they were the only ones she owned. She would sleep in Uncle John's room until she washed and dried them.

As she gingerly picked up the items to be washed and carried them out onto the porch, Jade remembered that today Elisha Collins would be buried. She would be expected to attend his funeral. All the mountain people would be there, although they hadn't liked the man any more than she had. Regardless, it was mountain custom to show respect for the dead. In the meantime she would wash the bedding, removing all scent of Kane Roemer.

She began by heating three big pots of water and carrying them out onto the porch so she could fill the big wooden tub that had hung on the wall. With a bar of lye soap in her hand she began scrubbing the linens. By the time she had them hung on the rope strung between two trees, it was time to change her clothes and go to the funeral.

After she had dressed in the plainest frock Maria had given her, she put an apple pie she had baked the day before into a basket and covered it with a white cloth. Then she set off for the Collinses' shack, the basket swinging from her arm. As she hurried along, trying to keep Kane from slipping into her thoughts, she became aware of the plodding of horse hooves coming up behind her. It was one of her neighbors going to the funeral, too, she imagined, and looked over her shoulder. She was surprised to see her old friend Long Feather. She hadn't seen him all winter, and she gave him a wide smile of friendship.

"Long Feather," she said, reining the mare in until the handsome young brave drew up alongside her. "It's been ages since I've seen you. Where have you been keeping yourself?" she asked as they rode along, side by side.

"In my village, of course. Where else would I be?"

Jade hid an amused grin. She had forgotten that Indians answered questions literally. A white man would have explained that he had been busy taking care of his stock, shoveling snow, running his traps.

"What brings you from your village today?" she asked.

"It is said in my father's lodge that you are now a married woman, and I have come to ask you if that is so."

"It is so, Long Feather."

"Is it also true that you don't live together as man and wife?"

Jade nodded. "That is also true."

"Is that not a strange marriage?" he asked.

"Again you are right. It is a very strange marriage."

"If you were my woman you would live with me in my wigwam."

"Yes, I know," Jade said, and then tried to change the subject by asking, "Have you chosen one of the maids in your village to be your wife?"

"I cannot do that as long as my heart yearns for another."

"Tell your heart not to yearn for a woman it can never have."

"It would not believe me. It knows that all things are possible."

"Not all things, Long Feather," Jade said gently. She drew a long breath of relief when the Collins shack came in view. "I have to leave you now, Long Feather," she said. "I'm going to Elisha Collins's funeral."

"I have heard about that man's killing. He was an evil man. He will have much to answer for when he stands before his Great White Father."

"He will at that," Jade answered gravely.

"So will the other two men who were killed."

"How do you know they were killed? All three deaths could have been accidents."

Long Feather shook his head. "No accidents. I think the mountain people know that."

Jade drew a breath of relief when she saw Virgil and old Tillie on their mules, also arriving for the funeral. "I must leave you now, Long Feather. Otherwise I'll be late for the funeral."

"I will see you again," the young brave said, his attention on Virgil. "I hear that you spend much time with that one."

"Some. He is a friend of mine."

Without further words, the Indian picked up his

little mare's hackamore and rode off in the direction of his village.

When Jade met with the schoolteacher and his aunt at the edge of the overgrown, trash-filled yard, Virgil raised a questioning eyebrow at Jade. "That was Long Feather," she explained. "I played with him and his sisters and cousins while growing up."

"He's certainly a stern-looking fellow," Virgil said as he helped his aunt off her mule.

"Yes. He's always looked that way, even as a young boy."

"I wouldn't want to meet up with him on a dark night," Virgil said, and pushed open the Collinses' door.

They nodded solemnly to people gathered in the small room, and then found seats and sat quietly, waiting for the funeral to begin.

"The boss is grouchier than ever," one of the cowhands said to Pete Harding, the drover. "He must have been on one big toot last night."

"Looks like it." Pete didn't add that he had not seen Kane in Laramie the night before. It was his opinion that the boss had spent the night with his wife, and that at some point they'd had a heavy argument. He'd have liked to feel sorry for his boss, for he could see that he was hurting, but it was hard to do that when a decent word hadn't left Kane's mouth all morning.

Kane sat a little mustang on top of a butte,

watching his men ride through an almost impenetrable chaparral. Overnight a small bunch of longhorns had returned to the shelter of evergreen scrub oak and had no intention of leaving the thicket if they could help it.

Finally, his patience gone, one of the cowboys drew his gun and began to shoot into the air. The loud reports startled the critters and they tore out of their hiding place, bawling their fright and anger.

Kane frowned. Some of the cattle were drifting toward the river instead of going toward the pen where the branding of calves was carried out. He squinted his eyes against the sun, peering down at the Platte a quarter of a mile away. Meltwater from the range and the mountain had flooded it beyond its banks. There could be some very dangerous spots in the swift-flowing water. He urged the little mount down the butte and struck off at a gallop, calling to his men, "Herd them away from the river."

The men were already doing that, and they turned most of the herd in the right direction. A dozen or so were running toward the river. They hit the water just as Kane arrived at the banks of the rushing water. A worried frown furrowed his forehead. Right in their path was a gravel bar. The water would be swifter there, with many nasty whirlpools. He could only sit helplessly and watch how the cattle fared. If he rode out there among them he'd be chancing his life as well as that of the little mustang.

The leader of the single-file line was swimming along fine, and Kane was beginning to think that they would make it safely to the other shore. Then, when the leader reached the gravel bar, he slipped and thrashed for footing. The heavy current took him and he was swept downstream. Like sheep the others followed him and all were swept away.

Kane could almost have wept. More cattle lost. Was there no end to it? Nothing was going right for him, it seemed. With slumped shoulders he turned his horse around and rode to join the others. He shortly came upon the cattle and men. The cowboys had managed to mill the cattle in a loose circle a hundred yards or so from the chuckwagon.

"Did you lose them, Kane?" Pete Harding asked as he rode up beside Kane.

"Yeah, every last one of them. They got caught in a current and were swept away."

"I'm sorry to hear that, Boss. We'll make sure the others are kept away from the Platte."

Kane had just swiped a shirtsleeve across his dirty, sweating face when Cookie rattled a striker around the inside of a triangle. As he rode toward the cookfire he wondered what the old cook had made for lunch. He hadn't had any breakfast and he was starving.

Cookie had thick beef sandwiches waiting for the men, plus a pot of strong coffee. Lunch was wolfed down in short order. When the men had rolled cigarettes and smoked, they mounted up again, driving the cattle along.

The sun was about to set when the ranch house and branding pen were sighted. Kane rode on as the cowboys once again drew the cattle into a loose circle for the night.

Maria had a basin of warm water, a bar of soap and a towel waiting for him on the porch. "You look beat," she said, watching him lather his face and neck.

"I am," Kane admitted as he rinsed the soap off his face. He groped for the towel and Maria put it in his hand. "The damned longhorns have grown as wild as deer over the winter. The cowpokes earned their pay today."

Maria looked at his red-rimmed eyes, the shadows under them, and scolded, "You look like the devil. How much whiskey did you drink last night?"

If it were only drink, Kane thought. Too much whiskey would have left him with an upset stomach and a pounding headache. But too much of making love to Jade left him wanting more and fighting the desire to ride back up the mountain tonight.

Chapter Eighteen

Jade sat on the porch, gazing down on the valley, which was shrouded in evening mist. Behind her in the cabin she could hear the slap of cards on the kitchen table. Her uncle and his cronies were playing their weekly game of poker. There was a difference now though. The Indian whores didn't show up to entertain the men anymore. Could Maria have anything to do with that? she wondered.

"Damn you, Kane Roemer," she whispered angrily. "You have ruined three people's lives and it doesn't bother you in the least. Surely someday you will pay for it."

Jade laid a hand on her stomach. If he had stayed away as her uncle had ordered, she wouldn't now be carrying his baby. A babe she had yet to tell her uncle about. She had put off telling him for fear of what he might do. In anger, he was capable of shooting Kane, killing him. And that must never happen.

Jade stood up and took down one of the lanterns hanging on the wall. She had to get away from her worrisome thoughts for a while. She stepped to the doorway and called to Big John that she was going to go visit old Tillie and Virgil for a while.

"You be careful now," John called back, "and don't stay too long. You know the little feller won't walk you home after dark."

Jade stepped off the porch, the unlit lantern swinging from her hand. She didn't need it lit yet, although dusk was falling rapidly and she would have to be careful not to trip over a tree root or a rock and go tumbling down the mountain.

It was almost dark when Tillie's Cabin came into view. Suddenly her heart seemed to jump into her throat. Back among the trees she had seen the dim figure of a man step from behind a pine and stand there like a statue. She flattened herself against the side of a boulder and held her breath as she watched the man. Then, as though he had never been there at all, he was gone. However, he had stood there long enough for her to recognize him. What was Virgil Clark doing out after dark? It was well known that the teacher never left the cabin once the sun had gone down. And he was walking away from the Clark cabin, not toward it.

When the old woman opened the door to Jade's

knock, she looked surprised and a little uneasy. "What are you doing out alone at this time of evening, child?" She swung the door wider for Jade to enter. "Virgil has retired for the night. Teaching the children puts a strain on him."

Why was Tillie lying about her nephew? Jade wondered as she took a seat before the small fire. Hadn't she just seen the man no more than five minutes ago?

She looked up at Tillie and said, "I just felt like taking a little walk. And"—she grinned—"since you're the only female who doesn't have a gaggle of children running around making an earsplitting noise, I chose you to visit."

"I'm right glad to see you, child. Can I make you a cup of tea?"

Jade sensed that her old neighbor was anxious for her to leave, and suspected it had something to do with her nephew. He might walk through the door any minute, thus proving her a liar.

"Thank you, Tillie, but I'm only going to stay a short time. Uncle John and his friends are playing poker and they'll be wanting me to bring them a fresh jug of whiskey before long."

The old lady didn't encourage her to stay longer, and after talking for several minutes Jade rose to leave.

"I think I'd better go." Jade picked up the lantern from where she had set it next to her chair. "I don't want to get caught out in the dark of the night," she said as she struck a match to the wick.

"Last night I heard a wolf howling farther up on the mountain."

"Do be careful then," Tillie warned as she walked Jade to the door. "Come visit when it's daylight."

Jade nodded that she would and, saying good night, she walked outside. By the dim light of the lantern she stepped onto the path that would take her home. Her eyes darted about, looking for signs of Virgil, or a wolf. She saw neither, yet she was glad to see the old cabin come into sight.

The poker game was still going on, and knowing that she had fibbed to Tillie about having to take more drink to her uncle and his friends, she sat down on the porch to savor the scent of pines and listen to the night sounds. And to wonder about the schoolteacher venturing out after sunset. Why would his aunt lie, saying that he had retired for the night?

The poker game broke up shortly. Even big, strong men didn't want to meet up with a pack of wolves or a female bear with young. The men trooped out onto the porch with Big John behind them. Good nights were said, and when John's company left he sat down in the chair beside Jade.

"Nice evenin', huh?" he said. "Soft and warm. Just the kind of night a feller would like to walk around in."

"You'd be surprised at who I saw walking around when I went to visit old Tillie."

"Who's that? The teacher?" Big John joked.

"You're right. That's who it was."

"Ah, you must be mistaken. Everybody knows the little feller don't go out after dark."

"Well, he did tonight. I saw him sneaking through the woods, being careful that no one saw him. What do you make of that?"

"Damned if I know." Big John played with his beard. "Do you think he's courtin' one of the young girls and don't want anyone to know about it?"

"I guess that could be it, but why would he want to keep it a secret? Unless he's up to no good with her. He doesn't strike me as being the sort to seduce a girl and then go off and leave her when the school term is over."

"That would be a rotten thing to do if it's true. Somehow I can't see him doin' that." Big John chuckled and added, "I don't think any of our girls would be interested in him in that way. He's so skinny and not very good lookin'."

"That's true." Jade laughed also. "But why has he pretended to be afraid to go out after dark all this time? We know now it's not true."

"I don't know. Maybe he is sniffin' around one of our girls. Or maybe he's meetin' one of the Indian whores. He wouldn't want anyone knowin' about that."

"I never thought about that, but it's a good possibility."

The subject of the teacher was dropped and Jade and Big John sat in silence. Jade was thinking that now was as good a time as any to tell her uncle about her condition. She took a deep breath and squared her shoulders.

"Uncle John, I have something to tell you."

When no more words were forthcoming Big John said, "Well, spit it out, girl."

Nervously playing with the ends of the sash tied around her waist, she said, "While you were gone at the rendezvous Kane came up here."

"I know that, Jade."

Startled, Jade asked, "How did you find out?"

"Do you think I'd go off and leave you without someone keeping an eye on you? I paid young Henderson and his brother to take turns watchin' you and the cabin." After a short, tense silence Big John added, "I know he spent the night here, too. It was just comin' daylight when he left."

"Are you mad? Why haven't you said anything to me about it?"

"I was plenty mad at first. I was tempted to go down there and shoot the bastard. Then I got to thinkin' that even though I don't like him, he's not the sort of man who would force himself on a woman. I figured that if you slept with him, it was because you wanted to."

Jade leaned her head back against the chair. "To my shame, I did want to. He brought me a hen to keep Pansy company, and he talked so nice I found myself liking him . . . a lot. I thought he felt the same way about me, but I was so wrong about that. Sometime in the early morning while I was asleep, he sneaked away. It's been a month now and I haven't seen him since."

Tears choked Jade's throat on that last utterance.

"I'm sorry, honey," Big John said tenderly. "I can still go down there and shoot him."

Jade knew by the seriousness of her uncle's tone that he meant what he said, and that would never do. "No, you mustn't do that," she said anxiously. "You'd be killing the father of the babe I'm now carrying."

The big man shot to his feet and paced the floor, his face twisted with rage. Alarmed, Jade watched him, afraid that he'd go hunting Kane, after all.

Finally the big man stopped and stood before her. "Do you have a mind to go live with him now?"

"I hope never to set eyes on him again," Jade said fervently. "If you don't mind having to support my little one, I'd like to remain here with you."

"Jade, girl"—John stroked a callused palm down her hair—"I'd like nothin' better than to help you take care of the little one when it arrives."

"Thank you, Uncle John." Tears glimmered in Jade's eyes.

"You're makin' me mad, girl, thinkin' I'd feel otherwise."

"I thought that you would be supportive, but I wasn't sure. My baby will be carrying Roemer blood in its veins."

"The little one can't help that," John joked and handed her his handkerchief. When Jade had wiped her eyes and blown her nose, he sat back down and asked, "When will you deliver the babe?"

"Sometime in December."

"You know, I've never been around a baby before," John said, a smile on his face. "I mean actually living with one."

"Neither have I, but I'm sure that together we'll make good parents. We'll raise him or her to be a good and honest person." In her mind she added, Not an unscrupulous person like its father.

But later as she slept, she dreamed of Kane and the last time they had made love together.

Chapter Nineteen

Kane had been riding fence all day, with the late June sun beating down on his head. It had barely risen when he'd started this morning.

Ordinarily one of the cowhands would be tending to this lonely chore; miles and miles of fence was all one could see stretching out across the range. He had seen an occasional roadrunner, a rattlesnake curled under a bush and a lizard sunning itself on a rock. Also an eagle flying high in the sky.

But it was the silence of the range that had made Kane take on the monotonous job of looking for breaks in the fence. He needed to be alone, to think, to mull over the way his mind had been working lately.

He no longer had a desire to go to Laramie at night and carouse with his friends. The whores no longer roused him no matter how hard they tried. His failure to get an arousal had embarrassed him, and he hoped they would not spread the word that Kane Roemer couldn't get it up anymore.

But that wasn't entirely true. He had only to think of Jade and he became as hard as a rock. That didn't count, though, he thought sourly. That one could make a wooden Indian's rod spring forth if she cozied up to him.

Was she doing that to the schoolteacher these days? The thought brought a dark frown to his face and a twist to his guts. "I'm gonna divorce that little witch when I can get around to it," he muttered.

He was thankful when he came upon a broken piece of fence. He could put his mind on something else for a while. He stepped out of the saddle and with a pair of pliers pulled the broken edges toward him. While he was wiring them together he remembered with a soft smile how his sister Storm had used to ride with him, making the chore an event with her cheery smile and light chatter.

He would like to go visit her, spend some time with his little nephew, Benny. He hadn't seen them all winter. But his brother-in-law had made it clear that he didn't approve of how Kane's marriage had come about. He had been surprised when he learned that Kane had taken Jade's virginity when he didn't love her. Kane felt sure that Wade had told Storm about it and that the next time he saw her he would get a good chewing-out.

When the mustang began sending a long shadow over the ground, Kane knew that it was nearing sunset, and he began looking for a place to make camp.

The course of the fence had taken him within a quarter of a mile of the foothills of the mountain. He turned his horse's head in that direction. There he would be sheltered somewhat from the wind.

Tired, dusty and hungry, Kane chose a spot in a stand of pine close to a stream of meltwater. He soon had a fire going, and after filling the battered coffeepot from the stream, he tossed in a handful of coffee grounds and set it on the fire to brew. He then unsaddled the mustang and staked him within a couple of yards of the fire. It took him but a few minutes to dress out the sage hen he had shot about an hour before, to spit it on a green cottonwood branch stripped of its leaves and to hang the fowl over the fire.

As he stared into the flames waiting for his supper to finish cooking, a wolf howled somewhere in the darkness, a melancholy chorus soon joining him. The little mustang's eyes rolled in fear as he strained against his tether. Kane rose and went to the frightened animal. He stroked its rippling neck and spoke soothing words to it. The touch of a human hand settled the animal down. Kane returned to the campfire and found that his supper was ready to be eaten.

The meat was tender and tasty, and Kane made short work of eating it. He rolled himself a cigarette and drank two cups of coffee.

By now the fire was dying out and Kane rolled up in his blanket, his loaded rifle at his side, his Colt within reach. He lay awake for a while listening to the wind in the pines, the flowing water and the howling of wolves. He drifted off to sleep finally to dream, as usual, of Jade.

The eastern sky was red with the rising of the sun when Kane came awake the next morning. He crawled out of the blanket, and when he stood up, stiff bones and sore muscles protested. He built up the campfire to reheat the leftover coffee while he washed up in the stream and took care of nature's call. When steam rose from the pot, he filled a tin cup with the bitter brew and ate two strips of pemmican.

Kane had rolled up his blanket, poured the remaining coffee over the campfire and was saddling the little mount when there came to him the muffled sound of a horse coming through the trees. He closed his hand over the mustang's nostrils to keep it from answering a nicker from the horse among the trees.

The sound of the hooves stopped suddenly, and Kane listened for the sound of footsteps. He was in that position when he heard the report of a rifle and felt the bullet strike him in the back. He went down on his knees, then fell flat on his stomach. As darkness overtook him, he heard the thunder of hooves racing away.

Wisps of mist lay in pockets on the mountain as Big John walked along, breathing deeply of the cool morning air. He could never quite decide which time of the day he liked better—the mornings with their freshness when the sun was rising, or the evenings when everything was soft and shadowy.

One thing he did know, however—there was no better place in the world than his mountains.

John had left his cabin an hour earlier to go hunting. For the past week he'd had a hankering for roast turkey—a tender young hen with a sage stuffing. He could almost taste it as he walked several yards to the side of the trail, slipping quietly through the trees and dense brush.

The sudden snap of a dry twig made Big John start. He stepped behind a tree and brought the rifle up. If he came upon a bear, he would certainly need it. When he heard the muted snort of a horse, he relaxed. He was about to go on his way when the crack of a rifle echoed through the woods. Damn, he thought, I'd better let that hunter know I'm here before he shoots me by mistake. He cupped his hands around his mouth to give a shout, then dropped them when he heard hooves pounding on the trail leading away from him.

That's strange, John thought. Why would a man shoot a piece of game, then race away from it? He decided this needed a little investigation, and stepping away from the tree, he walked in the direction from which the shot had come.

At first all John saw was the mustang lunging against his tether, trying to free itself. He walked toward the animal, speaking softly to it, wondering what had frightened the horse. It was then that he saw the man lying on the ground. The back of his shirt was wet with blood. Kneeling beside the wounded man, John lifted his face from the dirt and pine needles and exclaimed his surprise.

"What the hell," he muttered, recognizing the white, still face of Kane Roemer. "I think you're shot pretty bad, rancher," he said. Easing Kane's face back to the ground, he tugged the rancher's shirt from his trousers and shoved it up to his shoulders.

When he saw the gaping gunshot wound beneath Kane's right shoulder, Big John sat back on his heels, saying, "Whoever shot you, rancher, he did a good job of it. You're bleedin' like a stuck pig at butcherin' time. And I don't know if I can stop it." He grunted with the effort of hauling Kane up over his shoulder.

It took several minutes to get the mustang to stand still long enough to get Kane on its back. When at last it was done John yanked the stake out of the ground and mounted. He nudged the horse with his heels and sent it into a fast walk toward his cabin.

Jade saw her uncle coming and wondered where he had gotten the horse he was riding. When she spotted the limp body lying across the mustang's back, she started to step off the porch, thinking that another of their neighbors had been mysteriously killed. She paused in shock when John called out, "Go turn down the covers on my bed and heat a kettle of water. I found Roemer down in the foothills, shot bad."

Jade stared in disbelief, her heart beating painfully. She was unable to move until her uncle called impatiently, "Get on with it, girl."

When Kane had been laid on the bed and the shirt cut off his back, the blood drained from Jade's face. The wound was ugly. She clasped her hands tightly together as she watched her uncle examine it. He looked up at her after a moment and ordered, "Bring me the water, and then heat the poker. I've got to cauterize this wound, stop the bleeding."

"Is it bad, Uncle John?" Jade's voice quavered.

John looked up at her, surprised that her eyes were wet with unshed tears. He knew in that instant that his niece loved her husband. "Yes, it is, honey," he said gently. "But he's a healthy, strong man. I'm sure he'll pull through."

A silent prayer that Kane would be all right was on Jade's lips as she watched the tip of the poker turn a glowing red. "I love him, God," she whispered. "He is the father of the babe I carry. Although he doesn't love me, I feel sure he will love his child."

She picked up the poker with a heartfelt sigh and took it into the bedroom. Big John had undressed Kane and washed his face and back before pulling the covers up to his waist.

"Give me the poker, Jade; then stand back. I want to get this done before he regains consciousness."

"Can I help?"

"No. Not in your condition. You might mark your baby if you tried to help me. Go stand over there by the door."

Jade had barely reached the door when Kane gave a low groan of pain. It was done, she thought unclenching her fingers. She walked back to the bed and looked down at the seared flesh and flinched. She started to brush the hair off Kane's sweating face, then stopped as Big John spoke.

"I've got the bleedin' stopped, but the bullet is still inside him. I want you to ride down to Laramie and bring back the doctor to dig it out. Otherwise Roemer could die of lead poisoning."

Jade had never saddled her little mare more swiftly than she did now. She swung into the saddle and sent the little mount down the mountain at a reckless speed.

As the mare thundered along, Jade thought Laramie would never come in sight. She kept thinking of Kane, his face as white as the pillow his head rested on. He looked a different man from the one who had made love to her, so virile, so full of energy. His features, relaxed in unconsciousness, looked so vulnerable, so boyish. She had wanted to take him in her arms and comfort him after Uncle John had laid the hot poker on his bleeding flesh.

Jade remembered now, with bitterness, how Kane had used her the last time he came up the mountain—used her like a common whore. Only in her case he had carelessly left her with child. He hadn't even respected her enough to spill his seed onto the sheet.

She grew so angry as she remembered the past that she came to the outskirts of Laramie before she realized it.

Dr. Carl Simon's office was midway down the main street. As Jade drew rein in front of it, the doctor opened the door and stepped out onto the wooden sidewalk. "Well, good morning, Jade." He smiled up at her. "You're in town early, and your mount is all lathered up. Is someone sick up your way?"

"Yes. Kane Roemer got himself shot. Uncle John found him and brought him to our cabin. Uncle John has stopped the bleeding, but the bullet is still inside Kane. My uncle wants you to come dig it out."

"Yes, I'd better get up there and see what I can do."

After Dr. Simon disappeared into his office,

Jade hesitated, trying to come to a decision. Maria should be told about Kane. He wasn't going to be able to come home for some time and his housekeeper would be worried about him. A moment later she reined Cinnamon around and rode back out of town. When she came to the trail that broke off from the main one, she turned the mare in the direction of the Roemer ranch.

When Jade rode up to the ranch house, she spotted Maria inside a large wire enclosure, feeding her chickens. She swung out of the saddle calling Maria's name.

A wide smile curved the housekeeper's lips. "Jade!" she cried, "you've finally come to visit me." She left the chicken pen and embraced Jade. "Does John know that you are here?"

"No, he doesn't, Maria, but there's something that I think you should know. Kane was shot this morning up in the foothills. Uncle John found him and brought him to our cabin. I rode in to tell the doctor. He's on his way up there now."

Maria's face grew pale. "Is it a bad gunshot?"

"I'm afraid so," Jade answered, a tremor in her voice. "Uncle John has stopped the bleeding, but the bullet is still inside Kane."

"Who could have done such a thing?" Maria wrung her hands together.

"We have no idea. We've lost three neighbor men lately to mysterious deaths."

Maria took Jade's arm and led her to the house. When they entered the kitchen she said, "Sit down

and rest while I go gather up some clothing."
When Jade looked at her, a query in her eyes, Maria said, "I'm going back with you to look after Kane."

"I don't know what Uncle John will say to that."

"I don't give a damn what he says about it. I don't think he'll throw me off his mountain."

Jade turned her head away so that Maria wouldn't see her smile. Her stubborn uncle wouldn't show it, but he would be very happy to see Maria again.

Only a few minutes passed before Maria came from her bedroom carrying a bulging leather satchel. It took only another few minutes for her to saddle her mare and then they were off toward the mountain at a dead run.

Big John had stepped outside to water the doctor's horse at the watering trough. He paused at the bottom of the steps when he saw two riders galloping toward the cabin. He recognized Jade's mare immediately but had to peer a moment to make out her companion. His heart gave a lurch, and a broad smile curved his lips when he recognized Maria.

However, when the two women rode up to him and dismounted, his face showed no emotion. "Good mornin', Maria," he said, his voice cool and calm. "I suppose you've come to see your boss."

"Yes, I have," Maria answered, equally cool. "Also to nurse him while he's recovering."

"Me and Jade could do that." Big John frowned.

Maria shook her head and brushed past him as she stepped up on the porch, her satchel of clothes in her hand. "You could tend to his wound, give him his medicine, but he'll need to feel love, the touch of a gentle hand when he has to be bathed to bring down the fever that is bound to come."

With those blunt words Maria stepped inside the house, leaving the spluttering John behind. Jade was about to follow Maria to say that she would nurse Kane with loving hands when her baby stirred inside her. She took that tiny movement as a warning not to become too involved with the man who had no tender feelings for her. When Big John followed Maria into the house, Jade sat down on the porch and waited for the doctor to finish tending to Kane.

It seemed to Jade she had sat for hours listening to the low murmuring of the doctor and Maria, but actually only about half an hour had passed when Dr. Simon stepped out onto the porch and smiled down at her.

"How is he, Doctor?" She could not keep the anxiety out of her voice.

"He's had a narrow squeak, but he's gonna pull through with a lot of care. He's lost a lot of blood and it has to be built up so he can get his strength back. Now he's gonna be running a high fever. It's to be expected, so don't get alarmed about it. All he'll need is cold sponge baths and the medication I left for him."

Dr. Simon swung onto his horse. "Don't worry

about Kane. Maria will take good care of him."

Jade nodded and watched him ride away, resentful that no one thought she was capable of taking care of her own husband. She didn't stop to remember that no one thought she cared enough to take over the care of her husband.

Chapter Twenty

It was shortly after supper, near twilight, when Kane became restless with the fever growing inside him. Half an hour later he was burning hot to the touch and was tossing about, muttering incoherently. Sometimes he'd laugh loudly, then the next moment swear and complain. He fussed at his sister, Storm, railed at the old cowhand, Jeb.

Eventually Jade came in for her share of his restless discontent. One minute he was swearing at her, raging that he didn't want to marry her; then the next instant he would smile and say how he loved being married to her. In between he cussed out Big John and begged Maria for a drink of water.

Finally Jade had to leave the cabin for a while,

to get out of hearing distance of Kane's ranting and raving. As she paced about the yard there came on the warm air the impatient calls of mothers summoning their children home. A bittersweet smile curved her lips. One day she would be adding her voice to those of her neighbors, calling to a son or a daughter that it was time to come in. A child without a father or siblings.

Jade paused in her pacing when Maria called to her from the shadows of the porch. "Yes, what is it, Maria?" She hurried forward.

"Kane keeps calling out to you. Maybe if you sat and held his hand, spoke to him, he might settle down."

"Are you sure, Maria? I can't imagine him wanting me near."

"I don't blame you for feeling that way, and I must warn you that he still rants at you. But I feel that your presence would calm him."

"Of course I'll do anything that will help him."

Jade walked into her uncle's bedroom and found Big John gripping Kane's shoulder, holding him down so that he wouldn't turn over on his wound and start it bleeding again.

Big John looked up at her and said, "Sit down beside him and talk to him. See if you can get him to settle down. My arms feel like they're bein' pulled from their sockets. Roemer is one powerful feller."

Jade eased herself into the chair that had been pulled up beside the bed. She hesitantly took one of Kane's large hands and held it between her two small ones and said softly, "It's me, Kane—Jade. Are you in pain?"

Kane seemed to be listening, for his long, muscular body grew still. "Jade?" he whispered, his hand fastening on hers, gripping it so hard she was afraid he would crush the bones. "My sweet Jade?" he asked, as if for assurance.

"Yes, Kane, it's Jade. Try to sleep now."

The chair squeaked as Jade sat up and wiped the sleep out of her eyes. She groaned softly as she stretched, her body stiff from sleeping in the chair.

She hadn't slept that much, actually. Maybe three hours, but she had sat beside Kane all night. To her amazement she had found that as long as she held his hand and stroked his forehead, he slept like a baby. He even let her raise his head and spoon medicine between his lips. His fever had broken around midnight, and he hadn't wanted to let go of her hand while Maria changed the sweat-soaked bed linens. He had fallen asleep shortly afterward, a deep, natural sleep, his hand clasping hers.

Jade didn't know at what hour his grip had loosened, releasing his hold on her. She, too, had fallen into an exhausted sleep.

She stood up, blew out the lamp, whose light was no longer necessary, and, careful not to make a noise and awaken Kane, she slipped out of the sickroom and entered her bedroom. As she gathered up clean clothing, Maria never stirred. With the change of clothing draped over her arm, Jade walked carefully into the big room and just missed stepping on her uncle, who was rolled up in a blanket beside the hearth. Laying her clothes on a chair back, she filled the washbasin with tepid water from the big kettle and dropped a bar of her rose-scented soap and a washcloth into it.

Elmer and Pansy were setting up a hungry ruckus just as Jade finished her sponge bath. She hurried into her clothes, anxious to get to the animals before they awakened Kane.

It was a beautiful morning, the sky clear, the air fresh and crisp as Jade walked to the shed. Stepping inside it, she opened a narrow side door and shooed Pansy and Elmer into a wire chicken pen attached to the outside wall. When she had scattered cracked corn on the ground for them to peck at, she pitched some hay to the four horses whose heads were stuck over their stalls.

On her way back to the cabin Jade was hailed from down the trail. She smiled and waved and called, "Good morning, Virgil." When the teacher reined his mule in beside her, she asked, "What are you doing up so early? The sun is barely up."

"The early hours of morning are my favorite time of the day," Virgil said, climbing off the mule. "Especially when the weather begins to heat up and you hate to stick your head outdoors."

"I suppose you'll be leaving us before long, what

with school being out soon until fall," Jade said, leading the way to the cabin, where she sat down on the top step of the porch.

"Yes, I'm afraid so." Virgil sat down beside Jade. "I'm a city fellow and I can't get used to the ways of the mountain people. I admit I'm afraid of them, what with those men getting killed mysteriously."

"Some of our neighbors are frightening," Jade agreed, "but there are some who are God-fearing and wouldn't think of hurting a neighbor, much less killing him. And if you think about it, those men's deaths have made the mountain a better place to live. The widows and their children are happier and doing better than when their husbands were alive."

Virgil nodded. "Aunt Tillie mentioned that fact just the other day. She said it was a blessing those men are gone. But the truth is, I miss the comfort of city living. With the exception of missing you and Aunt Tillie, I can't wait to get back to that life."

"I'll miss our long talks, our rides," Jade said sadly. "I've never before had anyone to talk to about the books I've read. Most of the people up here can't read, and those who can have probably never read a book. They know nothing of the world outside these mountains."

"I hope that you will be able to see a part of that world someday, Jade. Maybe someday your husband will bring you to visit me."

"Ha! That one will never take me anywhere."

"I understand he got shot yesterday and that Big John brought him here to the cabin." Virgil looked at Jade as if to ask if it were true.

Jade nodded. "He's asleep in the cabin right now. The bullet that hit him barely missed his heart. But Dr. Simon says he will make it if he takes it easy and eats a lot of red meat to build up his strength."

"Will you be making his meals, tending to him?"

"Hardly." Jade gave a short laugh. "His house-keeper is here to take care of him."

"That's too bad. The two of you are missing the chance to get to know each other."

"That wouldn't make any difference, Virgil. Kane and I are like a bear and a cougar trying to get along."

"That's too bad," Virgil repeated. "You look so good together."

"Looks are deceiving, aren't they?" Jade laughed, standing up when the teacher did. "Have you picked a date when you will leave?" she asked, walking with him to where he had tied his mule.

Virgil shook his head. "No special date. But I'll be around for another couple of weeks or so."

"Then we must see each other as much as possible before you leave."

"My thoughts exactly," Virgil agreed as he mounted the mule. "Let's pack a lunch one day next week and have a picnic up at the waterfall in back of Aunt Tillie's place."

"I'd enjoy that." Jade smiled. "I'll bring my favorite book of poetry and we can take turns reading from it."

Virgil smiled and nodded and rode off up the mountain.

Kane awakened and stared at the log wall facing him. Where was he? he wondered, a frown creasing his forehead. He raised his head to look around and groaned. It hurt him to move. Why? What had happened to him and where was he?

He lay quietly, thinking back. He had left the ranch to ride fence. Near sundown he had made camp, eaten his supper, then rolled up in his blanket. The next morning he ate some pemmican, drank a cup of reheated coffee and rolled up his blanket. He was saddling the little mustang when he was struck down by a bullet. He couldn't remember what had happened after that.

Kane's thoughts were suddenly arrested by voices. A man and a woman were talking right outside the window near his bed. Although they talked in low tones he immediately recognized Jade's throaty voice. The man did not speak in the mountain people's vernacular and it took Kane but seconds to realize she must be talking to the schoolteacher. The man who, according to gossip, was seeing so much of Jade.

With an angry jerk of his body, he turned over on his back and gave a yelp of pain when pressure was put on his wound.

His outcry had barely faded away before Maria

was beside him. She was clad only in her night-gown and Kane knew that he had awakened her.

"How are you feeling?" Maria sat down on the edge of the bed and laid her hand on his forehead. "You have no fever, thank God. Are you in pain?"

"Only when I try to lie on my back. Where in the hell am I, Maria, and how come you're here?"

"Someone shot you yesterday morning. John found you and brought you to his cabin. He cau-terized the wound to stop the bleeding, but he was unable to dig out the bullet. Jade rode down to Laramie to send Doc up here, then rode to the ranch to tell me what had happened to you. Of course I came right on up here."

"You must be beat, taking care of me all night. I remember vaguely being sponged with cold wa-ter."

"I can't take credit for that. Jade is the one who sat up with you, bathed away your fever, gave you your medicine."

"She did?" Kane was astounded. "When that bullet hit me, it flashed through my mind that she was the one who had drawn a bead on me."

"Kane, what a thought!" Maria chastised him. "She might not like you, but it's not in Jade to shoot anybody. She nursed you because the touch of her hand and the sound of her voice were the only things that calmed you."

Kane shook his head, staring at Maria in dis-belief. "I must have been out of my mind with fe-ver," he said sourly.

"You had a high fever, all right. John had a devil of a time holding you down before Jade took over."

"I expect it's that schoolteacher she's talking to out there."

"You're right," Big John said as he walked into the bedroom. "He reminds me of a hound I used to have—always underfoot."

"Comes around a lot, does he?" Kane tried to speak nonchalantly, but there was a trace of anger in his voice.

Big John slid him a sly look. "He might as well move his bed in, he's here so much. I told Jade it didn't look right, him here so much and her a married woman."

"What did she have to say about that?" Kane narrowed his eyes at Big John.

"She said she supposed that I was right and that maybe she should start arrangin' to have her marriage annulled."

Kane's body gave a slight jerk; then he said sharply, "She can't get it annulled. As you know, we've slept together."

"Well then, damn it, I guess it will be a divorce. Ain't never been one of them in the Farrow family." Big John practically barked the words.

When the two men lapsed into silence, Maria looked at Kane and asked, "Are you hungry?"

"I'm starving," Kane said shortly.

"Good, I'll bring you something." Maria stood up and brushed past Big John as she left the room.

He made a fast turnaround and followed her. Kane was left alone with mixed emotions, most of them negative.

Anger boiled inside him, indignation that Jade, not he, would ask for a divorce. And last, an emotion that he would stubbornly deny—seething jealousy that his wife was laughing and talking to a man in a way she had never done with him.

Suddenly feeling sorry for himself, he called out with the whine of a spoiled child, "Maria, when are you going to bring me something to eat?"

Maria looked at Big John, who stood watching her, and shook her head. "He's the worst patient ever. When that wild horse took a bite out of his thigh a couple years ago, we were all ready to shoot him, just to shut him up."

"If I was hurt and bedfast, I'd want a lot of attention from you, too." The big man's eyes sent a message to Maria that made her blush a rosy red. He gave a knowing laugh when she pretended not to hear him. When she turned from the table with a plate of ham and eggs and biscuits in her hands, he was standing right behind her.

Caught off guard by his nearness, Maria froze, her lips slightly parted. Big John's eyes fastened on their red lusciousness and, without warning, he caught her to him and crushed his lips to hers. The plate, between them, pressed into Maria's midsection, but she wasn't aware of it. She was utterly lost in the hungry movement of John's lips. She was about to drop Kane's breakfast when Big

John broke the kiss and whispered hoarsely, "I've missed you, Maria."

With one hand Maria held on to his arm so that she wouldn't fall. Gazing up at John she said, "It's your fault that you have missed me. It was you who ordered that the Farrows and Roemers never see each other again."

"I know that, and it's the worst mistake I ever made."

"How do you plan on rectifying it?"

"Hell, I don't know, Maria. Roemer and Jade are so hardheaded, even if they cared for each other they'd never admit it. The thing is, Roemer really insulted Jade the last time he was here. After spendin' the night with her—in bed, you understand—he sneaked away when she fell asleep. A man only does that to a whore."

"He did that to Jade?" Maria was scandalized. "He's going to get a good tongue-lashing when I get him home."

"That won't change anything. I've been thinkin' on somethin'. What if we just let them hash it out between them, and me and you do what we want to?"

"And what is that, John Farrow?" Maria tried to look stern, but her twinkling eyes gave her away.

"You know what we want to do." John tried to pull Maria into an embrace again.

Maria pushed herself away from him. "I'd better get this food to Kane before he starts roaring again."

"Will you think on what I said?" John asked, reluctantly releasing her.

"Yes, I will, John," Maria promised as she left the room with Kane's rapidly cooling breakfast.

Chapter Twenty-one

Kane was sitting on the edge of the bed slipping his feet into his trousers. He had healed fast, as the doctor had predicted. Within two days he was sitting up, and the third day he was allowed to get up and move around a bit. And this fourth day he felt almost like his old self.

All this time Jade hadn't come near him. He had heard her talking to Maria and Big John, her laughter pealing out occasionally. And almost every day the teacher would come over and she would ride away with him, staying somewhere for hours before returning home.

A hatred for the man he had never seen had grown inside Kane. What kind of man was he, Kane asked himself, to court a married woman right under her husband's nose? And what about Jade? She was no better than the teacher, going off alone with him, doing God knew what. He gritted his teeth together, imagining what they might be doing.

"I don't give a damn what she gets up to," Kane muttered, walking into the main room, where he stopped short and stared. Jade was at her workbench kneading a large ball of sourdough. He had made no sound in his bare feet and she was unaware that he stood there watching her. He took advantage of the occasion to look his fill at what he thought was the most beautiful woman who ever lived.

The sun shining through the window cast a sort of halo over her bent head. His gaze dropped to her breasts. The three top buttons of her bodice had been undone due to the heat coming off the stove, and a good deal of cleavage was visible.

I don't remember her breasts being so full, he thought. In fact, her whole body looked riper. His gaze dropped to her softly rounded hips, hips that had cradled his a hundred years ago, it seemed. Had the schoolteacher experienced the wonder of lying between her soft thighs as she eagerly accepted his thrusts?

Kane barely managed not to groan aloud at the thought.

I must stop thinking such thoughts, he warned himself sharply. *She is divorcing me and will no doubt marry the city man and move away from the mountain. It's best if she does,* he thought with a ragged sigh, *for only then can I get on with my own life.*

While Kane was mulling over these things, Jade looked up and saw him standing there, watching her. Her hands grew still on the loaf of bread she was shaping as their gazes met. A tense silence grew between them, and it was several seconds before Kane broke it.

"It appears it is bread-baking day," he said, advancing into the room and sitting down at the table. "When Maria bakes bread we can smell it all through the house. To me the best aromas in the world are bread baking in the oven and coffee brewing in the early morning hours. It rejuvenates the body somehow."

"My favorite aroma is the scent of honeysuckle on a balmy evening when I'm sitting on the porch, relaxing after a hard day," Jade said, a dreamy look in her eyes.

Kane looked at her through narrowed lids. Had she sat with the teacher on such evenings? Was that what brought the soft look to her eyes? There was a honeysuckle vine at the corner of the ranch house, and he had breathed deeply of it when its perfume drifted up to his bedroom in the evenings.

He said none of this to Jade, however. What he did say gruffly was, "I never pay any attention to flower scents."

"You wouldn't," Jade snapped. "The smell of

horse manure would be more to your liking."

Damn her, Kane thought, watching Jade shove her morning's work into the oven. *She always manages to get in the last word, the last insult.*

But that's not entirely true, he corrected himself. Nothing could be more insulting than what he had done, sneaking away after having made love to her all night. She would never forgive him for that, he was sure.

Sighing, he stood up and walked over to the stove. He lifted the coffeepot and filled a cup with the strong brew.

With coffee in hand, Kane paused a moment, then, instead of sitting back down at the table, he walked out onto the porch. He eased himself into an old rocking chair there, being careful not to put any pressure on his back. Half an hour later, he saw Jade lead her mare out of the shed and ride off, disappearing in the bend of a trail that led farther up the mountain.

"I don't have to guess where you're going," he muttered sourly.

When twenty minutes or so had passed, the loneliness of the place began to bother Kane, and he wondered when Maria and Big John would return from their fishing jaunt.

The soft air, the birdsong in the trees, made Kane grow drowsy. He leaned his head on the chair back and closed his eyes. He didn't know how long he had slept when a cheery voice calling his name awakened him. He straightened up and then swore under his breath. How in the hell had she found him?

"What are you doing up here, Liz?" he asked impatiently as his old lover dismounted.

"I heard you had been shot, and naturally I wanted to come see how you were doing."

"Who told you where I was, and how did you find your way up here?"

"I rode out to your ranch and finally got it out of that old sharp-tongued Jeb. But all he would say was that you were with your wife up in the mountains. Then he had the nerve to say, 'Keep away from Kane. He don't need you now that he's got a wife.' The way I found out exactly where you were was easy. I hung around the Longhorn Saloon until one of the mountain men came in for a drink. I struck up a conversation with him, and when I said a friend of mine had been shot in his vicinity he said that he knew that man, that he was married to a neighbor's daughter. So when he left I rode along with him. Halfway up the mountain he pointed out the trail.

"Ain't I clever?" Liz smiled uncertainly as she stepped up on the porch.

"Yeah, you're clever all right." Kane gave her a flinty look. "Now be clever enough to realize that you're not wanted here and get back on your horse and ride away."

"You don't mean that, Kane." Liz smiled prettily at him, and before he knew it she was on his lap, with an arm around his neck. When he angrily tried to push her away, she jerked the low neckline of her bodice down, revealing a bare breast. Before he could stop her, she grabbed his hand and pressed it over her large bosom as she covered his mouth with a hot kiss.

That was the position Big John and Maria found them in. The roar John let loose startled the pair. As Liz jumped to her feet, hurriedly pulling up her neckline, Kane sat forward, saying, "I know this looks bad, but I can explain everything."

"My eyes don't deceive me, Roemer. I know what I saw. You're healed enough to get on your horse and ride the hell away from here."

"And take your slut with you," Maria said coldly.

"But, Maria, surely you believe me—" Kane began, but his longtime friend and housekeeper had disappeared into the cabin.

"I'm not going until I see Jade, explain everything to her," Kane said.

After a long pause John nodded. "She's over by the big falls lookin' for greens for our supper." He turned to Liz, and said, "You can leave now."

Liz didn't argue. She knew that here was a man who would bodily toss her onto her horse. She was mounted and gone in a matter of minutes.

Kane stamped on his boots, saddled the little mustang and went looking for Jade.

Jade had no intention of looking for greens when she rode away from the cabin. She had only told Maria and her uncle that when she ran into them fishing for trout. She couldn't tell them that she had to get away from Kane's presence, that she was always afraid he might coax her to make love again. It would take only one kiss and she would be like a soft piece of dough in his hands, allowing him to do as he pleased with her.

The sun shone hot on Jade's head, forming beads of sweat on her brow and making her feel uncomfortable all over. When she came to her favorite mountain pool she reined Cinnamon in beneath a large willow whose graceful branches hung over half the pool, and dismounted. The sun shimmering on the water looked so inviting to her, she was reminded that she hadn't been able to take a bath since Maria and Kane had practically taken over her home. She decided that she was going to take a sort of bath in the crystal-clear water.

After disrobing and folding her clothes neatly on the grassy bank, she dove into the pool. She swam slowly back and forth, erasing from her mind all bothersome thoughts. When her arms and legs grew tired, she knew it was time she left the pool and got dressed. Besides, Uncle John and Maria would be home by now and she wouldn't have to worry about Kane catching her alone.

As she pulled on her clothes she noticed the mare pricking her ears. What had Cinnamon heard? Jade asked herself as she listened intently. She couldn't hear anything, but that didn't mean that someone hadn't been spying on her. She swung into the saddle and rode away as quickly as the rocky, twisting trail would allow.

Kane, secreted behind a tall boulder, watched Jade ride away, held in shock. Her splashing around in the water had drawn him in the direction of the pool. He had dismounted when he saw Jade's slim body knifing through the water. His eyes kindled as he watched her, and he was seriously thinking of joining her when she suddenly stood up and left the pool.

His eyes fastened on the beauty of her body, her breasts, her hips. Then, with a twist of his heart, his eyes fell on her stomach. She was with child! He was sure the babe was not his, for she would have told him if he were the father. His hands clenched into fists and he thought hollowly that he no longer had to wonder if she had been making love with the teacher. The evidence was there, right in front of him.

Jade had cuckolded him. He swung into the saddle and, kicking his heels into the mustang's sides, headed down the mountain for home.

Chapter Twenty-two

Jade unsaddled her mare and turned her into the corral to join her uncle's stallion, the big work-horse and Maria's mare. Kane's mustang was missing, and as she lugged the saddle to the shed, she thought to herself that he must feel much improved to go riding.

As she approached the cabin, she heard Maria and her uncle in a heated discussion. "You're just making yourself believe that because you've been with the Roemer family so long," Big John was saying. "You feel obligated to believe that bastard wasn't at fault."

"That's not true, John. I know Kane well enough to know when he's lying. I also know how conniving that little bitch can be. She wants Kane and will go to any lengths to get him, no matter what. She's not above riding up here and throwing herself at Kane."

"That may well be, but I didn't see Roemer fightin' her off."

"Looks can be deceiving sometimes."

"I didn't see anything deceivin' about his hand on her breast."

"Yes, but—" Maria broke off when Jade stepped inside. She squirmed uneasily and refused to meet Jade's questioning look.

"How long have you been standin' out there, Jade?" Big John asked.

"Long enough to hear your conversation about Kane and some woman."

"I'm sorry you had to hear that. Me and Maria wasn't goin' to let on to you about Roemer and that slut."

"What about my loving husband? Is there more I should know about?" Jade managed to keep her voice calm, although she felt as if a part of her had died.

Maria and John looked at each other, and when Maria nodded, John said, "That's about it. We came upon them on the porch kissin' . . . and such."

Jade sat down at the table, fighting back the tears that stung her eyes. Was Kane never going to stop insulting her? It was beyond belief that he would carry on with a woman in his wife's home. Didn't the man she had married have any honor?

John's voice was rough, but the hand he laid on Jade's shoulder was gentle as he said, "Don't you dare shed one tear over that worthless man."

Maria sat down next to Jade and took hold of her hand. "Kane said that he could explain everything, and now that I've gotten over the shock of seeing that woman sitting on his lap, I believe that he could if we'd given him the chance."

"After I ordered him off the mountain, Roemer said he wasn't goin' to leave until he talked to you," Big John said. "Did he find you?"

"I didn't see him, so I guess he didn't look very hard." Jade looked at Maria and smiled. "I'm glad you didn't go with him, Maria."

"I'm not staying too long, Jade," Maria said, sliding a fast look at John. They had made no definite plans yet.

"I'll miss you when you're gone." Jade turned her palm over and squeezed Maria's hand.

"I'll come visit you, honey, and I see no reason why you can't come see me."

"Yes," Jade agreed, but she knew she never would. Kane wouldn't want her in his home. Besides, she couldn't hide her pregnancy much longer. So far she had managed to hide the slight swell of her belly with loose blouses.

"And, Jade," Maria spoke again, "don't give up on Kane. I know that sometimes he makes a person want to shoot him, but I want you to think about this: if Kane hadn't really wanted to marry you, there is no way in the world he would have.

He might not even realize that himself right now, but that fact will hit him in time."

Jade drew in a long breath and said stiffly, "I don't know what makes you think I want him. Can you give me any reason I should want a man like him?"

When Maria said helplessly, "I can't honestly think of any," Jade stood up.

"As far as I'm concerned I hope never to set eyes on him again." She stamped into her room and slammed the door behind her.

"I hate to see her hurtin' like that," Big John said.

"So do I. She's a sweet girl and doesn't deserve what Kane has done to her."

"She's a Farrow and she'll rise above this mistake she's made in her life and be a stronger woman for it. You just saw her take the first step."

Maria hoped that Big John was mistaken. He added, "Let's take a walk. I want to show you the little filly I caught in my last wild-horse drive."

When Jade heard them leave the cabin she released the tears that were burning her eyes and throat.

Maria would have gone past the shed to the corral, but John took her arm and turned her in the direction of the barn. "I want to stop in here a minute," he said. "I need to check out the stalls, see if Jade has spread fresh hay for the horses."

"You treat that girl like she was a nephew instead of a niece," Maria complained, then gave a loud grunt when she bumped into Big John's broad back in the semi-darkness. John wheeled around to catch her as she stumbled backward.

"I didn't see you." Maria laughed nervously, waiting to be released. "I—" Her words were cut off as strong arms wrapped around her waist and hot, urgent lips sought hers as if to devour them. Murmuring John's name, Maria lifted her arms to encircle his neck and to press him closer.

John's body trembled at her action, and he raised his hand and fumbled with the buttons of her bodice. Maria sensed that John had had little experience at undressing a woman. In fact, this might be the first time for him. She suspected that he had only dealt with whores before, and that they did their own undressing. She started to raise a hand to assist him, then stopped. Letting him do it on his own would set her apart from the women who sold their bodies.

Finally the buttons were undone, and John was feverishly pushing her bodice apart and easing it over her shoulders and down over her arms. Her camisole was pushed down to her waist next. John released her lips then and held her away so that he could gaze upon her large, firm breasts.

"I've wanted to taste them from the first time I saw you," he whispered huskily. Bending his head he flicked his tongue over each hardened nipple a couple of times before drawing one deep within his mouth. As he suckled it, Maria grew weak with the passion that was surging through her body.

John gripped her forearms to keep her from falling, then transferred his mouth to her other breast, drawing on the nipple. Maria felt an overpowering need to touch his maleness, to hold him in her hands, and she whispered her wish to him.

In seconds John had his fly open, and she gasped at the size of his manhood. It matched all the other parts of his big body—large, long and hard, and visibly throbbing. She took it in both hands and started to caress it. Big John stopped her. "Sorry, Maria," he said huskily, "but if you handle me now I might explode. When that happens I want to be inside you."

With one sweep of his hands Big John had Maria's clothes lying in a crumpled heap at her feet. He eased her down on a pile of hay and took off her shoes. Then, without taking his eyes off her, he shed his own clothing. As he stood over her, Maria couldn't take her gaze from the pulsating member that would soon enter her.

But John wasn't in any hurry. He dropped to his knees and began to kiss and lick his way down her body until he came to the thatch of soft, springy curls that protected what he had wanted for months. He gently parted that protection and flicked his tongue over the little nub hidden there until it grew swollen. He settled his teeth over it then and nibbled gently.

With a cry of pleasure Maria wrapped her legs around him. She wanted him inside her. Right now. She gently raised John's head from her and then took hold of his manhood and guided him to where his tongue had been before.

With a deep groan John grasped her buttocks and plunged inside her.

Maria braced her feet on the hay-covered floor and met each thrust with one of her own. Minutes passed as they rocked together, their bodies glistening with sweat. When John felt the tightening of Maria's body he intensified his movements, and with low cries of pleasure they shared the small death.

When both were breathing evenly again, Maria pushed at Big John's shoulders and laughingly said, "You're squashing me, you big buffalo. You can get off me now."

John raised himself on his elbows, taking most of his weight off her. Brushing damp hair off her forehead, he said with a rakish grin and a buck of his hips, "Can't you feel down there that I'm not finished with you yet?"

Maria smiled and bucked back at him. Sliding her arms around his neck she said softly, "Anytime you're ready."

"What if I'll be ready the rest of the day?" John looked at her hopefully.

"I think that would be very nice." Maria gave him an impish grin.

And so it happened. As the sun moved steadily westward, twice more they cried out a release of passion.

It was nearing sunset when finally, exhausted,

they lay side by side, their breathing returning to normal.

"It's just as well we've worn each other out," Maria said, turning her head to look at John. "We can't do anything tonight. Jade would hear us."

John smiled in amusement. "There are other ways we can pleasure each other, Maria. Ways that don't make noise."

"There are?" Maria looked puzzled.

"Remember what I did before I entered you?"

"Yes." Maria blushed.

"You can do the same thing to me."

Maria's blush deepened. "I've never done that before."

Big John laughed and hugged her to him. "There's so much I've got to teach you."

"Well, for now we'd better get up to the cabin before Jade comes looking for us," Maria said as she sat up and pulled her camisole over her head.

"What are we goin' to do about us?" John asked, stuffing his shirttail inside his trousers.

"Do you have anything in mind?" Maria looked at him when she finished buttoning up her bodice.

"Yes, I do," Big John said firmly. "I want us to get married the way we originally planned. Will you marry me, Maria?"

"Do you need to ask, John? I would be honored to have you as a husband."

"No, the honor will be mine, having a woman like you for a mate." John took her in his arms and tenderly kissed her.

"The question is, when?" Maria asked.

"I don't know." John scratched his beard. "Things have gone plumb wrong between Jade and Roemer. I guess we shouldn't do anything until something is settled between them. I've got this deep-down feelin' that they're gonna work out the differences between them and have a happy marriage. But in case they don't, I'm of the old sayin' that no two women should live under the same roof. Jade has been mistress of the cabin ever since she was a little girl, and you, as my wife, should be mistress of your home. Besides," John added with a laugh, "my place is only big enough for two people to live in it comfortably."

"You're right about everything," Maria agreed. "I think what we should do is wait awhile and see what happens between those two muleheads. I'll come up often to visit you and you can come down to see me."

"I reckon," John said, "but it's gonna be hard as hell not to be with you every day."

"I know. I'm going to hate leaving you tomorrow."

They were silent as they left the shed and walked toward the cabin. The filly was forgotten . . . if there ever was one.

Chapter Twenty-three

It was high noon in mid-July as Kane sat his little mustang on a knoll, straining for some sound of his herd in the still air. The sky was turning darker by the minute, and in the distance lightning flashed and thunder rolled.

We're in for one hell of a storm, he thought *and the cattle are bound to stampede. But where in the hell are they?*

Kane hadn't gone out with his men that morning. Last night he had ridden into Laramie, planning to get roaring drunk, to drive Jade's image from his mind for a few hours, to dull the misery that thoughts of her brought him.

He had succeeded, but he'd paid dearly for it on awakening this morning. His stomach rolled and his head ached so, he couldn't bear to raise it from the pillow for a couple of hours.

He didn't feel much better now and didn't look forward to trying to stop a stampede.

As Kane sat the little mustang, trying to decide which direction to ride, there came a fierce bolt of lightning, followed by a deafening roll of thunder. Before it died away he heard the terrified bawling of cattle and the thundering of six hundred hooves. A second later he saw them. They were headed straight for the river, with the cowboys frantically trying to turn them away from sure danger.

The rain came with slashing force just as Kane was ready to put spurs to the mustang. Swearing, he yanked his slicker from behind the cantle and quickly pulled it on. He was charging down the knoll then, yelling at the top of his lungs, "Turn them bastards! Try to mill them! Make the circle as tight as you can!"

But the frantic cattle refused to be circled. However, the cowboys had managed to turn them away from the Platte. They were now heading straight for the foothills, their eyes rolling as they bawled their fright. As the rain beat against his face, almost blinding him, Kane gave a sigh of relief. The longhorns couldn't continue running once they were hindered by trees. Also, the storm wouldn't be so frightening to them and they would gradually quiet down.

He and the cowhands followed them, though,

to make sure they didn't try to go up the mountain, where they might fall and break their legs, or maybe slip in the mud and go tumbling to their deaths.

Kane swung out of the saddle and stepped beneath a tree to roll himself a cigarette. As he struck a match and held it to his smoke, he noticed that there were longer intervals between the lightning and thunder now. The storm was moving off. As he dragged on the cigarette the rain slowed to a drizzle, and by the time he threw away the butt, it had stopped completely. The cowhands would have no trouble driving the tired cattle back down to the range.

Kane didn't follow them. He took off the slicker and hung it on the saddle horn to dry: then, with reins dangling over his shoulder, and the mustang following behind, he started up the mountain. He didn't understand his sudden urge to see Jade. It came over him as strong as the storm that had battered his face a short time ago. He intended only to see her from a distance. It wouldn't be wise to meet her face-to-face. There was no telling what he might do if that happened . . . like grab her into his arms and kiss the breath out of her.

He was drawing near the mountain settlement when he heard much laughing and talking. The merry sound didn't come from the Farrow cabin, for it was set apart, quite some distance from the others.

A barefoot boy of nine or ten came down one of

the rocky paths, a fishing pole on his shoulder. "Hey, young man"—Kane smiled—"what's going on up there?"

"They's givin' the teacher a farewell party up at old Tillie's."

Kane nodded his thanks and the boy walked on, leaving Kane with an alarmed look on his face. Would Jade be going away with the teacher? "Of course she'll be going with him, you dunderhead," Kane muttered harshly. "She's carrying his baby, isn't she?"

Kane led the mustang up the path to the old woman's cabin, which was situated high above the others. He had to see this man who had won Jade's heart. When he came within a hundred yards or so of the merrymakers, he wrapped the mustang's reins around a pine branch. Then, careful not to be heard, he continued on, stopping when he came within sight of the old cabin and the people sitting around it.

His eyes went straight to Jade and lingered on her for a long moment, as he thought that she was lovelier than ever with her face thrown back in laughter. He started scanning the group then, looking for the teacher. He hadn't any idea what the man looked like, but he felt that he would be good-looking, clean shaven, and wouldn't be dressed like the mountain men.

Kane looked somewhat confused when he finished his survey. The only male who looked different from the men who inhabited the mountain was a little runt of a man sitting next to Jade. He felt certain she wouldn't be interested in him.

He gave a start and stared in disbelief when one of the women looked at the small man and said, "We're sure gonna miss you when you're gone, Virgil. Ain't we, Jade?"

"We certainly will," Jade said, smiling at the teacher. "I've been trying to talk Virgil into staying longer, but he insists that he has business to take care of back east."

Kane's first reaction of astonishment quickly turned to one of blinding rage. If the teacher was going to leave, Jade probably meant to pass the baby off as her husband's. *You'll not get away with it, lady,* he vowed silently, turning around and walking back to the little mount. *I'm going to Laramie tomorrow to speak to a lawyer about divorcing you.*

It was not quite sunset when the party for the teacher broke up and Virgil set out to walk Jade home. They walked at a brisk pace, for Virgil wanted to get home before dark. Even though there had been no more strange deaths in the small community, he was still reluctant to be out after dark.

"I truly will miss you when you've left us, Virgil," Jade said. "You've made the past months bearable for me."

"It pleases me that I did, Jade. I only feel sorry that you needed me. It's hard to believe that your husband can't see your worth, could treat you so shabbily."

"I guess it's because we're two such different personalities that we always clash."

"Jade, I want you to know that if you ever want to leave the mountain, you'll be more than welcome to come to me. You'd like living in a big city. I'd take you to operas; we'd eat in fancy restaurants. Your beauty and intelligence are wasted here. You are not appreciated. You deserve so much more."

Jade slid Virgil a startled look. What was he saying? Did he have romantic feelings for her? She wanted to laugh out loud at the thought. She stood a head taller than he, could beat him in a wrestling match. But he sounded so sincere about whatever it was he was offering her, she choked back her mirth.

"Thank you, Virgil, that is very kind of you," she said as they came within sight of her cabin. "I'll remember that."

"Just let Aunt Tillie know if you want to come to me and she'll get a letter off to me."

Jade was relieved to see her uncle sitting on the porch. What if her companion planned to kiss her good-bye?

She held out a hand to Virgil and said, "I consider you one of my best friends, Virgil. I hope you have a safe trip home."

"Thank you, Jade." The small man took her hand. "Remember what I told you."

"I will." Jade smiled and watched him hurry away from her. Another fifteen minutes and it would be dark.

"When is the little feller leavin'?" Big John asked as Jade sat down on the top step.

"Sometime tomorrow morning." She looked up at the big man. "You never really liked him, did you?"

"Well"—John stroked his beard, which was much shorter these days and was always neatly groomed—"I didn't like him or dislike him. I didn't like his prissy ways or the fact that he's so cowardly. When he left you he was practically running, he was in such a hurry to get home before dark. I don't care for a man who has no grit about him."

"Unlike my husband, I suppose," Jade said sourly. "Would you say he has grit?"

"That one!" Big John snorted. "He has enough grit for two men."

There was respect in her uncle's voice and Jade said, "But you don't like him either."

"I did at first. Roemer's the sort of man I always had in mind for you to marry. A strong man who would take care of you." After a pause he added, "He's the first man I was ever mistaken about. I never thought for a minute that he'd turn out to be a low-down cur."

Jade made no response to her uncle's angry description of Kane as she gazed out at the darkening twilight. What could she say? she asked herself. She couldn't deny what he had said.

She sighed. Lord, but she wished that she could say that he was mistaken about her husband. She wished also that she wouldn't dream about him tonight.

Chapter Twenty-four

Jade let the small garment she'd been working on fall to her lap. As the neighbor women chatted among themselves she examined the many needle pricks on her fingers. Maria had only recently taught her how to sew, and she was not very proficient at it yet. No matter how hard she concentrated on it, her stitches were always uneven.

She leaned her head back against the trunk of the cottonwood she sat beneath and let her gaze wander over her friends. How different they were from the way they'd been a few months back. They were almost unrecognizable, as were their children. They still wore the same worn clothing, but their clothes were clean now and neatly mended. The mothers no longer wore defeated looks but now went about with smiles on their faces and confident looks in their eyes. Bruises and broken bones had healed, and better yet, so had their souls. They were beginning to believe that there was a God after all.

It hadn't been discovered yet who had helped Carter Oates and Boris Greene and Elisha Collins depart this world. And that kept all the other men from laying heavy hands on family members. There was the dread that they too, might meet with untimely deaths.

A peal of rich laughter rang out, and Jade smiled. Only Maria made that full-bodied sound when something tickled her. Jade was still surprised at how fast the mountain women had accepted her dear friend. She didn't believe that being Big John Farrow's lady friend had anything to do with it. There was a sincerity about Maria that drew people to her, made them trust her.

Jade closed her eyes. She was sorry that her problems with Kane were still keeping Maria and her uncle from getting married. It was clear they loved each other. It wasn't right that they should have to be apart so much.

Her lips twitched in a slight smile. They didn't know that when Maria visited, Jade was aware of Maria's quietly leaving the bed that she shared with her and slipping into Uncle John's room. How much longer could that go on, she wondered. The strain of being kept apart must be wearing on them.

But why should it be that way? Jade's eyes popped open with an idea. There was no real reason they couldn't get married as soon as possible. If they waited for her and Kane to come to some kind of understanding, they might never get married.

Jade sat erect and broke into the conversation of how best to make wild-grape jelly. "Maria"— she smiled at her friend—"we'd all like to know when you and Uncle John are going to get married. I think you and Uncle have courted long enough."

Startled by the question, Maria could only stare at Jade while the other women looked at her expectantly. While she was trying to think of something to say, Janie Collins spoke up.

"We've all been wonderin' about that, too, Maria. Big John is a lusty feller who wants his lovin' regular-like."

Jade was almost sorry she had brought the subject up, Maria's face had grown so red. But she and Uncle John had to be jarred into thinking about their future. She knew her uncle claimed that no two women should live under the same roof, but in this case, it wouldn't be two females vying to be mistress of the cabin. She would gladly hand over the running of the household to Maria. It wasn't as if Jade knew all that much about operating a home. She barely knew how to cook.

"What about it, Maria?" Kathy Greene asked. "Should we set a date right now?"

"Why . . . I . . . I don't know," Maria stammered. "I'd have to talk to John first."

"Talk to me about what?" Big John walked up behind the excited women.

With a mischievous twinkle in her eyes, Kathy Greene answered. "Maria was wonderin' what you would think about gettin' married right away."

John sat down beside Maria and looked into her eyes. "Is that what you were thinkin', Maria?"

"Well . . . well . . . sort of." She smiled crookedly. "I am getting tired of climbing this mountain to see you."

As the excited women waited expectantly, John looked at Jade. "What do you think, girl?"

"I think you two should stop wasting time. It was my idea that you get married as soon as the arrangements can be made."

"All right!" John slapped his knee. "We'll do it. Just name the day, Maria."

Everyone started talking at once, each woman expressing her opinion of when the wedding should take place. The women were so caught up in planning the wedding, they didn't notice when John and Maria stood up and walked away.

Maria and John walked in silence until they came to the small waterfall several yards behind the cabin. John helped Maria sit down on a flat rock, then eased down beside her. Putting an arm around her waist he said, "I don't know anything about plannin' a real marriage. There wasn't anything planned with Jade and Roemer. I just marched the preacher in and it was done."

"Sometimes I think you were wrong in doing that, John. Being forced into marriage only made them dislike each other all the more. Sometimes I think they'll never get together."

"I agree I made a mistake there, but I do believe they'll settle their differences before long. Now, let's think about ourselves. What goes into plannin' a weddin'?"

"Well, first off, we have to decide where it will take place."

"I'd like for it to be here, where we're gonna make a life together," John said.

"Yes"—Maria smiled—"that's the way it should be. However, Kane might want us to get married at the ranch. We are almost family."

"Ha." John snorted. "Most likely he'll try to talk you out of marryin' me. That rooster don't like me no way."

"I think he does like you, John. He's just hard-headed and doesn't like to be forced into doing anything." She gave John a coaxing smile. "Now tell the truth; don't you kind of like him?"

"Liked him fine until I caught him and Jade in the barn. He took advantage of her innocence, and that is hard to forgive. He didn't care for Jade, and that was an insult to the girl, as well as to me. I took him into my home and saved his life. I don't like the way he thanked me for that."

"I know." Maria sighed. "And I'm ashamed that Kane would do that. It's not like him to dishonor you and Jade that way. That's why I keep thinking that if he'd only admit it, he cares deeply for Jade and couldn't keep himself from making love to her. Of course, that doesn't excuse what he did."

"Did you know that Jade is with child by him?"

"You mean . . . ?"

"That's right." John didn't let her finish her sentence. "He sneaked up here and wormed his way into her bed. It broke Jade all up when she woke the next mornin' and found him gone. She thought that everything was all right between them and that she'd be going back to the ranch with him."

"Damn him!" Maria exclaimed angrily. "I've half a mind to not even invite him to the wedding."

"That's up to you, honey. Now, when should we tie the knot?"

"I don't care. You name the day."

"What about Saturday? That's two days away and will give you time to fetch your things up here and get settled in." When Maria only nodded agreement, John put an arm around her shoulders and said, "I know it's a big step for you, Maria, but we're gonna have a good life together."

Maria laid her hand on John's. "I don't doubt that for a minute, John. It's just that I've lived with the Roemers a good part of my life. They are truly like family. I consoled Kane and his sister, Storm, when they lost their parents."

Maria sighed and leaned her head on John's

shoulder. "Damn that Kane. He's always doing something that drives a person crazy."

"He's a grown man, Maria. It's time you stop coddling him. Once he's left on his own, maybe he'll do some hard thinkin' and be more considerate of others."

Maria sighed. "I hope so. I like to think that when his baby is born, he'll realize that he loves its mother and they will become a family."

"We'll just have to wait and see," John said, standing up and helping Maria to her feet. "Now let's go tell them gabbing women what we've decided."

Kane leaned against the wooden pillar of the porch watching Maria ride away with the man who was responsible for disrupting the carefree lifestyle he had enjoyed all his adult years.

He rued the day he had ridden up the mountain that autumn day and become a captive of Farrow's green-eyed niece. Even as angry sparks flew between them, he'd had the driving desire to possess her slender body. He had been unable to control that desire.

But he had paid dearly for the most satisfying lovemaking of his life. He'd never imagined he'd be forced into a shotgun wedding. Big John's decree that he and Jade wouldn't be living together had been welcome news to him. His life would continue as usual, he had told himself.

How mistaken he had been. Nothing had been the same since. His wife had become an obsession with him.

What puzzled him the most was her relationship with the schoolteacher. He couldn't understand how Jade could care for the man enough to sleep with him, yet not seem disturbed that he was leaving her behind to raise his child alone.

Maybe caring didn't enter into it, Kane thought. Maybe it didn't matter to his wife whether she loved her bed partner or not. He wondered if she had already chosen the man who would replace the teacher. His fingers balled into fists. He would be the laughingstock of the community if she had one lover after the other. For sure he must speak to the lawyer about getting a divorce.

He stared unseeingly out across the range. Big John Farrow hadn't been satisfied with forcing him into a marriage he didn't want; now he was taking away the woman who had been Kane's mainstay ever since he'd lost his parents. He supposed that although it went against the grain, he owed it to Maria to attend her wedding. He would attend her marriage and then get off that mountain for all time. He wouldn't even look at his man-crazy wife.

Old Jeb hailed him from the corral, and Kane stepped off the porch, grumbling. "What the hell does he want?"

* * *

Norah Hess

As Jade pressed the pink lawn dress that Maria would wear when she became Mrs. John Farrow in just a few hours, she couldn't help thinking how different this wedding would be from her own. There was laughter and excitement in the planning of her uncle's marriage, and there was so much love between him and Maria.

A soft sigh escaped her as she set the cooled iron back on the stove, then, with a towel to protect her hand, picked up the handle of a heated one. There had been none of that in her hasty marriage. There had been only nervous tension on her part and stony dislike on Kane's.

Jade asked herself why she hadn't stood up to her uncle, refused to marry the overbearing rancher. Things would be very different if he hadn't let his temper rule him when he'd caught her and Kane in the barn. For one thing, she wouldn't be carrying Kane Roemer's baby. It was doubtful he would have come up here again if he hadn't thought he had the right to.

She wondered if he would show up for Maria's wedding. She hoped so. It would mean so much to Maria. Kane and his sister, Storm, were like family to her.

What was Kane's sister like? Jade wondered. Was she as arrogant as her brother? Would she think that a mountain man wasn't good enough for her longtime friend? And what did she make of her brother marrying that man's niece?

Maria had mentioned once how close the sister

and brother were, that Kane had practically been a father to Storm since she was sixteen years old. Kane had probably taught her to think as he thought. No doubt she would look down her nose at the plain, uneducated mountain women with their patched clothes and careworn faces.

"Enough thoughts wasted on the Roemers," Jade murmured as she finished pressing the wedding dress. "I must decide what I'll wear for the wedding." Most of the dresses Maria had given her no longer fit. There was one, a light green muslin, which she might be able to squeeze into. It had always been a little loose on her.

As Jade set the two irons on the back of the stove to cool, she heard Maria and her uncle approaching the cabin. They were coming from the waterfall, where they had gone to bathe. She smiled as she watched them through the window. The soon-to-be-married couple walked hand in hand, her uncle carrying their wet towels and the small basket that held two different kinds of soap, a rose-scented one for Maria and a bar of yellow lye soap for Big John. Before he had fallen in love with the attractive woman at his side, he'd have never carried the basket, which he looked upon as a woman's job.

Jade thought to herself that she hardly knew this new John Farrow.

Jade walked out onto the porch, leaving her very nervous uncle to be calmed by his soon-to-be bride. It was nearly time for the preacher to arrive; their friends and neighbors would come shortly afterward. She started to step off the porch to check the long table constructed of boards laid across two sawhorses and covered with a white tablecloth Maria had brought with her. But then she stopped.

Two riders were coming up the mountain. She immediately recognized Kane and the white stallion he was riding. Her excitement at seeing her onetime pet turned to rage. Kane had deliberately chosen the handsome horse just to torment her that the animal was no longer hers.

Jade forced her attention to the other rider and her eyes widened. Kane's companion was a woman. It must be his sister, Storm. He wouldn't dare bring any other woman here. Her palms grew moist with nervous sweat as the couple drew nearer. What had Kane told the beautiful woman who sat her mare with such ease? She imagined he had told her the whole sordid story of his forced marriage to the wild mountain girl.

When the horses were reined in and the riders dismounted, Jade braced herself for some cutting remark from Kane. What she received was a cold, condemning look at her stomach as he brushed past her and walked into the cabin. She looked at his sister, expecting to see the same censuring regard. She blinked when she was greeted with a warm smile and an outstretched hand. "I'm that rude man's sister, Storm," she said, her eyes twinkling. "I don't know why in the world you married the aggravating clod."

"I don't know either." Jade laughed. The sister and brother were as different as day and night. "Actually," she amended, "my uncle made Kane marry me. I guess you know that."

"Yes, I was told that, and I found it hard to believe. I have never seen my brother forced to do anything; he's that stubborn."

"You've not met my uncle yet. He can be a pretty fierce man sometimes." Jade laughed again.

Storm made no response as Maria came flying through the door, calling out to her.

Jade watched the two embrace and wished she'd had that kind of womanly affection in her life. She knew that her uncle loved her deeply, but he wasn't the sort to hug and kiss. She watched Storm closely when she was introduced to her uncle. Would she be friendly to him as well?

Big John received the same genial smile and handshake Storm had given her. He likes her, Jade thought, otherwise he wouldn't be smiling so widely. She turned away from them and unintentionally gazed straight at Kane. His eyes swept coldly over her, lingered a moment on her stomach; then, with a curl of his lips, he turned his back on her and stepped off the porch.

For a moment she was tempted to go after him, to grab his arm and demand why her pregnancy offended him. He seemed to think it was all her fault, that she had gotten with child on purpose.

She started to follow him, then stopped. The preacher, astride his swaybacked horse, was approaching the cabin. The wedding guests wouldn't be far behind, so now wouldn't be a good time to start a row with him. But they would have it out before the day was over, she promised herself.

Reverend Hart had barely been introduced to Storm when the mountain people began to arrive, the women carrying covered dishes they had prepared for the wedding supper.

For a time it was total confusion as everyone talked at once, met and shook hands with Storm. During the laughter and loud talk, Jade pulled Storm aside.

"We weren't sure if you would be here, Storm, so Maria asked me to stand up with her. It would make her so happy if you stood up with her instead. You're like a daughter to her."

"If you're sure, Jade," Storm said eagerly, "nothing would please me more."

"It's settled, then. But let's don't say anything to Maria about the switch. When the time comes, just go up and stand beside her."

Storm nodded with a happy smile, then asked, "When is your baby due?"

"Sometime in December."

"How does my big brother feel about becoming a daddy?"

Jade gave a bitter little laugh. "He hasn't said, but the looks he gives me say that he isn't at all pleased."

"He'll change his mind once he sees the little one," Storm predicted, and before she could say more, the reverend was announcing that it was time to start the ceremony.

Everyone gathered beneath the shade of a large cottonwood at the corner of the cabin. The preacher motioned Maria and Big John to come forward. Jake Jefferson—John's longtime bachelor friend—and Storm followed them and took their places beside the couple.

Maria gave a start, and happy tears formed in her eyes when she saw Storm standing beside her. The Reverend opened his Bible, and with the words, "Dearly beloved, we are gathered here today," he began uniting the beaming pair in holy wedlock.

When he said to John, "You may kiss your bride now," a loud shout went up, and everyone jostled each other to be the first to congratulate the newlyweds.

Storm kissed Maria and hugged Big John, and then Jade kissed them both. "I'm so happy for you, Uncle," she whispered, her arms around his waist, her head resting on his chest.

"If you were happy, too, I'd feel much better." John's big hand stroked her head. "Does it bother you that he's here?"

Jade stepped back and shook her head. "I'm glad he came, for Maria's sake. I'll just ignore him. I see him talking to Maria now. I imagine he'll be leaving soon."

"How are you feelin'?" John tilted her head with one hand and scanned her face. "You look a little pale. Is the heat gettin' to you?"

"I'm a little tired, that's all." She looked up at John, an impish twinkle in her eyes. "Old Tillie has invited me to stay with her a few days so that you and Maria can honeymoon by yourselves. I expect she'll be ready to go home soon."

"Now, Jade, that's not necessary," John protested, but Jade sensed that his objection was a little weak.

"I know that, Uncle John, but you and Maria deserve a few days without me underfoot."

"Now don't go thinkin' that way, girl," John began, but then was interrupted by his best man. Jade left them and joined the women, who were setting out the food to start the celebration. John had decreed that there would be no alcohol, that he didn't intend for the men to get drunk and start fights on this most important day of his life.

Jade had no appetite. While the others were crowded around the makeshift table filling their plates, she slipped away, walking toward the tree where Satan and Storm's mare were tethered.

The beautiful white stallion whickered a welcome to her and nudged his head against her shoulder when she came up to him. "I knew you wouldn't forget me," she said softly, scratching his ears. "He may think he owns you, but we know better, don't we?" Did she dare take him for a ride? She chewed on her bottom lip. I'm going to do it, she decided and tightened the cinch, which Kane had loosened.

She was shortening the stirrups when an arm circled her waist and a rough hand was clamped over her mouth. As she struggled fiercely, furious with Kane, she realized it was not her husband who was holding her squirming body as he mounted the nervous stallion, bringing her with him. The arm around her waist was that of an Indian. What did Long Feather think he was doing? she thought angrily as the stallion was nudged into motion.

When they had traveled out of hearing distance of the wedding party, the Indian kicked Satan into a hard gallop. Jade ceased struggling and grabbed hold of the horse's mane to keep from falling off. She told herself that she must save her energy for what might happen once they arrived wherever he was taking her.

When they entered the foothills, the Indian veered to his right, away from the community and the Indian village. When they had ridden about a mile, the rough fingers were removed from her mouth, but the arm remained tightly around her waist. Jade turned her head to demand of Long Feather where he was taking her, and then gasped in surprise and dismay. It wasn't her longtime friend who held her so tightly; the Indian was a stranger to her. "Who are you?" She gasped as he pulled the stallion to a halt in a small pine grove. "You had better turn me loose before my uncle,

Big John Farrow, tracks you down and kills you."

Ignoring her, the Indian swung from the saddle and jerked her down beside him. "If you try to run away I will shoot you in the legs," he threatened. He gave her a hard push in the back, ordering, "Go sit with my braves beside the campfire."

Jade noticed then several Indians sitting around a small fire, staring curiously at her. Back in the shadows hovered four Indian women, their eyes reflecting suffering and resignation. Were they camp followers, or were they slaves kidnapped from another tribe? At any rate, from the way they jumped to attention when the leader spoke to them, she knew that she would get no help from them. Even if they wanted to help her escape, they would be afraid to.

Jade ran a fast glance over the men and decided by their ragged appearance that they were renegades. She had heard of such groups breaking away from their tribes because their chiefs didn't want to make war against the white man.

She wondered if their hatred would extend to her. If so, in what way? Would the women be allowed to beat her? Or worse yet, would she be passed among the men, to be raped by each one of them? She put a protective hand over her belly. She would lose her baby if that happened.

I mustn't even think of that, she was telling herself, when a familiar figure approached the fire. Her heart leaped with hope, for it was her long-time friend, Long Feather. She started to call out to him, but a slight shake of his head told her to be silent. She relaxed a bit. Somehow he would help her escape.

Long Feather, like his companions, was almost naked, wearing only a breechcloth around his waist. When had he left his people? she wondered. He had never hinted to her that he was dissatisfied with his life on the reservation. How worried and upset his parents must be.

Jade stopped thinking about Long Feather's parents when the leader of the renegades rose and moved to stand before her. Although inside she was a bundle of raw nerves, she made herself unflinchingly return his hard glower. When he abruptly turned away, she couldn't believe that she had stared him down. For the moment, she warned herself. His intent to rape her was clear in his black eyes.

Unless, she thought, he satisfied himself with one of the women he now strode toward. Pity for them stirred in her breast as they cowered away from the harsh-featured brave. There was fear and dread in the face of the one he grasped by the arm and dragged into the deeper shadows. When squeals of pain rent the air, the men at the fire laughed knowingly and made remarks to each other. Jade was just as glad she couldn't understand them.

Some fifteen minutes passed, and the moans of pain continued all the while. Jade gave a sigh of relief when the man came striding back to the campfire, taking his time to replace his stained breechclout. With a few guttural words, he motioned toward the three other squaws who stood waiting, dread and hopelessness in their eyes. The men were on their feet immediately. It was all Jade could do not to voice her relief when Long Feather reached her first. An argument erupted at once between him and the leader. Fierce words were exchanged, and only when Long Feather snatched a knife from his waistband did the leader back down.

Jade stumbled twice as she was jerked along toward a jumble of boulders. But she knew no harm would come to her and that Long Feather's roughness was put on for the benefit of those who watched them so enviously.

They passed the woman whose cries of pain had made Jade's blood run cold. The squaw was limping along and a trickle of blood ran from the hem of her doeskin shift down both calves. Just before Jade was pulled behind a tall boulder she glanced over her shoulder and swore under her breath. The leader had given the squaw a hard push in the direction of a kettle set over the cookfire. It was clear he intended that she cook their evening meal. She wondered with pity how long the woman could live with the harsh treatment meted out to her. Already she looked more dead than alive.

Long Feather drew Jade down beside him and

said in low tones, "Let loose a loud cry, as though you are in pain."

"I don't know if I can do that," Jade whispered back.

"I'll help you," her handsome friend said and gave her a hard pinch in the side.

The nipping of her flesh was so sudden, so unexpected, Jade let out a screech that rivaled cries coming from the three squaws being brutalized by the other braves.

"Damn you, Long Feather," Jade hissed, "that hurt."

"I intended it to, and I'll do it again if you don't cry out every time I tell you to."

With a meek look Jade said she understood. "Can you get me out of here?" she asked, looking pleadingly at Long Feather.

"I think so. I have a plan that I believe will work. But before I tell you what it is, let out another scream."

Jade nodded, then threw back her head and let loose a shriek that rebounded up and down the valley below.

A slight grin stirred the Indian's lips, and then he became very somber. "I may have to fight Broken Nose to get my way, but I'm going to try to keep you to myself, claiming that I'm not through with you. If all goes well tonight, when the camp sleeps we'll slip away."

"Isn't that chancy? Won't they hear our horses?"

Long Feather shook his head. "We're not going

to take our mounts. We must walk if we're to be successful in getting away. My plan is to get to the river, where I have a canoe hidden in some reeds."

"Isn't that a long way around to get home?"

"A little, but it's the safest way. Broken Nose will be unable to follow us because he won't know whether we went upriver or down. Now, scream again."

Dusk was coming on, and Jade had sounded many cries of pain by the time Long Feather said that it was time to return to camp. "But first you must look ravaged," he added, and took hold of her sleeve at the shoulder and nearly ripped it off. He next rent two long slashes in her skirt, then stood back to study her. After a moment he put both hands in her hair and ruffled it with his fingers until it was all atangle. He took hold of her hand then. "Don't forget to limp painfully as I drag you back to the campfire."

Jade gave him a sour look. "Why do I get the feeling that you enjoy being a little rough with me?"

"Now why would I do that?" Long Feather grinned and promptly gave her a shove that sent her stumbling toward the campfire. He was right behind her, reminding her to limp and to look as though she were in pain.

Jade noted that everyone had returned to the fire. Long Feather laid rough hands on her, pushing her down to sit on a flat rock several feet away from the others. "I'll go get us something to eat," he said in undertones.

While she waited for his return, her eyes skimmed over their companions. The men looked relaxed as they lolled around the fire. They had evidently sated their lust for the time being. She looked at the women serving them their supper. Poor things, she thought. Although they looked ready to drop in their tracks, they didn't dare complain.

Jade's body suddenly stiffened. Broken Nose had left the fire and was walking toward her. She was ready to call out to Long Feather when he, too, saw the ugly brave approaching her. He dropped the two wooden bowls that one of the women was about to fill for him, and with his hand on the knife at his waist, he ran after the man.

Jade held her breath when he grabbed Broken Nose's arm and spun him around. She didn't understand the angry words they exchanged, but in the end Broken Nose wheeled around and stalked back to the fire.

"I guess we'll not get any supper," Jade said to herself, but quickly decided that she would gladly go hungry if that was what it took to keep her safe from the cruel Indian.

But to her surprise Long Feather was also returning to the fire. She watched in amazement as he picked up the two bowls and motioned to one of the women to fill them for him.

"What is it?" Jade asked when a steaming bowl was handed to her.

"Venison stew." Long Feather sat down beside her and dipped his fingers into his bowl. "You'll have to eat with your fingers. Indians don't have forks or spoons."

Jade nodded and followed her friend's example. "What did you and Broken Nose say to each other?" Jade asked when the edge of her hunger had softened a bit. "He looked fierce when he left you."

"He insisted it was his turn to have you, and I insisted that I wasn't finished with you. That maybe tomorrow I would be."

Jade sent up a silent prayer. "Please, God, let us escape tonight."

Full dark had settled in when, after they had finished every scrap of their supper, Long Feather jerked Jade roughly to her feet. "We'll go back to our place in the boulders now and wait."

As Jade stumbled along behind him, Broken Nose called out something to Long Feather. "What did he say?" she asked when they were once again behind the tall boulders.

"He was reminding me that tomorrow you would be his."

"I'd rather die first," Jade said in all sincerity. "If it should happen that we can't get away tonight, and if you can't protect me from him, promise me you'll put your knife through my heart."

"I feel sure we'll escape, but I promise I will kill

you rather than see you suffer under his hands."

A full moon floated in and out of gathering clouds as Jade and Long Feather waited for the renegades to finish taking turns with their women hostages and retire for the night.

Chapter Twenty-five

Kane sat off by himself watching the children at play. Amusement curled his lips when two young boys, around eight years old, he judged, got into a fistfight. One of the battlers outweighed the other by about ten pounds and was a couple of inches taller. But the smaller one was giving back as good as he received.

Kane was suddenly wishing that the baby Jade carried was his. He had always liked children and enjoyed the time he spent with his nephew, Benny.

He picked up a dry stick and absentmindedly broke it into pieces as he stared unseeingly at the boys and girls at play. If he was ever to have a family, he must divorce his present wife first.

However, with that accomplished, who else could he marry?

He went over the daughters of his neighbors and promptly dismissed them. They were a silly, giggling bunch without too much between their ears, and the older ones with whom a man could have a decent conversation were already married. That left only the whores and man-hungry Liz, the biggest whore of them all.

"Your wife isn't giggly and simpering," Kane's pesky inner voice pointed out.

"That's true," Kane agreed, "but she has a tongue that can cut a man to pieces."

And speaking of her, where is she? Kane wondered. He hadn't seen her in the past half hour. He stood up and walked over to where Maria and Storm and Big John were sitting in the shade of a cottonwood. "Do any of you know where Jade has taken herself off to?" he asked. "I want to get some things settled between us."

Storm shook her head, and Maria said, "The last I saw her, she was talking with old Tillie."

Big John spoke then. "She left the old woman about twenty minutes ago and walked in the direction of where the horses are tethered. She probably wanted to say howdy to her old pet, Satan."

Kane's face took on the look of a dark thundercloud. "Damn it," he growled, "I don't want her around the stallion. I worked hard to get him to accept me. If she starts mollycoddling him, I'll have to start all over again." The three grinned in amusement as he strode hurriedly away.

Kane immediately saw that the white stallion was missing and rage consumed him. Jade had dared to take him for a ride. As he hurriedly saddled Cinnamon, Jade's mare, he promised himself that she was going to get a good dressing-down when he caught up with her.

Satan's tracks were easy to follow. His left front shoe bore Kane's initial. But how far did she intend to ride him? Kane wondered uneasily. He had covered at least five miles and still hadn't caught up with her. What was more, slanting shadows were beginning to penetrate the forest, touching the tree trunks. Dusk was a short time away and soon he would be unable to track the stallion.

He rode another couple of miles before the sun went down and twilight descended. He knew that he could become lost and ride in circles all night when real darkness set in.

Reluctantly, Kane reined Cinnamon around, his anger and impatience growing. Did Jade plan to keep Satan hidden until he gave up and left? he asked himself. Then he dismissed the idea. She would know better than to try that.

So what was she up to? He was still musing on that question when he arrived back at the Farrow cabin.

All the wedding guests had gone home, and Maria, Storm and Big John were sitting on the porch.

As Kane swung off the tired mare's back, Jade's uncle stood up and asked anxiously, "Where is Jade? Didn't you find her?"

Kane shook his head. "I followed her more than five miles before I had to turn back because of darkness."

"Something is wrong here," Big John said, concern in his voice. "Jade is a levelheaded young woman and would never do anything that would worry me. I'm goin' to light a lantern and we'll go examine the area where the horses were tied up. I've got a feelin' that some dirty work has gone on."

The ground was riddled with hoofprints and boot tracks, including marks made by Jade's small shoes. After closely studying the churned-up dirt and gravel and finding nothing out of the ordinary, Big John said, "There's nothin' to do but wait for mornin' and take up her trail again."

When the big mountain man, with sagging shoulders, turned back toward the cabin, Kane said, "Leave the lantern with me. I want to look around a little more."

But after another ten minutes of closely scrutinizing every inch of the area, Kane decided he was wasting his time. He was about to go back to the cabin when he stopped short. Almost hidden beneath Jade's footprint was the imprint of a moccasin. He had seen no Indians here today.

Jade had been abducted by an Indian! The thought hit him like a kick to the stomach.

When Kane hurried up to the porch, Big John jumped to his feet. "What is it, Roemer? Did you find something?"

"Yes." Kane dropped down weakly onto the top step. "An Indian has her, John. I found his moccasin print."

"Long Feather, by God." Big John slammed his fist into a porch post. "When I catch the bastard, I'll kill him with my bare hands."

"Who is Long Feather?" Kane and the women asked in unison.

"He's a damn Indian Jade has known most of her life. She grew up playin' with him and the other Indian children. When they grew older, Long Feather decided he wanted her for his wife. He was always hanging around, but we haven't paid much attention to him since Jade got married and came up expectin'."

"Do you think he will hurt her . . . force himself on her?" There was a savage look in Kane's eyes.

"I don't think he'll hurt her. He cares for her too much. But the other, I don't know. I pray that he doesn't."

Kane jerked to his feet. "I'm going to bed down in the barn," he said, his voice raw with the roiling emotions inside him. "As soon as it is daylight, I'm riding into that village and I'll tear it apart until I find my wife."

John and Maria looked at each other with raised eyebrows. It was the first time they had ever heard him refer to Jade as his wife.

"You'll be wasting your time going there," John said. "He'll not take Jade there. His chief is a very honorable man and would make him release her."

"Then where would he take her?"

Big John shook his head helplessly. "I have no idea. Maybe somewhere in Utah."

With unshed tears glittering in her eyes Maria asked, "Will you still try to find her, Kane?"

After giving her a look that said she had asked an inane question, Kane answered, "I'll take up the stallion's tracks tomorrow and follow them until I find her."

"Take my sorrel," Big John said. "The mare is fast for short runs, but she doesn't have much stamina. Red can go all day and not tire."

"Let's hope it doesn't take me all day," Kane said brusquely as he stepped off the porch, heading for the small barn.

Kane didn't sleep more than a few hours that night. He had made a discovery that still had his mind reeling. He realized now that the little wildcat was the kind of woman he'd unconsciously been looking for all his adult life. All the many other women he had known had been necessary only to his male drive. He loved his wife totally and would love her child when it arrived. His abominable behavior toward her had driven her into another man's arms. And now, because of his foolish pride, she was out there somewhere, and God knew what was happening to her.

*   *   *

The moon had gone down and the night was pitch dark when Long Feather laid a hand against Jade's lips before gently shaking her shoulder. Her eyes flew open and she would have cried out if his hand was not covering her mouth.

"It's time we left," he whispered, removing his hand when he saw that she recognized him. He helped her to her feet and allowed her to stand a moment to let the stiffness ease out of her muscles and limbs. Then, taking her hand, he led her away, leaving behind the snoring Indians and exhausted women.

They traveled for an hour at a trot before Jade began to slow down with weariness. Hunger was making her feel nauseous, and her legs ached.

"Can't we stop a minute?" she called breathlessly to Long Feather.

Long Fellow slackened his pace somewhat, allowing her to catch up to him. "We must take advantage of the night. I'm aware of your condition, but if Broken Nose catches us, I will die immediately, while your death will be a hard one and a long time in coming. Even if you managed to survive his harsh treatment, you would lose the baby sleeping beneath your heart."

"I'm sorry, Long Feather," Jade apologized. "I'm afraid I haven't been thinking ahead. Move on. You won't hear any more complaints from me."

As they moved on, Long Feather kept his pace slower, which helped Jade somewhat. But by the time the eastern sky began to lighten, she had a sharp pain in her side and she stumbled often. It was an effort to put one foot in front of the other.

She bumped into Long Feather, unaware that he had stopped. "We must hide now," he said. "Our feet are leaving dark traces in the dew-laden grass, and if Broken Nose is already on our trail he'll see them."

Jade could only nod and follow him as he started loping along. She hadn't enough breath to speak her understanding.

A short time later, when they came to a bare, gravelly patch, Long Feather turned his steps upon it. He reminded Jade to watch where she put her feet, to do as he had taught her in their youth. He led her then to a thicket of young pines. Weaving his way to its center with Jade close behind him, he stopped.

"We'll wait here and watch to see if Broken Nose passes by. Lie down now and get some rest." He reached into a pouch attached to his breechclout and brought out a strip of pemmican. "Here," he said, "chew on this. It will stave off some of your hunger."

Jade curled up on the pine needles and instantly fell asleep, the pemmican gripped in her hand. Long Feather sat down at her head and leaned his back against a tree trunk. As he kept watch his hand gently stroked Jade's hair.

The eastern sky was just turning pink when Kane stood up and ran his fingers through his hair, dislodging the hay sticking to it. After he had brushed off his clothes, he walked outside to wash up in the water trough. He was drying his face on his neckerchief when Big John emerged from the shadows and stood beside him. The dark smudges beneath his eyes told Kane that the big man hadn't slept any better than he had.

"I brought you a beef sandwich," John said, pushing a cloth-wrapped package toward him. "You can eat it as you ride along. I don't know if you noticed, but I've got Red saddled for you over at the corner of the shed."

Kane hadn't noticed, and, glancing over his shoulder at the big waiting stallion he said, "I'm obliged, John." He was thinking how ironic it was that now that they might never see Jade again, he and the mountain man would become friends.

When Kane swung into the saddle John laid a hand on his knee. "Bring her back, Kane," he said, half pleading and half commanding.

"Nobody wants her back more than I do, John," Kane said. Reining Red around he headed him down the mountain. When he rode down into the foothills, he found the whole area in a heavy fog. That didn't concern him overly. He knew in which direction to ride. Before long, the sun would come up to clear away all traces of the thick mist.

As he had predicted, an hour later the air was clear and he had no problem picking up Satan's hoofprints. How much farther, he wondered, until he caught up with the red bastard and put a bullet through his heart?

Kane figured he had ridden another five miles when he heard voices—voices of Indian women. He reined Red in beneath a wide-spreading cottonwood and swung to the ground. Dropping to his knees, he crawled through tall grass for several yards before coming upon a sight that made him swear under his breath.

Four Indian women sat beneath as many trees, their hands tied behind their backs, a long rope looped around their necks and then tied to a tree. He carefully scanned the area and saw no men, no horses. He asked himself what kind of depraved man needed so many women to satisfy his lust.

When he felt reasonably sure that there were only women in the camp, he stood up and walked toward it. The chattering stopped immediately when he appeared before the women.

"Do any of you speak English?" he asked as they stared at him fearfully.

One of the women, looking older than the others, answered hesitantly, "I do . . . a little."

"Where is your man?"

"Braves no kin to us." The woman spat on the ground. "We are their captives. They hunt Long Feather. He ran away with white woman who Broken Nose captured."

Kane gave a start and then asked, "Broken Nose, not Long Feather, brought her here?"

"That is right. Long Feather took her away while

everyone slept. Broken Nose much angry."

"Were Long Feather and the woman riding?"

"No. They walk."

Kane drew his bowie knife from his boot and, kneeling down, cut the rawhide strip that bound the woman's wrists, then unfastened the rope from around her neck. As she looked at him in wonderment he said, "All four of you are in bad shape. Do you think you can manage to get back to your people?"

All four heads nodded eagerly. "We can," their spokeswoman answered, "even if we have to crawl all the way. Broken Nose and his followers evil."

Kane handed her the knife. "Cut your companions loose and get out of here as fast as you can." He started to walk away and then paused. He took the sandwich from his vest pocket and handed it to the woman, who was already cutting through the ties binding the woman next to her. "It's not much," he said, "but it will take the edge off your hunger."

He walked away then with heartfelt thanks following him.

Chapter Twenty-six

During the two hours that Long Feather had kept watch, he had seen no sign of Broken Nose and his followers. Then, just as he was thinking it was probably safe for him and Jade to continue on to the river, he heard the distant pounding of hooves. He glanced at Jade and decided that she slept too deeply to be startled awake.

He drew a wicked-looking knife from his waist and laid it down beside her. If they were discovered and captured, he would stab Jade in the heart with it rather than let her suffer untold agony at Broken Nose's hand.

As the hoofbeats drew nearer, Long Feather's nerves stretched to the breaking point. Then, in a matter of seconds, the small band flashed past the thicket. His tension didn't ease, however. When Broken Nose found no trace of them, he might pass this way again, returning to the camp, and decide to investigate the thick stand of pines.

An hour later he heard the renegades returning and held his breath, not letting it out until the band had ridden past. Broken Nose's face was dark with anger, and Long Feather pitied the women when the cruel man returned to camp. They would bear the brunt of his anger.

Long Feather let another half hour pass before gently shaking Jade awake. "We can go now," he said when she opened her eyes.

"Is it much farther to the river?" she asked as he helped her to her feet.

"Maybe another four miles. How are you feeling? Do you think you can make it? I can carry you if necessary."

"I'm tired, but I can do it if we don't have to run."

"I don't think we'll have to, but we shouldn't delay either. The sooner we get to the river and onto the water, the safer we will be."

The sun rose higher and hotter. Jade felt blisters rising on her heels, and each step was pure agony. Every time she wanted to rest awhile, however, she remembered the Indian women and what they suffered day and night at the hands of Broken Nose and his men, and she kept plodding along.

The sun was well up in the sky when Jade and Long Hair heard the murmur of running water. A moment later they were looking at the Platte. Jade was so thankful tears ran down her cheeks.

Long Feather frowned when he gazed at the river. It had been an unusually wet summer and the Platte was a wild, rushing torrent of water. It could be very dangerous in some spots, he knew, with deep eddies and rapids, maybe even white water farther down. But since it was equally dangerous to stay on land, he went to where he kept his canoe hidden.

He pulled the canoe out of the reeds and onto land. When he handed Jade into it she teetered in the middle, before carefully sitting down. There was the muted crunch of gravel then as he pushed the lightweight vessel into the water.

When he picked up the paddle and directed the canoe downriver, Jade asked with a wary frown, "Shouldn't we be going upriver?"

When Long Feather made no answer, only stared straight ahead, Jade said angrily, "I know you heard me. What crazy notion do you have in your head?"

"It is not a crazy notion," he answered fiercely. "You have known for years that I want you for my woman. You are a foolish girl who would not listen to me and instead married a paleface who does not love you. I am taking you to my mother's people. After your baby is born you will become my wife."

In her anger and disbelief Jade had not noticed that the water had grown swifter and rougher.

When she stood up and threatened to jump out of the canoe, her eyes widened in horror. Only yards away the river was rushing madly over huge jagged rocks, and spumes of white water were spraying the air. There was no way in the world Long Feather could stop the fragile vessel from capsizing.

Kane picked up the trail he wanted in a short time. Moccasin prints mingled with the ones made by Jade's small shoes. She and the Indian were running; he could tell by the distance between the footprints. After an hour or so he came to a place where it looked like they had paused. Probably so that Jade could rest. How hard it must be on her to run in her condition, he thought angrily, wishing he could get his hands on the Indian. He prayed to God she didn't lose her baby.

He had ridden another hour when he heard the distant sound of hoofbeats. They came from several horses and he imagined it was the renegade bunch that had gone out to run Jade and Long Feather down. He kicked his heels into the sorrel and steered him down into a deep gulch where flooding rains had washed a jumble of large boulders. He steered Red behind the largest one and, swinging to the ground, he placed a hand over Red's nostrils. He didn't want the animal to whinny and give away his hiding place.

The riders were silent as they rode past at a walk. Kane ventured a quick glance through the foliage and breathed a sigh of relief when he didn't see Jade among them. When the last hoofbeat had faded away he swung back into the saddle and urged Red up the steep bank. Then he began looking for the tracks he had been following, which had mysteriously disappeared.

He had almost given up hope of finding them when suddenly at the end of a patch of gravel he picked them up again. He shifted his gaze to a pine thicket and knew that Jade and the Indian had hidden there from their pursuers. He rode on, hope building within him.

Half an hour later he came to the river. For a long moment he sat studying the waters, a worried frown creasing his forehead. Had Long Feather been foolish enough to try swimming across the fast-moving water? He knew that Jade could swim, but in her condition, and hampered by full skirts and petticoats, it would be difficult for her, if not impossible, to get safely across.

As he sat, wondering what to do now, his eyes fastened on Jade's small shoe prints and he gave a start. He had spotted the marks left from a canoe being dragged up on the bank. Harsh oaths ripped through his lips. The crazy Indian was trying to navigate these treacherous waters.

Fear and dread gripping his chest, Kane kicked the stallion into motion, guiding him downriver. Even a fool wouldn't try to paddle upstream, bucking the swift water.

The riverbank became steeper as he followed

the bends of the river. When he spotted the tossing canoe and the fierce rapids it was headed toward, the bank was about forty feet above the water, and it was a sheer drop down to the river.

Kane felt as if his heart had stopped beating. How was he to get to Jade, to save her from almost certain death? He groaned when he saw her stand up just before the canoe hit the white water dashing over the jagged rocks. As he watched helplessly, Jade tumbled out of the vessel. He saw the Indian grab at her and miss as she was carried away. Her mouth was open and she was shouting something that wasn't audible to him over the roar of the water.

Kane was desperately hurrying the stallion on when he saw the canoe smash against two rocks and break in half. "May God forgive you. I don't know if I can," he ground out as the Indian's broken body was flung upon a tall rock.

Kane continued to follow the river for a couple of miles, calling Jade's name over and over. There was no response.

Finally, he had to accept the fact that he would never see Jade alive again. He sagged forward in the saddle, his head hanging, blinded by hot, flowing tears.

Despair filled his heart when he turned the sorrel homeward. As the tired horse plodded on, he reached into his vest pocket and fingered the wedding ring he had carried around for months. He started to throw it into the waters that had taken Jade from him, but something made him return it to his pocket.

Chapter Twenty-seven

The sun shone hot on the old man astride his mule. He had left his cabin early this morning to fish in the Platte. He hadn't known of the rains that had swelled the river and he was highly aggravated that he would be unable to catch any fish in it today. He was now making his way homeward.

He had gone only a short distance down the riverbank when he reined the mule in. His attention was caught by the tail end of a canoe caught among the rocks in the madly rushing water. He shook his head, wondering if anyone had survived the breaking up of the vessel. He peered downstream and gave a start. The limp body of an Indian lay sprawled on a tall rock sticking up out of the water.

"He's a goner, Jake," the old man said to his mule. "I wonder if there was anyone with him."

He nudged the mule on up the river. The bank was beginning to grow steeper when he heard a groan coming from a small arm of the river. Urging his mount toward the edge of the river, he shortly came upon a small cove about four feet wide. It was filled with debris from the flooding water. When he had studied the backwash a moment he gave an exclamation of surprise.

"By God, Jake, I can see a woman's head and shoulders half layin' on a piece of log."

He slid off the mule and splashed through the water to reach the woman. He stared down at her pale face. "She looks in a bad way," he said to himself. "She'd never make it to my place. I'll have to make camp here where maybe I can help her. I wonder what she was doin' with an Injun," he muttered, pulling the unconscious woman out of the refuse.

He called to the mule to come to him. When the animal obeyed him he lifted the woman onto Jake as gently as he could, and then climbed on behind her.

As soon as he came to a wooded area, he reined the mule in and slid to the ground. He carefully pulled the woman into his arms and carried her to the shelter of a cottonwood. After laying her down on the ground, he removed a slicker from behind the cantle and hurried back to her. When he had spread it next to her, he dragged her onto it. With practiced hands, he then pressed and probed her entire body.

He found she had three broken ribs. When he stripped the wet skirt and petticoat off her, he found many gashes up and down her legs and thighs and on her back.

And finally, with shock, he discovered she was expecting. He laid his whiskered cheek on her stomach and listened intently for several minutes. When he lifted his white head he said softly and solemnly, "Miracle of miracles, the baby is still alive."

But the young mother-to-be was in a bad way and he didn't know what to do for her. In his little cabin ten miles away he had herbs and roots and bark with which to doctor her. But out here all he had was a canteen of water, a pint of whiskey and his fishing pole and line.

"I can clean her up a little," he thought out loud, and, taking the kerchief from around his neck, he sparingly poured water from the canteen to wet it. After he had wiped her face clean, he dabbed at her cuts, getting them reasonably clean. He hated leaving her in her underwear, but until her clothes dried, he had nothing else to cover her up with.

Next the old man cleared a wide place of leaves and pine needles and built a small fire. Then he went deeper into the woods to search for the blazing star plant. When steeped in hot water for a while, it made a fine medicine to treat different ailments with. Indians and white men alike swore by its power.

It didn't take long to find a blazing star plant. They grew in abundance in the shade of the foothills.

Fifteen minutes later its roots were scraped clean and steeping in a chipped granite coffee cup. The old man hurried about then, turning over rocks, looking for worms. When he found one he threaded it on his fishing line and dropped it into the river. He didn't have much faith in catching any fish in the turbulent waters, but in five minutes he had snagged a three-pound bass.

Back at the fire again he checked on the woman and found that she hadn't moved, but the rise and fall of her chest told him she was still alive. He set aside the tea to cool, then scaled and gutted the fish. Wrapping it in reeds he had broken off at the river's edge, he buried it in the ashes beneath the fire's red coals. The fish would be ready to eat in less than half an hour.

He had just finished unsaddling the mule and hobbling him in a patch of grass not far from the fire when the young woman began to moan fitfully. He hurried to her, afraid she might start tossing around, causing one of the broken ribs to puncture her lungs. When he knelt beside her, long lashes swept up and alarmed green eyes stared up at him.

"Who are you?" she asked weakly.

"You can call me Lize, the feller who pulled you out of the river. I spread your dress and petticoat in the grass to dry out."

The injured woman looked bewildered. "Why was I in the river?"

"I was hopin' you could tell me that. I think the canoe you was in got all broken up in the rapids. There's a dead Injun back there. I imagine he was paddlin' the canoe."

When she stared at him blankly, as though she didn't know what he was talking about, he asked, "Who are you, young lady? Where do you come from?"

"I'm—" She stopped and stared at him helplessly.

"Well?" Lize prodded when she didn't continue. "What's your name?"

A tear slid from the corner of her eye. "I don't know," she answered in near panic.

"What do you mean, you don't know? Everybody knows his name. Where do you come from? Was you with that Injun?"

"I don't know the answer to any of your questions," she answered, her tears falling freely now.

"Well, I'll be danged." Lize sat back on his heels. "You must have got a hard knock on your head that made you lose your memory. I've heard tell of that but I never seen it afore. I guess we'd better pick you a name until you remember your own. You got any preference, any handle you like?"

When he received a negative shake of the head, Lize thought a minute and said, "I'll call you Lass. I used to have a sister named that. She's been dead twenty years now."

Jade gave him a wan smile, then started to sit up. She gasped and laid her head back down. "It hurts me to move," she said weakly. "It hurts just to breathe."

"That's because you've got some broken ribs. I'm gonna have to tear your petticoat into strips to bind them up. Your things are most likely dry by now."

Jade heard a ripping sound and turned her head toward Lize. He was tearing her undergarment into wide strips.

Although rheumatism had gnarled the old man's fingers, they were gentle as he tightly bound Jade's rib cage. "There, now"—he grinned at her— "do you feel better?"

"I feel ever so much better," she said, returning his toothless smile. "I can breathe deeply now. Is my dress dry?"

"It may be a little damp, but I think we can get you into it."

It was a slow process, trying not to disturb the rib bindings and the bruised shoulder and arms as Lize eased the dress down over her battered body. She flinched visibly several times as the material scraped against deep cuts.

When he had done up the last button, he asked, "Are you hungry?"

She nodded her head vigorously. "I could eat that old mule of yours if you cooked him."

Lize let loose a cackling laugh. "You don't want to eat Jake. He's got to carry you to my cabin up on Rock River tomorrow. How does fresh-caught fish sound to you?"

"It sounds wonderful. I don't know when I've eaten last, but my stomach says it's been a while."

"Let me help you sit up then and I'll bring you your supper. Now grab my shoulders and I'll ease you up to rest your back on the tree trunk."

Jade felt weak as she sat upright, but not in too much pain. What aches she had were forgotten when Lize brought her the steaming fish still wrapped in reeds. With the two of them sharing the bass there was soon nothing but bones left.

"It was absolutely delicious, Lize." Jade leaned her head back, a sated smile on her face.

Lize picked up the cup of tea that had been sitting beside him. "Now, you're not gonna like the taste of this," he said, handing her the cup. "It's awful bitter, but there's nothin' better to ward off infections. Drink about half of it now and I'll give you the rest at bedtime. It will help you sleep."

Judging by the face Jade made on swallowing the tea, it was indeed bitter. When she handed the cup back to him she said with a sour smile, "I guess if it tasted good, it wouldn't work."

"I reckon. That's what my old maw used to say," Lize replied with a grin.

When he lingered beside her, his brow wrinkled in thought, Jade asked, "Was there something else you wanted to say to me?"

Lize looked at her, then glanced away. "I don't see no weddin' ring on your finger, so I don't know if you're married or not. But the thing is, girl, you're in a family way."

Jade stared at Lize, speechless, shaking her head dazedly. "Are you sure?" she gasped finally.

"Yes, child, you are." Lize looked into her distraught eyes. He took her hand and laid it on her stomach. "You can feel for yourself."

Jade did as he had suggested, then whispered hoarsely, "What if it's that Indian's child?"

"If it is, you'll love it regardless, and we'll raise it no matter its color."

"Ah, Lize." Jade took his hand and squeezed it gently. "Are you sure you want to be burdened with a crazy woman and maybe a half-breed child?"

"The way I look at it, when a man comes to a time in his life when it looks like he can't have too much of a future, it would be good to know he had a past worth remembering. Now, I ain't done much with my life, never even bothered to take me a wife and have some younguns. I didn't want to be bothered by them. Maybe the Man up there is givin' me a chance to do somethin' worthwhile.

"But that's not the onlyest reason I want to help

you with your child when it comes. I get mighty lonesome sometimes, especially at night in the winter when the snow is up to your rump and the temperature drops below freezin'. There was a time, years back, when none of that would have bothered me. I'd just climb on my old mule, who was young then, and mosey on over to the fur post and spend the evenin's with my trapper friends. But no more.

"So you see"—he gave Jade one of his toothless smiles—"I'm thinkin' of myself, too."

"Nevertheless, I'll benefit more than you will."

"Let's just say that we're even and leave it at that," Lize said and picked up his fishing pole. "I'm gonna try my hand at catchin' another fish for our breakfast tomorrow mornin'."

Jade eased herself over onto her side and gazed into the fire. The only sound in the starless night was the crackling of the fire and the old man's soft snoring close beside her.

Should she be thankful that he had found her? she asked herself, or would she be better off dead? Was it a good thing or a bad one that she couldn't remember her name, her past? Maybe there was some shame in her past life that she'd be better off not to recall.

When she finally fell asleep she had decided to count her present blessings and live each day as it came. In all truth, that was all she could do. Wasn't it?

Chapter Twenty-eight

Maria sat on a tall, flat rock in the shade of a big cottonwood. She had been there since breakfast, three hours ago, watching John and two of his friends adding two rooms to their cabin.

She laid a gentle hand on her stomach. The extra rooms would be needed come next spring. She still couldn't believe that at the age of forty she was going to have a baby. It was a lucky thing she and John had decided to marry when they did, for she knew now that the babe had been conceived even before their wedding.

The father of her unborn child paused and drew an arm across his sweating face. He looked over at Maria and gave her a tender smile. She smiled back, thinking that her pregnancy couldn't have come at a better time. It had helped dull some of the grief John felt over losing Jade. It was only recently that he had come to terms with the loss of the niece he adored and picked up the threads of his own life.

Maria sighed softly. She didn't think she would ever forget that day when Kane rode up to the cabin, a broken man. There had been no need to ask if he had found Jade.

But John had asked him anyway and Kane's answer had drained the color from his face. John's face had contorted with the pain gripping him and he had walked away. No one had seen him for a week. To this day she didn't know where he had been, nor what he had done in his distress.

And poor Kane. How was he handling his pain? She hadn't seen him since he'd brought them the awful news.

Maria's sad reflections were interrupted when the oldest Henderson boy came running up, out of breath. "What is it, youngun?" John asked, his face anxious. "Is somethin' wrong up at your place?"

The boy shook his head, paused a moment to catch his breath, then said, "It's old Tillie. I guess she's dyin'. She wants to see you right away. I think you'd better hurry. Maw said she didn't think the old soul has long."

John grabbed Maria's hand and they hurried after the boy.

Silence and loneliness emanated from Tillie's

cabin as John and Maria approached it. It was as if its old owner had already departed, to go on to a better life. They stepped through the door, which had been left open to catch any breeze that might come along.

The pleasant odor of herbs and bark and apples drifted to Maria, and she remembered hearing that the old woman had cured many mountain people of their ills with the herbs and roots she gathered in the foothills.

Mrs. Henderson and another neighbor woman stood up, relinquishing their chairs beside the bed to John and Maria. John picked up the fragile, arthritic hand lying still on the sheet, and as he gently stroked it said, "I have come as fast as I could. Did you want to tell me something?"

Tillie nodded and gave his hand a slight squeeze. "I'll be . . . leaving these mountains . . . soon and . . . before I go I . . . must let . . . its people know . . . who did all the . . . killin's.

"Virgil done . . . them," she whispered, making all four people gasp. "My nephew is not . . . what he seems to be. He doesn't have many tender feelin's in his makeup . . . but he has always been fond of me . . . I was the only one in his family who . . . ever showed him any affection."

Tillie paused as if to gather strength to continue her broken sentences. "For years I have seen what . . . our women have had to bear from . . . brutal husbands. I made the decision that . . . before I left this . . . old world I was . . . gonna do somethin' about it. I wrote to Virgil, telling him I needed his help.

"You know the rest," she finished weakly. With a soft sigh she closed her eyes. Those in the room knew that the soul of the old woman had left her body. Maria, the only Catholic among them, made the sign of the cross and folded her hands in silent prayer that God would forgive Tillie Clark for her part in the taking of three lives.

Big John let the other two women sob softly for a few minutes; the old woman had been a fixture in the mountains all their lives. She had helped each one of them into the world.

He rose and pulled the sheet up over the wrinkled face, then, sitting back down, said, "Ladies, there's something I want you to consider. Don't you think it would be wise to keep Tillie's secret to yourselves? As long as certain men around here still think there's a killer among us, a man who is keeping his eyes on their behavior, they will continue to treat their families in a more decent way."

"Thank you, John. I've been thinkin' the same thing," Mrs. Henderson said, relief in her voice. "But I didn't know how you would feel about it."

"All right then, what Tillie just told us won't go any further than this room."

Both women nodded agreement and Mrs. Henderson said, "If you'll get hold of Reverend Hart and set the men to diggin' Tillie's grave, we'll prepare her for burial."

*   *   *

Later, when John and Maria were walking home, John shook his head in disbelief. "Never in a million years would I have thought that the little feller could be a cold-blooded killer."

"Well, from some of the stories I've heard, he did the women around here a great favor. As far as I'm concerned, those men he did in had already lived much too long."

"That's a fact," John said, then sighed. "I wish we could have found Jade's body, buried her in our cemetery. I have dreams of her lyin' somewhere all alone, exposed to the weather and varmints."

Maria put her arm around his waist and hugged him. "I know. I think of her and her unborn baby all the time. And, John"—she looked up at him—"I can't help worrying about Kane, wondering where he went to lick his wounds. He was half out of his mind with grief when he left us."

"Feelin' guilt too, I imagine," John said gruffly, not yet ready to forget the shabby treatment the rancher had given his niece.

Maria nodded. "That too."

The rising sun had reddened the crest of the mountain when Kane stepped out of the cave that had been his home for the past two weeks, ever since he had ridden away from Big John and Maria.

His mind dull with pain and grief at losing Jade, he had unconsciously kept to the foothills to escape the glaring sun. He didn't know how far he had ridden that day, or the next.

On the third day, late in the afternoon, he came upon a branch of the Platte. He realized then that he had ridden close to fifty miles—a distance great enough that there wouldn't be anything in the area to remind him of Jade.

The sorrel was tired and Kane was gut hungry. He remembered there was a small fur post a few miles down on the Platte where mostly Indians brought their furs to trade for food, bright cloth and gaudy beads for their wives and sweethearts.

Kane counted the money he carried in his vest pocket. He had plenty for supplies. Tomorrow he would find that post and lay in some grub. But what was he to eat now? His stomach rumbled, reminding him how hungry he was.

At that moment he spotted a disjointed flock of geese paddling around the edge of the branch, foraging in the tall reeds. He slowly dismounted and unstrapped his Colt so it wouldn't get wet. He dropped down on all fours and carefully crawled through the tall grasses. Before he knew it, he was in the shallow water, an unsuspecting goose only a foot away. In an instant, he had the squawking fowl by the neck.

Half an hour later he had built a fire, dressed the goose and had it spitted over the flames. As its juices dripped and hissed on the red coals, saliva filled his mouth. It was hard not to start consuming his supper before it was fully cooked. When he did finally remove it from the spit and tore off a leg, he knew he had never tasted anything so good.

While Kane had been feeding his ravenous hunger he heard from a distance the rumble of thunder. Damn, it's gonna rain, he thought, tossing a bone into the fire. "We'd better look for some shelter, Red," he said to the sorrel as he got to his feet.

Unlooping the reins from a tree branch, he headed farther up into the foothills, the horse clomping along behind him. A few years back he and his drover, Pete Harding, had come to this area to hunt the bighorn sheep. They had remarked on the several caves they'd seen while hunting. He hoped to find one of them now.

A streak of lightning and a crash of thunder split the air at the same time Kane saw the dark opening of a cave. The nervous horse almost stepped on his heels as Kane hurried toward it.

The shelter was high enough and deep enough to accommodate Red, and as Kane unsaddled him the rain came. "It's a real gully-washer, horse," Kane said as he stood in the cave's opening, looking out at the slashing rain coming down in sheets, the lightning flashing and streaking across the dark sky.

When a large cottonwood lost its top to a jagged streak of lightning and fell smoking to the ground only a few feet away, Kane quickly moved farther into the cave.

The incessant rain kept up its patter all night.

Kane roused several times, awakened by the claps of thunder that seemed to shake the ground beneath him. But at least the inclement weather kept at bay his haunting dreams of Jade, in which he took her in his arms, not in passion but in tenderness.

The following morning he had set out early for the fur post. He had no trouble finding it, a dirty, godforsaken place.

As he stepped up on the porch a dog slunk out of his way. Nothing but fur and bones, it lay down, behind a chair, out of the way of an occasional kick by some drunken Indian or trapper. He wondered who the big-boned animal belonged to and how long it had been since it had last eaten.

He found the proprietor alone in the dark, foul-smelling post and was thankful. He didn't want to answer nosy questions, to state his business or where he was living. To his relief, the bald-headed owner was as untalkative as Kane. Their conversation was limited to the specifies of his order. When everything was amassed on the rough counter, Kane remembered his need of a lantern and kerosene.

Once everything had been shoved into a gunnysack, with the exception of two horse blankets folded over his arm, Kane paid the bill and walked outside.

He was ready to step off the porch when he noticed the dog again. It lay in the same spot, its head between its paws. When Kane hunkered down beside it and said softly, "Who do you belong to, fellow?" he received a weak wag of its tail.

Kane's heart went out to the animal. It looked as defeated as he felt. He fastened the grub sack across Red's broad rump, then returned to the porch and picked up the dog. It was so light he had no problem climbing into the saddle with the dog in his arms.

The first thing Kane had done on arriving back at the cave was to feed the dog the leftover goose. Although more than half of it had been left from his supper, the dog, which he named Bones, demolished it within a minute.

Kane grinned his amusement, remembering how during that first week with him the dog had consumed a whole deer. He was still a voracious eater, making it necessary for Kane to go hunting once a week to keep a supply of meat for his new companion. Bones was a large animal, a mixture of hound and God knew what else. And there was no doubt he loved his new master. Every look, every wag of his tail said so.

Bones came running up now, whining and nudging Kane with his nose, and he realized the dog was trying to tell him something. "What is it, fellow?" he asked. When Bones struck off through the trees, Kane decided he'd better follow him. Something had upset the hound.

He caught up with Bones at the edge of a small clearing. Kane grinned. Evidently the dog didn't like Indians, for there were five of them gathered around a small fire. From their unkempt appearance he suspected they were renegades. He was about to turn around and go back to camp when he heard the stamping of hooves. He peered in that direction and saw several horses tethered among the trees. His eyes widened in disbelief when his gaze fell on a pure white stallion.

"By all that's holy, there stands Satan," he whispered. He started to move forward, to announce to the group that the white was his and he wanted him back. He realized then that his Colt was back in the cave. He spun around and ran as quietly as he could toward camp. Bones followed him, whining a protest. "Quiet," Kane commanded. "They're gonna hear you."

Hurrying into the cave, Kane picked up the Colt, checked to see that it was fully loaded, then started off at a lope to where the Indians were camped.

He swore long and hard when he found the camp empty and the Indians racing away, Satan ahead of the others.

"I'll get you, you rotten thieves." He shook his fist at the retreating backs. "If it takes the rest of my life, I'll track you down."

Chapter Twenty-nine

Crouched behind a boulder, Kane blinked against the white glare of the sun, squinting his eyes and scanning the area for a glimpse of the Indians and his stallion. Finally, he was rewarded by a spiral of wood smoke reaching up among the trees.

His heart began to pound. He had been trailing the renegades for over a week. Each day he would think that this day he would catch up with them. But each time he came upon their camp he found it deserted. Sometimes he found the ashes of their campfire still warm. It was as though they had a sixth sense that told them he was coming.

They had somehow learned that his only interest lay in the white stallion and that they had no fear of him ever catching up with Satan, who ran like the wind.

One day last week he had spotted the renegades up on a ridge. The leader, astride Satan, was several yards ahead of the others. Kane put his thumb and middle finger to his lips and gave the whistle that always brought the stallion to him.

It had worked, but he would never do it again. The big animal had tried his best to pivot and come to him, but the Indian had lashed his head and neck so cruelly with a short whip that Kane didn't whistle again. The brutal slashing could catch the stallion in the eyes, blinding him.

Kane didn't rush right in on his prey but sat thinking. At last he had them and he didn't want to chance fouling up everything. The renegades were tricky. If they had seen him coming they might be waiting for him to ride into a trap they had prepared.

"I'll never know hiding behind this rock," he muttered and stood up. He looped the reins over a bush and started toward the smoke that still drifted up and into the treetops. He made no sound; not even his feet rustled the dead leaves on the forest floor.

Kane stopped just short of the Indians' camp. A movement a couple of yards away had caught his eye. He squatted down behind a tree and held his breath. Only a few yards away a sentry had been posted to alert his companions to any sign of danger.

As Kane wondered how he was to slip past the guard there came the lonesome cry of a whip-poorwill. The next instant he knew it was no bird call, for suddenly the Indian was no longer there and a thundering burst of hooves filled the air. Forgetting personal danger he ran headlong to where the renegades had camped.

He found only the fire and some half-eaten sage hens. Furious tears glinted in his eyes. He had been so near to recovering his stallion. In desperation he brought his thumb and middle finger to his lips and did what he had sworn never to do again. The clarion whistle would bring Satan to him if it were at all possible.

There was no sound of returning hooves. His shoulders drooping in defeat, Kane turned around and started back toward the little sorrel. The animal whinnied a soft greeting, and Kane was reaching for the reins when he heard the fast, hard beat of a single horse's hooves. He knew that it was Satan trying to get to him.

Drawing his Colt, Kane leaped out onto the narrow trail just as the white stallion, blood running from a dozen whiplashes, galloped into view. Surprised and shocked at seeing Kane, the renegade leader tried to run him down. But the horse stopped short and refused to move, no matter how hard he was hit between the ears with the whip handle being used on him.

The Indian's eyes gleamed with cunning hatred as he swung from the saddle, placing Satan between them. Kane ground his teeth in frustration. The Indian was going to use the stallion as a shield while he shot at his enemy. He knew the white man wouldn't chance hitting his horse.

"What you don't know, you bastard," Kane growled savagely to himself, "is that I'm a crack shot, that I can knock a fly off a horse's ear."

Kane forgot all else—the blazing sun, the sweat running down his face. His whole attention was on where the Indian would show his face.

It didn't happen that way. The Indian, thinking to take him by surprise, suddenly jumped from behind Satan, the pistol in his hand blazing. A bullet whipped past Kane's ear and buried itself in a tree trunk behind him. With a grim smile on his face, Kane took careful aim and shot.

The renegade clutched his chest, the color slowly leaving his face. His lips loosened and his jaw dropped. His body began to sag and his eyes widened with fear. He took a faltering step, stiffened, then crumpled to the ground.

Without a glance at the dead Indian, Kane went to the stallion. Satan was blowing softly, his head hanging. Kane put his arms around the animal's bloody neck, and speaking softly to him, said, "There's a waterfall nearby, old fellow. We'll soon get those whiplashes cleaned up."

Kane led Satan back to where the sorrel waited, then led both animals the few hundred yards to where a small fall of water tumbled over a mass of smooth boulders. After removing his boots and laying aside his vest, hat and holster, Kane led both horses into the refreshing fall of water, relishing its coolness when it fell on his heated body.

Satan nickered his pain a few times as the cold water hit his wounded flesh, but stood still and let Kane wash him down with the kerchief he had taken from around his neck. "I'll put some salve on those cuts when we get back to the ranch," he soothed, then led both animals out into the sunshine to dry off. He walked back into the water then and vigorously scrubbed his hair, which now hung to his shoulders, and did the same to the short beard he sported.

"I guess I look pretty much like a mountain man now," he muttered as he stepped out onto the forest floor, water streaming off his clothes.

The horses were chomping at a patch of lush grass. Knowing that they wouldn't go far from him, he stretched out in the grass to let the hot August sun dry his clothes, and to give the stallion a much-needed rest. In minutes he was fast asleep.

Early in the morning, before the heat had grown fierce, Jade had left the cabin to look for service-berries. She would add them to venison suet in the making of pemmican.

They needed supplies, but she suspected that Lize didn't have the money to buy them. She felt guilty every time she partook of the meals the old fellow provided—mostly fish and sage chickens. There hadn't been any bread for the past two days but she hadn't mentioned that fact. It would have embarrassed him greatly if she had.

How lucky she had been that Lize had found her. He had taken care of her as if she were his granddaughter. He had insisted she drink a bitter concoction of herbs and roots and God knew what else to build up her strength. He had healed her cuts and scratches with some kind of herb salve. She didn't think it was necessary to continue wearing the bindings around her ribs, but he insisted she wear them at least another week.

"Did you know," the old man had asked, "that when a woman is delivering her baby, every bone in her body, except the jaw bone, stretches? I want them ribs to be fully mended and strong when your time comes."

The way Lize took care of her and bossed her around reminded her of someone, but of course she couldn't remember who.

As her nimble fingers plucked the berries off the bushes she thought of the dreams she'd been having lately. A man, tall and lean, would come out of the night and slide into bed with her. She would reject him at first, but then his caressing hands moving over her body would eventually coax her to press up against him.

Jade blushed furiously as she recalled what went on then, what a wanton she had become, following his lead in their lovemaking. Then, always just before his thrusting body brought her to the peak of shattering fulfillment, she awakened. She would lie in the darkness, aching and empty inside, wondering if she had known that man in her past. For although she had grown to know the muscular body so well, his face was still a mystery. He never allowed her to touch him there.

Jade mopped at her sweating face with a white rag she took from her pocket, then went and sat down under the shade of a tree. As she examined her scratched hands she wondered if she had known her night lover in the past. Was he the father of her baby, or had the dead Indian planted his seed in her?

So many questions, she thought with a sigh. Hard ones to answer when all she could remember was what had happened since the old man pulled her from the river and brought her to his cabin.

What a dear man the old trapper was, she thought. He so looked forward to the birth of her baby, and also worried about how he would support it. She leaned her head against the tree trunk, her mind weary from all the unanswered questions. The silence around her was profound; even the old mule stood motionless. She was about to doze off when a rustling in the forest had her sitting forward. An Indian, she thought immediately. No, she amended. No red man, young or old, would break twigs and scatter rattling stones.

Her heart jumped and raced. Maybe it was a bear hunting the serviceberries. She was ready to get to her feet, climb on Jake and ride toward home as fast as the mule could carry her when she eased back down. It wasn't a bear that emerged from among the trees, but one of the biggest dogs she had ever seen. He stood looking at her, his brown eyes inquisitive, as though to say, "Who are you?" He wagged his tail, the act saying that she shouldn't be afraid of him, then bounded off into the forest.

Who owned him? she wondered. As far as she knew Lize didn't have a neighbor within ten miles. The animal looked too well fed and cared for to belong to any of the trappers that did business at the fur post.

Jade stood, picked up the pail of berries and scrambled onto the mule's back. Lize would be worrying about her right about now. The way he fretted over her was worse than a hen with one chick.

Arriving back at the cabin, Jade found the old man scaling fish and she held back a sigh. Fish again. Had the poor old fellow run out of ammunition for his rifle? Would there be no more meat on the table?

She smiled at him as she passed into the small log building. What was to become of them? Would they starve to death? she wondered as she washed the berries and spread them on the table to dry. Later Lize would crush them and mix them with the suet he kept in a small crock for the purpose of making the pemmican. They already had at least a pound of pemmican wrapped up in oiled paper. Was that to be their main staple from now on? she wondered.

Jade's spirits were low when she stretched out on Lize's bed that night. He had insisted that she use it the first day he brought her home with him. Her lips curved in a tender smile as he snored from his pallet of hay across from her. When she was feeling better after a few days, she had tried to persuade him to take back his bed, but he had insisted that she use it.

"In your condition you don't need to be sleeping on the floor," he said, ending their discussion.

A few minutes later Jade was also asleep, and she soon found herself in her dream lover's arms. Because she was in low spirits, she clung more tightly to him than usual, and her kisses were more urgent. He responded, his lovemaking tender but demanding. With her arms and legs wrapped tightly around him, her hips lifting to each thrust, she knew suddenly that this time she was going to receive full satisfaction.

At last, after several wonderful minutes, she began nearing the crest of her passion. She cupped her lover's face in her hands and looked full into her husband's mocking eyes.

"Kane!" she called out, sitting up in bed as she woke from her dream.

When her body stopped trembling, she lay back

down, wide awake. As she stared at the ceiling, every aspect of her past came flooding back to her. She was married to Kane Roemer, carried his child inside her. She loved him, but he didn't love her. She remembered being taken by a bunch of Indian renegades and that Long Feather, an old friend, had rescued her. She remembered the river and falling into its raging waters.

Her uncle and Maria came to mind then. Poor Uncle John, how he must worry, not knowing where she was, whether she was dead or alive.

She slid out of bed. It was important that she get home as soon as possible, to let her uncle know that she still lived. As she lit the stub of a candle the thought came to her that she and Lize weren't going to starve after all, for she was going to take the old man back with her. I wish I had a cup of coffee, she thought, but was afraid she would waken Lize if she made it.

Lize was awake, however. He had been ever since her outcry. He sat up now and asked in a sleep-roughened voice, "Is somethin' wrong, Lass? Are you in some kind of pain?"

"No, Lize, everything is fine." She turned and smiled at him. "I've never felt better in my life."

"You sure sound happy."

"I am. I had a dream that brought back my memory."

"Do tell!" Lize exclaimed and, pulling on his trousers, joined her at the table. "Who exactly are you then?"

"My name is Jade Roemer. I'm married, and the little one I carry inside me is my husband's."

The eastern sky was turning gray by the time Jade had made a pot of coffee and related everything about herself to her friend. She ended her story by telling him how it came about that her uncle had made Kane marry her.

"He can't stand the sight of me and has made no claim on the baby. So you and I will be living with my uncle and his new wife."

"But, Lass," the old man protested, "I can't go piling in on strangers."

"Five minutes after you've met Big John Farrow he'll not be a stranger to you. He's like that when he takes to a person, and he's going to love you for saving my life."

"Well now"—the old man looked flustered—"I don't think anyone ever loved me. Maybe my maw did."

"I love you." Jade's eyes twinkled. "What do you think about that?"

"I think you must still be teched in the head, girl." Lize tried to look stern, but he had to grin. He didn't say any more for a while, but Jade had seen the relief that momentarily flashed in his faded blue eyes. She knew he was thinking that he wouldn't have to worry about trying to keep food on the table.

"Now whereabouts in the mountains does your uncle live?" Lize asked, breaking the silence.

"It's not far from Laramie."

Lize nodded. "I've heard tell of that town. It's a far piece from here. It will take us a couple days to get to your uncle's place."

"What will we do about another mount? I don't think either one of us is up to walking that far."

Lize sat for a while, his brow furrowed in deep thought. He spoke finally. "There's a young trapper friend of mine who has been wantin' to buy my traps for over a year. I've been hangin' on to them, figurin' to lay a line this winter, but I reckon that won't be necessary now.

"I can get enough from him to buy you a pretty good piece of horseflesh. I'll go to the fur post as soon as the sun comes up."

It was around seven when Lize climbed up on his mule and rode off, at least forty traps fastened to his saddle. They were in excellent shape, much better than a person could buy today, he had bragged to Jade. She watched him fade out of sight among the pines and then turned her hand to straightening up the sole room of the cabin.

When she had made up the bed she hauled the hay pallet out behind the cabin. She folded its sheet and blanket and carried them inside to put them on a shelf that also held the old man's worn towels, two pairs of trousers and two shirts. Beside them lay three pairs of rolled-up socks.

The poor old fellow doesn't have much, she thought as she picked up the broom and began sweeping the floor. Then, returning the broom to its corner, she wiped the bread crumbs off the table. They had each had a chunk of hard sour-dough bread for breakfast.

When Jade had the room neat, the way Lize liked it, she brushed down her dress, thankful she had washed it the day before, and went outside to sit on a stump while she watched for Lize's return.

She had sat for only about a half hour, wondering what they would eat on the two-day journey, when she saw the old man coming through the trees. A little Indian pony followed him on a lead rope. She thought she had never seen Lize's toothless smile so wide as he swung to the ground and held up a gunnysack for her to see.

"I done real good, Lass, girl," he said. "The damn young fool offered me more than I was gonna ask for the traps. I got in here some trail grub and a couple horse blankets for us to sleep on. And what do you think of this little hoss? I got him off an Indian for ten dollars, saddle and all. I think he's stolen and the brave wanted to get rid of him."

"Well, I certainly hope the owner doesn't catch us and put a bullet in our heads." Jade grinned at him.

"That's not likely to happen," Lize said, then asked, "When do you want to get started?"

"We might as well start right now. I've straightened up the cabin already."

The old man nodded. "We might as well. We've got the whole day ahead of us." When Jade stepped up to her new steed, Lize helped her to mount. Then, handing her the reins, he said gruffly, "You ride on ahead. I'll catch up with you directly."

Jade nodded and reined the pony around, sending him down the trail he had just traveled. She knew that Lize wanted to be alone when he said good-bye to the cabin he had built so many years ago. She felt sure he wouldn't be leaving it now if he weren't destitute and could no longer support himself.

Chapter Thirty

The hot afternoon sun shone down on Kane's head as Satan entered the foothills, with Bones trailing along behind. The dog never left his side, asleep or awake.

As they headed up the mountain, the stallion whinnied a soft sound of pleasure, and Kane wondered with a sigh what the big fellow was feeling. Was he reminded of the carefree years he had spent in the area, or was he remembering the wild, young girl who had tamed and loved him?

Kane was suffering at the memory of the beautiful young woman he had treated so cruelly. He would feel his pain, his guilt and his love for her as long as he lived. There would be no pleasure in his life anymore. He would throw himself into the running of the ranch.

And for whom would he be doing that? he asked himself. He would have no son to pass it on to. All chance of that happening had died when Jade lost her life in the river.

Kane was thinking that his nephew, Benny, would reap the benefit of his hard labor, when among the trees he saw the Farrow cabin.

He smiled. Already the place showed signs of Maria's touch. There was no more trash in the yard, but lush, green grass that extended to where the pines and trees took over. There were flowers blooming in beds along the cabin's walls, and if he wasn't mistaken, the red blooming rosebush at the corner of the building used to grow alongside his own porch.

When he grew closer Kane wasn't at all surprised to smell the aroma of a baking apple pie drifting through the open door. He had sniffed that spicy aroma too many times not to recognize it.

He guided Satan onto a gravel path, outlined with big rocks, which led to a hitching post that had recently been erected. Maria wasn't going to put up with horses tramping down the new greenery of her yard, he thought with a grin.

He sighed as he swung out of the saddle and ordered the hound to sit. He dreaded seeing Maria and Big John. Seeing them would bring back too many painful memories.

As he stepped onto a narrow path that led to a new porch, he saw Big John coming up from the pasture where he kept the wild horses he captured.

The big man spotted him and called a greeting. Maria evidently heard him, for she appeared at the door, her face beaming a welcome. John stood back, smiling as his wife made much over Kane, exclaiming how thin he had become while he was away. When she finally ran down, Kane and John shook hands, John saying, "I see you got the white back."

"Yes. And the redskin who stole him won't be stealing any more horses."

"Come on in and tell us all about it," John invited. "Maria just took an apple pie out of the oven a short time ago." He smiled at his wife. "Maybe she'll give us a slice of it to go with our coffee."

As Kane ate a piece of pie, drank two cups of coffee and related how he had tracked the horse thief down and killed him, dusk was settling in. In that time Jade's name wasn't mentioned, for which he was thankful. But Big John's eyes still wore a look of grief at losing his niece. He, like Kane, hadn't forgotten her for a minute. He never would.

When Kane was taking his leave of the happy couple, who had followed him out onto the porch, he couldn't help sliding Maria a sly look and saying, "That rosebush looks like one at the ranch."

Maria blushed a bright pink. "I didn't think

you'd mind, Kane. I was afraid you'd forget to water it and it would die."

"I was only teasing, Maria." Kane bent his head and kissed her cheek. "You can have anything you like from the yard, or from the house, for that matter."

"Thank you, Kane, but the rosebush is plenty."

Maria and John walked him to where the stallion and hound waited for him. "Where'd you get that dog?" John looked warily at the big animal.

"I found him at a fur post, half-starved. He looked as down as I felt, so I took him along with me.

"Well, take care of yourselves," Kane said, climbing into the saddle.

"You, too, Kane," Maria said, her eyes a little wet. "And come visit us often."

"I will," Kane answered. He reined Satan around and, with a word to the hound, cantered off through the trees.

Maria and John watched him until he was out of sight. "He won't, you know, come back again," John said as they walked back to the cabin.

"I'm afraid you're right," Maria agreed sadly. "He's changed so. He's not the laughing, carefree man I used to know."

"No, nor will he ever be. The heart has been taken out of him."

The day after Kane's visit, Maria and John were sitting on the porch enjoying the flowers and birdsong after their noon meal. Maria suddenly sat forward and peered off through the trees. "I've never seen that man on the mule before," she said. "Is he a distant neighbor I've not met yet?"

John stood up and walked to the edge of the porch. "No, he and the mule are strangers to me," he began and, then stopped short and shaded his eyes against the sun. "There's a woman trailin' along behind him.

"Maria!" he exclaimed, jumping off the porch, "by all that's holy, if my eyes ain't deceivin' me, it's Jade!"

"Are you sure, John?" Maria stepped down beside him. When the old man's companion kicked her heels into her little mount and galloped to the front, John yelled, "Jade!" and ran toward her.

Jade was off the horse before it came to a full stop. She flung herself into her uncle's arms.

"Ah, girl"—he hugged her fiercely—"I never thought to see you again."

Jade gave a shaky laugh. "I never expected to see you either, since I forgot that you even existed."

"What do you mean?" John held her away and searched her face.

"I had amnesia for a while. I got knocked in the head when I fell out of a canoe." She walked over to the mule and laid a hand on Lize's knee. "This is Lize. He saved my life. He pulled me out of the river, bound up three broken ribs, tended to my cuts and bruises and made me drink some vile-tasting tea until I was mended. As soon as I got my memory back I hurried home."

While John wrung Lize's hand with heartfelt thanks, Jade turned to Maria, who also folded her into a warm embrace. "You look tired, honey," she said, releasing Jade. "Let's go inside and I'll set out some ham and beans for you and Lize. You can tell us then in more detail all that has happened to you."

John and Maria exchanged amused smiles as Jade and her old friend ate like two starved wolves. John said later to Maria that it didn't look like they had been eating too high on the hog lately.

When the meal had been topped off with pieces of pie and some coffee, Jade and Lize sat back and told their remarkable story.

"I always knew that Long Feather meant trouble, hangin' 'round you," John said angrily. "I can't say that I'm sorry he's dead."

"I feel bad about it," Jade said. "He did save me from those renegades. God knows what might have happened to me if he hadn't. Anyway, you don't know how good it feels to see you, Uncle John, to be back in the mountains again. Along with my dear friend." She smiled fondly at Lize.

"You can't be more glad than I am to have you back." John squeezed her hand. "And, Lize, I'll never be able to thank you enough for bringin' her back to me."

Lize ducked his head, blushing. "I'm right glad to have done it," he finally got out.

"And we've got room for both of you," John said. Then he went on to explain about the two rooms he had added onto the cabin.

"Jade," Maria said, "you know that you and Lize are welcome here, this will always be your home, but before you decide, I think you should ride down to the ranch and let Kane know that you're still alive. He's awfully torn up, thinking that you are dead. You'll find him a different man from the one you knew before."

"Are you saying that he felt bad at my disappearance?"

"Feelin' bad don't describe it," John said. "He went out of his head for a while there. He disappeared for a month. No one knew where he was." He gave Jade a grave look. "He feels deeply for you, Jade."

Jade looked doubtful, remembering how hateful Kane had always been. "I'd like to believe that, but I just can't see him having any tender feelings for me."

"Give him a chance, Jade. Ride down to the ranch and watch his reaction when he sees you."

"Do you think that I should?" She looked hopefully at Maria. "I don't think I could bear it if he rejected me again."

"He'll not do that," Marie assured her. "Chances are he'll never let you out of his sight again."

"Well, Lize"—Jade looked at the old man, who

was taking it all in—"do you feel like doing a little more riding?"

"After that good meal I could ride another twenty miles. Even farther if in the end you get back with that gent you're so loco about."

As they prepared to leave John said to Lize, "You may not like ranch life. If it don't appeal to you, just hotfoot it back up the mountain. Like I said before, there's a room waitin' for you here."

Jade's nerves were raw as she and Lize neared the ranch house. What if Uncle John and Maria were only partially right? What if Kane did feel bad about her disappearance, even felt some guilt because of his shabby treatment of her? It didn't necessarily mean that he loved her, wanted her to live with him.

I'll feel like such an idiot if he only shakes my hand, says that he's glad I'm alive, then waits for me to leave, she thought.

She was tempted to turn the horse around and return to the mountain. But the thought of her unborn child gave her the courage to continue.

Jade squared her shoulders and rode on, raw emotions roiling inside her. She would face Kane Roemer with her head held high. After that she would follow his lead; unless, of course, he ordered her off the ranch. That would be another matter. She would demand her baby's rights then, and declare that if he wanted her off his ranch he would have to bodily throw her off.

Which he might do, she thought with a sinking heart.

When Jade and Lize rode up to the big house and tied their mounts to the hitching post at the edge of the yard, Cookie stepped out of the cookhouse and stared at Jade, too astounded to speak for a moment.

"You're alive!" he finally gasped, coming toward her, a wide smile splitting his wrinkled face. "Man, oh, man, there will be rejoicing tonight!" He held out a flour-covered palm to shake her hand. "That is if the boss don't drop dead from shock when he sees you," he added.

"Well now, we wouldn't want that to happen, would we?" She smiled back at the cook. When she saw him eyeing Lize, she said, "Meet my friend, Lize."

The two old men shook hands, but it was clear they hadn't taken a liking to each other. Jade didn't take the time to wonder why: she was too concerned about facing Kane.

"Where is your boss, Cookie?" she asked.

"Out on the range somewhere." The cook looked to the west, where the sun was about to go behind the mountain. "He and the men will be in most anytime now. Why don't you go on up to the house and wait for him? Unless you'd like a spot of coffee first?"

Cookie's last suggestion appealed to Jade. She didn't want to be sitting in Kane's house waiting for him when he returned home. She would rather he invited her into his home.

"We could do with a cup of coffee, Cookie," she said, sitting down at the table. "Thank you."

Jade smiled as the cook poured the coffee. It was plain he was full of questions. Consequently, she kept up a barrage of them herself to ward the cook's queries off. How did he like the hot weather they'd been having lately? Did he think it would rain soon? Was grass plentiful for the cattle?

Lize sent Jade an amused grin. He knew what she was up to and began to throw in his own questions. How many head of cattle did the ranch run? How many men did Roemer have working for him? How far was it to Laramie?

Cookie gave up trying to question Jade. She and the old coot had too many of their own to shoot at him. Just as he sat down to catch his breath a large dog bounded into the room.

"I've seen that dog before!" Jade exclaimed. "Who does he belong to?"

"He's the boss's hound. He found him at some fur post or other. Kane will be comin' in soon. The animal never strays far from him."

The oversize dog approached Jade, his tail wagging, a look of recognition in his soft brown eyes. She patted his head with nerveless fingers, panic tightening her throat. She would be facing Kane soon, and her future, good or bad, would be settled.

* * *

Tired and hungry, his throat parched from eating dust all day, Kane rode up to the ranch house, wondering who the mule and Indian pony belonged to. As he stepped out of the saddle Cookie came out onto the narrow porch of the cookhouse, a wide smile on his face.

"Boss," he called, "there's a young woman here that you'll be glad to see."

"Damn it!" Kane swore under his breath. "What makes the old fool think I'll be glad to see Liz Curtis? Can't he remember what a hell of a time I had getting rid of her?" His dust-grimed face was stern when he stamped into the kitchen, his angry eyes telling Cookie he would deal with him later.

Kane had taken only a couple of steps when he stopped to grasp the back of a chair. His knuckles turned white as he stared at Jade. "Is it you, Jade?" he half whispered.

Her heart was beating so hard it threatened to burst out of her chest. Jade stood up and gave him a shadow of a smile. She wasn't sure yet what he was feeling. Surprise, she knew, but what lay beneath that? "Yes, Kane, it's me."

Kane opened his mouth, then closed it. He had become aware of the two old men watching him with avid interest. He cleared his throat and said, "Let's go to the house. We've got to talk."

He stepped aside to let Jade precede him outside. They were silent as they walked the short distance to the house. When Kane took Jade's elbow to assist her up the stairs to the porch, his hand trembled. Jade gave him a sideways look, wondering if he was as nervous as she was. If he was, she feared it was from a different cause from what had set her own pulse to racing. All he had to do was touch her and she became as weak as water.

The house smelled musty inside, as though no one had lived in it for some time. It was neat and tidy as Maria always kept it, but in the family room, where Kane steered her, a thick layer of dust lay on everything.

Kane directed her to the leather couch and sat down beside her. "Jade," he began, "when I thought you were lost to me forever I was forced to face the truth. I love you. You're the only woman I will ever love. I know I treated you shamefully and I'm sorry for that."

He took her hands and, holding them tightly, went on in a cracked voice, "Will you forgive me and let me spend the rest of my life proving how much you mean to me?"

Jane looked deep into his earnest eyes. She believed that he did love her, but what about the unborn child they had created?

She took a deep breath and asked bluntly, "What about the baby? It will be coming along sometime in December."

"I swear to you, Jade, I will love it as if it were my own. It was my fault that you turned to another man."

Anger flashed through Jade and she wanted to slap his face. She felt insulted that he thought she could possibly make love with skinny Virgil Clark. But as old Tillie had pointed out once, "Men don't have a lick of sense when they are in love."

"I believe you, Kane." She laid her palm against his unshaved cheek. "Although I didn't know it, I've loved you as far back as when you took Satan away from me."

"Did you really, Jade?" His hands tightened painfully on hers. "You're not lying, are you?"

"No, I'm not. And I'm not lying when I say that the baby is yours, you foolish man. It was conceived the second time we made love. I've never been with another man."

The look of relief that shot into Kane's eyes before he gathered her in his arms told her how he had suffered, thinking she carried another man's child. Reaching into his vest pocket, he withdrew the gold wedding band that he had kept near his heart for so long. "Will you live with me, be my wife in all ways?" he whispered as he placed it on her finger.

"Yes, Kane, I promise. You'll never get rid of me."

"As if I'd want to, my wild little savage," he said huskily, sweeping her up in his arms and carrying her to his bedroom.

When he stood Jade on her feet, they tore at each other's clothes, tossing them every which way in their hurry to make up for all the wasted time. When they stood naked in front of each other, desire swelled Jade's breasts, and Kane's maleness jutted out proud and hard. Too weak to stand any longer, Jade sat down on the edge of the bed and swung her feet off the floor. Kane sat down beside her and stroked the slight swell of her stomach.

"I'm half out of my mind with wanting you, but I'm afraid I might hurt our baby."

Jade looked at the heat in his eyes and made a decision. He might very well get carried away and forget to be careful the first time he took her.

She came up on an elbow and, bending her head to his lap, ran the tip of her tongue over his erection. When he gasped and jerked, she smiled and drew most of his length into her mouth.

"Oh, God, yes," Kane moaned as she wound her tongue around him. As she felt him grow and harden, filling her mouth, Jade reveled in the fact that she could do this to him. His reaction fired her own passion, and she sucked and nibbled him, moaning low in her throat. All the while Kane stroked his fingers around her working lips, whispering, "Yes, yes, yes!"

Kane pulled himself away from her just before reaching a groaning climax. He slumped against Jade, gasping for breath as his manhood jerked and pumped out his spent passion.

Jade stroked his head while she waited for his breathing to return to normal. When finally he leaned up and looked down at her, awe in his eyes, he said with a crooked smile, "You almost killed me. I could feel your mouth drawing away all my strength."

"Didn't you like it?" She gave him a siren smile.

"You know I did, you little witch." He smiled down at her. "You can do that anytime the notion hits you. What made you do it this time?"

She stretched lazily, arching her back, pushing her body against him. "I was afraid that the first time you would be so filled with passion, you might forget yourself and thrust too hard and fast. I overheard a couple of mountain wives one time laughing together about how they did that to their husbands whenever they were too tired to be ridden half the night. They said it took the starch right out of their men."

"Well, my wise little wife"—Kane chuckled—"it only half worked on me. I have plenty of starch left." Straddling her, he grinned and said, "You slowed me down but nothing in this world is going to keep me from loving you for the rest of this night and the rest of our lives."

Epilogue

Jade presented Kane with a son two days before Christmas. They named him John after Big John Farrow, his great-uncle.

Maria delivered a baby girl, whom they named Emilie. But old Lize soon had everyone calling her Lass.

Lize hadn't liked ranch life, as Big John had suspected he wouldn't, and he settled in at the Farrow cabin up on the mountain.

Over the years Jade had two more children, another boy and then a little girl. Although Kane loved his sons, was proud of them, baby Melody had gripped his heart the first time he looked down at her and saw the small image of his wife's face.

Maria and Big John had only one daughter. They grew gray together, their love for each other growing stronger as the years passed.

Old Lize died at the age of ninety-three. He was laid to rest in the mountain cemetery. LOVED BY ALL was carved on his wooden tombstone.

The mountain wives were far from being coddled by some of the husbands, but they were no longer beaten. The mysterious deaths—which had taken on the quality of legend among the mountain folk—were a warning few men failed to heed.

Raven
Norah Hess

When Raven's two-bit gambler husband orders her to entertain a handsome cowboy at dinner, she has no idea of the double dealings involved. How is she to know that he has promised the good-looking stranger a night in her bed for $1,000, or that he has no intention of keeping his word? Cheated of his night of passion, Chance McGruder can't get the dark-haired little beauty out of his mind. So he is both tantalized and tormented when she shows up at the neighboring ranch, newly widowed but no less desirable. What kind of a wife will agree to sell herself to another man? What kind of a woman will run off with $1,000 that isn't hers? What kind of a widow can make him burn to possess her? And what kind of man is he to ignore his doubts and gamble his heart that when she gives her body, it will be for love.

___4611-3 $5.99 US/$6.99 CAN

Wild Fire

NORAH HESS

The Yankees killed her sweetheart, imprisoned her brother, and drove her from her home, but beautiful golden-haired Serena Bain faces the future boldly as the wagon trains roll out. But all the peril in the world won't change her bitter resentment of the darkly handsome Yankee wagon master Josh Quade. Soon, however, her heart betrays her will. His strong, rippling, buckskin-clad body sets her senses on fire. But pride and fate continue to tear them apart as the wagon trains roll west—until one night, in the soft, secret darkness of a bordello, Serena and Josh unleash their wildest passion and open their souls to the sweetest raptures of love.

___52331-0 $5.50 US/$6.50 CAN

Trapped in a loveless marriage, Lark Elliot longs to lead a normal life like the pretty women she sees in town, to wear new clothes and be courted by young suitors. But she has married Cletus Gibb, a man twice her age, so her elderly aunt and uncle can stay through the long Colorado winter in the mountain cabin he owns. Resigned to backbreaking labor on Gibb's ranch, Lark finds one person who makes the days bearable: Ace Brandon. But when her husband pays the rugged cowhand to father him an heir, at first Lark thinks she has been wrong about Ace's kindness. It isn't long, however, before she is looking forward to the warmth of his tender kiss, to the feel of his strong body. And as the heat of their desire melts away the cold winter nights, Lark knows she's found the haven she's always dreamed of in the circle of his loving arms.

___4522-2 $5.99 US/$6.99 CAN

KENTUCKY BRIDE

NORAH HESS

Fleeing her abusive uncle, young D'lise Alexander trusts no man...until she is rescued by virile trapper Kane Devlin. His rugged strength and tender concern convinces D'lise she'll find a safe haven in his backwoods homestead. There, amid the simple pleasures of cornhuskings and barn raisings, she discovers that Kane kindles a blaze of desire that burns even hotter than the flames in his rugged stone hearth. Beneath his soul-stirring kisses she forgets her fears, forgets everything except her longing to become his sweet Kentucky bride.

___52270-5 $5.50 US/$6.50 CAN

Dorchester Publishing Co., Inc.
P.O. Box 6640
Wayne, PA 19087-8640

Please add $1.75 for shipping and handling for the first book and $.50 for each book thereafter. NY, NYC, and PA residents, please add appropriate sales tax. No cash, stamps, or C.O.D.s. All orders shipped within 6 weeks via postal service book rate. Canadian orders require $2.00 extra postage and must be paid in U.S. dollars through a U.S. banking facility.

Name_____
Address_____
City_____State_____Zip_____
I have enclosed $_____ in payment for the checked book(s).
Payment <u>must</u> accompany all orders. ❑ Please send a free catalog.
      CHECK OUT OUR WEBSITE! www.dorchesterpub.com

TANNER

Norah Hess

Roxy Bartel needs a husband. More important, her son needs a father. But the lonely saloon owner cannot forget Tanner Graylord, the man who, eight years before, gave her love and a child, then walked out of her life. And now he is back, hoping she can believe that he has never stopped loving her, hoping for a chance that they might still live a life in each other's arms.

DEVIL IN SPURS

NORAH HESS

Raised in a bawdy house, Jonty Rand posed as a boy all her life to escape the notice of the rowdy cowboys who frequented the place. And to Jonty's way of thinking, the most notorious womanizer of the bunch is Cord McBain. So when her granny's dying wish makes Cord Jonty's guardian, she despairs of ever revealing her true identity. In the rugged solitude of the Wyoming wilderness he assigns Jonty all the hardest tasks on his horse ranch, making her life a torment. Then one stormy night, Cord discovers that Jonty will never be a man, only the wildest, most willing woman he's ever taken in his arms, the one woman who can claim his heart.

____52294-2 $5.50 US/$6.50 CAN

ATTENTION ROMANCE CUSTOMERS!

SPECIAL
TOLL-FREE NUMBER
1-800-481-9191

Call Monday through Friday
10 a.m. to 9 p.m.
Eastern Time
Get a free catalogue,
join the Romance Book Club,
and order books using your
Visa, MasterCard,
or Discover®

Leisure
Books

LOVE
SPELL